the RUSH

AS ABOVE BOOK TWO

To Mr. Stone for being the
stone that's kept me rolling

<u>**Character List:**</u>

Not all of these characters will make an
appearance in this book, but will be around.

As Above band members

Rex Thompson— vocals, guitar, songwriting

Finland Montgomery— guitar, backup vocals, songwriting

Tobias "Toby" Jeffers— bass, rhythm guitar

Mac Thompson— drums, nickname designator

Sentry Security

Ian— Head of Security, Rex's detail

Lugh— Second in command, Toby's detail

Peach— Fin's detail

Jordan Kauffman— Mac's detail

Jonathon— The floater

and more ...

A Note from the Author

Hello, again.

If this is your first Rae Stone book, thank you for picking up The Rush. If not it's not your first, then thanks for returning.

This book is a little different than the last and while all the issues are handled with as much care as possible, this story is not as smooth as The Moment. There is content included that might be uncomfortable to some readers, and very real for others.

Maybe you're one of them.

One of the cycle breakers, the misfits.

The survivors.

I'm glad that you are here.

I knew back when I was writing The Moment that Fin and Cedar would end up together. Arcade scene, anyone? I knew there would be a struggle, an imbalance of power, a give and take that neither of them seemed to want to give up. But when I finally sat down to write this book, I had no idea it would be so … *raw*. Hence the note.

While this work is strictly fictitious, I have done my best to represent a certain level of trauma that is purely character driven. This is the story that they wanted to tell and it may not be for everyone. That's okay.

A full list of content warnings can be found at the back of the book, after the acknowledgements.

Keep in mind that this book is a spicy romance, includes a lot of *fucks,* and is meant for audiences of 18 years or older.

I hope you enjoy :)

Blurb

"*WHAT CAN I SAY? Pain and lust make good music.*"

As his generation's *best guitar soloist* and *As Above's* lead guitarist, Finland Montgomery has everything he's ever asked for.

Women? *Check.*

Whiskey? *Check.*

Headliner status at the biggest music festival in the country? *Double check.*

But the one thing Fin never accounted for was a familiar face to come crashing into his life and becoming the focal point of his fascination.

Hardheaded tattooist, Cedar Jones, is no stranger to flirty advances and assholes with complexes. They're present at every ink shop. Every concert. A problem that has easily been defeated with feisty remarks and her trusty bat.

Until a particular guitarist looks at her like there's more behind his seemingly empty promises. Like maybe he's *different* than those that came before him.

When passions collide, *the rush* begins and a nightmare threatens to tear them apart, can Cedar and Fin learn to trust each other among the flames of her past?

This is the second interconnected standalone in the As Above series and can be read on its own but, as always, I will recommended that you read in order :)

Contents

Prologue

Cedar

*S*EVENTEEN YEARS OLD

I have a ticket in my hand.

A piece of paper that screams admittance, along with the lanyard around my neck, boasting the band's handwritten insignia down each side in silver sharpie I can still smell. The cheap material comes together right over my heart and attaches a little plastic badge that includes my name scrawled neatly.

Cedar Jones- VIP

The ticket was a gift.

An early graduation present from my dad who absolutely hated the music that I listened to and would never admit I got my love of rock from the bad boy turned father—but loved me enough to get them for me anyway.

Jeremy was supposed to be here with me for our anniversary. We've been seeing each other for just short of a year and I had to put in long hours to scrounge up enough tips at the café his parents owned to buy him a ticket. I didn't want to come alone, yet here I am standing in the autograph line with nerves fluttering up and then down in my stomach.

Alone.

Almost feeling out of place, which never used to be the case when music was involved.

In a bar too small for an event this size that happens to be filled to the brim with people who look like bikers, prison tattoo artists, and straight-up misfits. Not that I would know what prison tattoo artists look like, but that's my best guess, considering I've seen the rest hanging around my dad's shop. Noise fills the space between the postered and weathered walls, songs filtering low through the shitty speakers that are easily drowned out by the shouting and cussing.

I probably should be scared, but I'm not.

Considering the brand-new ring through my nose and the itchy doodles tattooed on my exposed thigh that I let Jeremy use as a practice pad for the tattoo gun we pieced together from garbage scraps, I feel more at home than I ever have.

So why do I feel so damn nervous? Sick almost.

Feet shuffle the line closer to the fold-up table littered with the band's merch—one of the tee shirt's I'm already wearing—and get us a few steps closer to what I'm really after.

The guitarist's autograph.

To go with the shirt I have tucked into the belt loop of the ripped pants—jeans I picked just to show off the ink—that I'm planning to give to Jeremy for our anniversary, if he ever shows the hell up, in hopes that this time he'll be convinced I'm serious about our relationship. And maybe he'll even tell me he loves me.

Where the hell is he?

Pushing up on my Chuck-clad tiptoes to see over the crowd piling in, I try to get a closer look at the band members from our favorite band, *The Saltwater Skulls.*

Sinking my teeth into my upper lip when I come up empty, despite Jeremy's promise to show, I fall back to flat feet and take another step closer to the men accepting items to sign and hands to shake. Only a few more feet and I'll be able to see their faces as they reach out to the patrons in front of me, and that fills me with fluttering giddies I wish I could share with Jeremy. He'd be so excited right now.

The line moves at a snail's pace, but I can finally see the man I'm after—the one everyone on Myspace claims is the next young Hendrix with chiseled features—and I'm filled with nerves beyond belief at the smirk on his thick lips and the crazy waves of jet black hair I'd really like to run my hands through. Even if it was just to see if the strands were as soft as they looked.

Not much older than me, Finland Montgomery is already covered in amazing tattoos I wish I could draw, has rings through his nose and lip, and according to the internet, is only five-nine. But judging from where I'm standing, his sitting position puts his head up past my shoulders. And I'm not short for a chick.

The internet lies sometimes.

"Dudette." My attention snaps away from the end of the line, where Fin puts his Sharpie to another CD case and makes my stomach do a weird little somersault, to my right, where the lead singer of *The Saltwater Skulls* sits, hand extended expectantly. "What do you want me to sign?"

"Oh, um..." I shake my head and turn my hip away from his grabby hands. "No thanks."

"Whatever then." He scoffs and swings his reach out to the person behind me who happily hands over a trucker hat for the singer's endorsement. "Next!"

What a douche.

Another step forward and another awkward exchange with the drummer where I refuse his signature and gain myself a scrunched up nose, and a shrugged dismissal.

"Cedar?" I whip around at the voice, my stomach lifting for the first time since the show started, and settle my sight on the one person I wanted here the whole damn time the music played.

"Jer!" I move to step closer to him for the hug I know he'll gladly accept, only to pause before I let myself out of the line I've been waiting in for over an hour.

"What the fuck are you doing?" It takes a minute for the hard set of Jeremy's gaze to sink in, his harsh tone causing scoffs to echo around me.

"I was trying to get you something." I shake off the weird mood he seems to be in and flash him a smile I know he likes since he's told me as much.

"I told you I couldn't come, and you did it anyway." Jeremy shakes his head, his long blond hair falling around his slim shoulders as he bites me with his words.

"What do you mean?" My smile falters, my brows furrowing.

"I told you!" He pushes aggressively closer to me with raised words, gaining himself a few mean-mugs from the people whose toes he stomps on as he closes the distance and wraps a hand around my bicep. "I sold the ticket to fix the broke-ass car you had to fucking have." His grip on me tightens, and it's almost as if the room does the exact opposite of all the novels I've read—y'know, where the couple touches and the room fades away?

No. I feel all of the eyes swing on us. Judge us.

I didn't want the car. He did. I have the bike my dad and I are rebuilding—albeit slowly, with each paycheck that has a few extra dollars—stored in the garage, just waiting for me to graduate so I can afford the more expensive pieces to get Frankenstein up and running.

Jeremy's a good guy.

At least, that's what I tell people when they ask about him and why a twenty-year-old is into a seventeen-year-old.

He's not like that, I tell my friends when he calls and gets angry with me for the things that I've done. Because I did do those things.

Like forget about the car because I was so excited to see my favorite band play tonight.

Or forget to put the tattoo gun away after trying to dry ink myself as practice because my hand isn't as heavy as his when he inks me and leaves me aching.

"Yo, you good?" The deep graveled voice rings around in my brain, breaking the trance Jeremy's molten gaze has put me in and has my attention swinging from my angry boyfriend to the man with the waves and the talented fingers.

My stomach drops.

"Oh, um—" I tug gently at my arm and meet Fin's hardened eyes, but Jeremy's grip is tighter than normal, his boney fingertips digging into my skin and refusing my release.

"Yeah, bro," Jeremy sneers, interrupting me for the thousandth time. "We're great." He yanks on me, effectively pulling me out of the line and away from the autograph I was desperate to get for him with shuffling feet and heated words. "I'm taking you home."

"Hey, wait," Fin calls out as Jeremy rushes us into the crowd and farther away from the table with the band I've been following since they hit the underground scene a year ago.

"What the hell do you think you're doing, Cedar?" Jeremy shakes me as he pushes me into people, pulling me in front of him to lead us through a sea of people packed like sardines where shoulders land on my chest and elbows bruise my arms.

"I was just trying to—"

"Get him to fuck you?" he hisses into my ear and releases my bicep, only to plant a hand on my lower back and push me into the crowd. "Make *fuck me* eyes with the guitarist?" I land in a throng of people as he spits the words at me, some of whom grab at my arms to catch me and help keep me upright.

"S-s-sorry," I mutter to the ones that right me, one particular set of haunted eyes landing on mine in a way that makes my skin crawl and my stomach twirl in knowing.

"You okay, miss?"

I don't get to answer the older woman with crow's feet and a Harley tee, though.

Because that same bruising grip is back on my upper arm and swinging me into a face contorted with such rage that I don't recognize the boyfriend I thought I had.

"I asked you a *goddamn question!*" Anger splits open my gut and when Jeremy's grip encases both arms and yanks me closer, so close that he screams spittle on my jaw, that red hot feeling splinters off into a deep-seated fear for the first time in my life. "You want him to fuck you?"

My wide eyes water. And my mind goes blank.

Because while I wasn't aiming for Fin to sleep with me, I did think he was cute. And I'd told Jeremy as much.

Which made me guilty … right?

"You think he'd give it to you better than me? Huh, Cedar?"

Despite the fight my dad made sure I knew was in the Jones's blood since before I could conceptualize the reason that might cause a need for it, I stand there and stare as Jeremy spews hatred right in my face in front of a crowd of strangers.

Where did my caring boyfriend go?

The boy that drew me pictures and took me to the park for walks?

That same face that hovered over me for the first time, took my virginity, is now so distraught with misplaced rage that I'm actually afraid he might hurt me for real.

"Yo, dickweed." Jeremy's nostrils flare—a sure sign that he's beyond reasoning—and he squeezes me harder with bared and gritted teeth.

"So he's coming to rescue you now?" he sneers at me, his breath washing over me and turning my stomach enough that I might actually vomit on him. "Fuck *off*," he yells in my face, making me jump.

"I said *hey.*" Large hands land on Jeremy's shoulders and spin us, his grip breaking free in time for the fist to land square on his nose and send him careening to the floor.

This time, no one catches him.

No one helps keep him on his feet like they did me.

In fact, the horde separates for Jeremy's landing against the sticky concrete, then closes in around him like he's not even there.

I watch in shock and horror as bodies and feet move and Jeremy doesn't get up.

"So, you wanted that autograph?" I lift my teary eyes from the floor where my boyfriend is engulfed in the growing crowd and meet a set of blue eyes that sparkle beneath a lifted brow. Fin flips his handy Sharpie between his lifted fingers much like my stomach does, that smirk tight, but lifted in the corner of his lips.

I do want the damn autograph.

I really, really do.

For myself.

And I think he knows it. Because he sticks the cap end of the marker between his teeth and tugs the writing end free.

I let the Saltwater Skull's guitarist gently brush my long black hair back from my shoulder and spin me until he can rest the heel of his hand just above my shoulder blade and the swipe of his marker tickles my skin beneath the shirt I spent two weeks allowance on.

"Just ... say..." he narrates as he scribbles. "No ... to..."

Drugs. Great. He's writing stupid shit on my shirt.

Goddamnit. This whole thing was a mistake.

I jerk away from the guitarist's stupid joke and spin to see where my boyfriend ended up in the crowd, only to be blocked by a hard chest clad in a Stones's tee.

"Jerks ..." I sigh at his words and let my sight trail up Fin's frame to meet his chiseled features, where I find the jerk winking and capping his marker. "Like that one." He thumbs over his shoulder, but steps into my path when I go to walk around him. "I suggest you forget about that asshole and call a friend. He's not coming back."

Chapter One

Fin

A FOUR-DAY MUSIC FESTIVAL is the last official stop on the Road Trip tour Leo cooked up for us.

For now.

That and a damn wedding.

The *Wedding of the Century*, if you ask the press. Or the fans. Or happen across it on every social media platform from here to the other side of the globe. So much so that it has drowned out all the other shit the band has been through in the last year—including the scandal, the independent label our manager Leo started when our band leader fired the last guy, and the complete destruction of a record tycoon.

Because As Above's beloved eternal bachelor—Rex *mother fucking* Thompson—is getting married.

To a normal chick.

But the festival.

One bigger than anything As Above has done yet. Complete with a tattoo convention going on from the moment the gates open till they close again four days later.

The most grueling of shows, hellbent on testing the fanbases of each artist and band with hot temperatures, long lines for port-a-potties, and expensive-as-hell beer. It is also trying for the artists who like to attend these kinds of things—most often flying in the night before, living out of an RV parked in the back of the stadium turned fortified stage, and rocking out with some of the greats beside some of the up-and-comers.

Which is actually not all that bad for us when I think about it that way.

And happens to be my favorite part of touring.

Just stickier. Trickier. Louder. And a helluva lot more fucking fun wrapped in four way-too-short days.

Lounging back in the mesh metal chair with spread legs and an iced coffee keeping me company in this heat when I'd rather have the steaming shit, I look out over the terrace at the mingling patrons of the local café and spot the As Above tees from several feet away.

The girls who wear them can't be much older than eighteen—if at all—and have been sneaking giggling glances my way for the last half hour. Or at least long enough for most of the ice to melt in my cup and make me wish it was a regular cup of Joe.

Continuing my scan of the crowded patio, I catch sight of the distinct flash of orange hair that lets me know my bodyguard is in fact near, but keeps to himself like he has the majority of the time he's spent with me as his detail.

Which is fine with me, considering he sticks out like a sore thumb unless he can be mistaken as a member of the road crew backstage with the rest of 'em. Y'know, with all the ink, the metal in his face, and the highlighter orange hair that earned him the nickname he's had for so long, I forget what his real fucking name is—Peach.

And right now, I'm trying to blend in and enjoy the few moments of peace before the gates of hell break open.

It's not every day a guitar veteran—award and all—like myself can walk out in public without being bum-rushed for autographs or pics.

Or followed for miles by desperate paparazzo like Rex has been since the wedding announcement went viral.

Blending into the crowd has been my game since joining As Above and I continue to test it every chance I get. Like right now, my bodyguard perches at the entrance to the café with his sketchbook in his lap and his eyes scanning like mine.

I'm in my white short-sleeve button-down and light jeans—the exact opposite of what I wear on stage, and in videos, around the fans, and at the after parties. Add in the backwards hat and I am the opposite of all those scenes in the movies where the 'hide in plain sight' character thinks that a black tee and a dark blue hat pulled low around the eyes is a great disguise.

Pfft.

Truly testing the theory, I let my gaze swing back over to the table with the girls donning shirts from my own damn band and make eye contact with the one that looks like she might be the ringleader. She jerks her gaze from me to her friend, her face flushing and her loose hair flying in the wind, then stands the fuck up and makes me regret testing the universe.

Her friend stands with her and they shuffle in cut-offs and Chucks over to my table with sheepish grins and tight grips on their tiny purses.

"Hey," the ringleader says, and I let my gaze flicker past them to see my bodyguard stand from his station and stretch his arms high above his head. "Are you, um ..." She wrings her hands in front of her as her nervous eyes flit over my chest and finally meet my eyes when her friend nudges her with an elbow. "Are you George Clooney's brother?"

I balk. Like eyes nearly fall out of my skull and roll around on the mesh metal table separating me from the way-too-young girls in front of me.

"You just, um, look like him." The friend steps forward when all I do is stare and hammers me again.

"Just not *like* like him."

Expectant eyes settle on mine, waiting for an answer I shouldn't *have to give.*

"Ladies." I clear my throat in an awkward chuckle and lean forward to rest my tatted forearms on the table. "How old are you?"

"Um..." The ringleader looks to her friend, then swings her gaze back at me when I lift a brow. "Nineteen."

I make a buzzer sound in the back of my throat, making the friend jump. "Try again."

"Ohhh kayyyy." Ringleader rolls her eyes and drags out the syllables. "We're sixteen."

"Didn't your parents ever teach you not to talk to strangers?" I flash my forearms to show both covered in ink. "Especially tattooed ones?"

"Well, duh." Ringleader rolls her eyes. "It's just that Nanny loves your brother's movies, and we just wanted an autograph."

"Nanny? What kind of name is that?"

I should not have asked that.

I really shouldn't have.

"What the hell do you call *your* grandmother?"

Even. Fucking. Better.

I hang my head and close my eyes because I am clearly having a nightmare. When I bring my gaze back up, the murder twins are still standing there, staring at me like I owe them an answer to a question that makes me double my age and non-existent if it were true.

"Listen." I clear my throat again and fish a pen from my pocket as I extend a hand and await the thing they want signed—because how can I deny an old lady some excitement? "I'm not his brother." I shake my head when the two jump and clap excitedly like I didn't just say I was not who they were looking for and slap a café napkin against my palm. "But you should really look up the band on those damn shirts."

I sign the stupid napkin with an eye roll and offer it over with enough of a grip to keep the thin paper from flying away in the wind.

"Thanks," they say in unison as they snatch the signature from me and take off in giddy fits.

"And don't talk to strangers," I call after them but all I get is ignored as they pick up their cups from the table—the ones they'd left unattended—and take off down the street.

"Clooney, huh?"

"Shut up, Peach." Turning in my chair, I snarl at my bodyguard when his stupid mug snorts down at me like this shit is funny.

"No, I'm definitely not going to do that." He laughs and lands a heavy palm against my shoulder in a slap that tells me exactly how long he's going to remember me being mistaken for George Clooney's non-existent brother.

Which is until the end of fucking time.

Rolling my eyes, I push to stand from the chair that protests my weight considering the size and age of it, and throw a bill on the table even though I already paid for the coffee-flavored shit I didn't finish.

Peach's *ahem* and subtle head tilt to his right send my gaze floating over to see several of the patrons watching me like a hawk. Like maybe I'm someone worthy of chasing down for an autograph if only they could place my face.

Time to go.

I jut my chin at my bodyguard in acknowledgment and follow his lead out into the street, down the next block and stop next to the bikes we rode in on.

First requirement of being on my detail?

Must ride.

Second—you watch my back, I got yours. But remember it's my life and I lead that shit.

Peach has been great ever since I laid it down and hasn't gotten in my way yet. He even learned how to ride just to keep up.

Flashing my bodyguard a gloved finger when he looks at me expectantly, his bike already between his legs, I snag my helmet and switch it out with the hat I shove into my back pocket.

Mounting the machine, I snap the visor down over my eyes and turn the key until the engine is roaring beneath me. Vibrations travel up my body and loosen my muscles as I lean into the beast and kick us out onto the pavement with only a mild amount of burnt rubber in my wake.

I let loose a breath as I speed out of town onto country roads, hammering the throttle with a refreshing freedom that can only come from three things—wicked fast speeds in the open air, on stage with an axe in my hands, and a damn good and kinky woman willing to try a little something new. And while the rush for each is different, they each get my dick hard.

Okay, that last one gets my dick real hard, but we're not there now.

Chuckling at the thoughts in my own head, I ease the bike into a turn and amp up on the gas on the exit, the wind whipping through the thin shirt on my chest. Loose and grinning, I glance in the rearview and catch sight of Peach keeping on my tail. Close enough not to lose me, but not so close that he'd run me over if I went down.

Good.

We drive like that, through the back roads of a town I don't know, until the sun is setting behind the wide open fields and the sky is painted in a crazy combination of blues, purples, and reds.

I slow my speed until we come up on a road that might as well be dirt, and I pull off to fish out my phone and snap a picture of the landscape before the colors fade. With my bike still between my legs, I lift up the visor and snap a selfie from above me, my helmet and bike taking up most of the frame—including the bird I flip the camera—and post both pics online with a single hashtag.

Where am I?

Securing the phone back in my pocket, I take a glance back at Peach, whose helmet lifts, and we take back off into the fading sunlight.

Chapter Two

Fin

BY THE TIME WE make it back to the venue, the stage is already erected tall enough to be seen over the stadium seats from our bikes. We ease through the wide opening off to the side of the turnstiles at the main gate that will be locked up before shutting down tonight to keep out the campers and squatters. But for now, people rush around to get ready for the next four days of craziness.

Vendors hurry to stash extra supplies and finish setting up, security are roaming around with scowls as they watch each person's badges that come and go, checking passes and tickets to confirm identities as Peach and I ride right by all of them. Past the multitude of canopies where some set up tattoo equipment while others flash their best merch to be sold at the highest price and we ride right on through the concrete throughway to the main stage that was a soccer field only a few hours ago. The grass has been covered by festival mats that bump beneath my tires, meant to keep the real sod underneath from being destroyed by the tens of thousands of feet that are about to stomp the shit out of it, the gallons of beer from seeping in, and the weird amount of piss that will more than likely leak through anyway.

Coming up to the stage where all kinds of techs move equipment about, I spot my band's long-haired and blue-green eyed vocalist off to the side with his ass planted and legs dangling down off the platform, his torso curled around a guitar and a pen pinched between his teeth.

I pull the bike right up under his feet, kill the engine, and toe the kickstand down for me to dismount the machine.

"Sup, fucker," I say once my head is free of my helmet and I can shake out the dark waves on top of my head, Peach parking his hog beside mine and cutting the noise.

Rex snorts and flips me the finger but doesn't look away from the notebook in front of him as he retrieves his pen and scribbles something on the paper.

My ears ring from the sudden silence that's not altogether that silent with all the work going on around us. I work my jaw to pop my ears and hop up onto the stage next to my bandmate and brother.

Rex works a few cords on the instrument in his lap, the sound short and sharp without the amp hookup, but when you've got talent and have done this as long as we have, you hear it anyway. Almost as if the amplification is coming directly from the speaker.

"Take a ..." Rex scribbles another note on the page and flips the book in my direction, the thing landing with a splat between us. "Look." His blue-green eyes flick to mine, his pen back between his teeth.

"Looks like hieroglyphics to me." I snag the notebook, holding it up and turning it to the side with a lifted brow. "What language is this?"

Knuckles land on my bicep and have a laugh bursting from between my lips.

"Lyrics, you dickhead." Rex shakes his head of wild curls, a smirk tipping the corner of his pierced lips. "I already know my handwriting sucks."

I snort and right the book so I can actually try to read the words scribbled in weird angles that completely ignore the lines on the page.

Oh, shit.

These are good.

"This isn't another damn ballad, is it?" I squint at the lettering that mushes together and give my band brother more shit simply because he always deserves it.

Because the last set of ballads this fucker wrote knocked everything else As Above has written to date out of the water.

"Shut up and tell me what you think," Rex says, but I'm already nodding my head and searching the page for the key to start humming the music once I find it. The lyrics are abstract and generalized, but if anyone knows anything about the tatted man next to me, they'd know exactly who these raunchy lovesick lines are about.

"This about her?" I ask without taking my eyes off the words, the cords already playing in the back of my mind despite the soft but irritating feedback that filters through the speakers right behind Rex.

I also don't wait for the answer.

Because of course it's about her. The new up-and-coming designer that has stolen his heart and brought him back from the dead. Rex's fiancé and baby momma, Aria Scarlett.

Soon to be Aria Thompson.

Jumping to my feet, I search for a loose instrument cord and throw it Rex's way. "Plug it in."

The feedback whirrs at the contact but clicks when he seats the jack in the input of the guitar and that pen is back between his teeth when he strums the pick over the cords.

Left hand to the fretboard, Rex's fingers engage the strings for the right notes, playing the chorus of a brand new song as I walk-think over mats and wires.

I nod along as I read the shit on the page and mash it together with the cords he plays, which continues in my head even when he stops playing.

"I just don't know ..." He's on his feet and at my side with a finger to the words as I pause in my steps and notice the spot he's talking about.

"Speed it up," I say, my sight bouncing around to the tune building in my head. "And come in with the hook here." I point at the line, the one that leads to the slam of the music. The one where the beat drops and comes back harder than before.

Rex nods and steps back to reposition the strap over his torso and plays the section over again, but faster and harder than the first time.

Goosebumps rise on my skin as the notes ring loud through the venue, truly testing the speaker system and giving the techs a freebie to witness the great As Above in full-on writing mode.

"God *dayum*," someone says when the guitar stops and a silence falls over the stage.

Rex looks at me then, his smirk notched up, and meets my eyes.

"God *dayum* is right." I spin to the audio tech frozen in his spot with his jaw mopping the floor. "Get this man a fucking mic."

Chapter Three

Cedar

BASS THUMPS OVER THE speakers and echoes across the open floor to bounce off of the mostly brick walls of the tattoo parlor and reverberates right back to my eardrums.

Like a heartbeat outside of my body, the organ in my chest races to catch up with the rhythm as each roll of my hips spurs the beat faster, harder.

Closer.

Closer to that delicious edge where my brain stores all the feel-good chemicals that make stressful shit seem so much easier, and further from the compartments of my brain where the body aches and the overwhelm are kept. Further from the responsibility of planning a bachelorette party, where the knots in my back have knots that make leaning over to work so much worse, and definitely far away from being able to squeeze into a bridesmaid's dress I know I'm going to hate along with the ink show that has to happen before any of that.

And definitely far away from that nagging voice in the back of my head that sounds an awful lot like judgment for my life choices.

The organization of a four-day tattoo convention coupled with the biggest rock show in the history of ever is some of the worst planning I've ever had to do.

But it's what you do when no one knows you've tatted the neck of a bigshot rockstar and frontman like Rex fucking Thompson. And plan on marrying him to his future bride, who happens to be your bestest friend.

That's right. Cedar Jones—aka *moi*—is officially an ordained minister.

Who would have seen that shit coming?

"Oh, baby." The breathy words bring me back from the to-do list ranking itself from highest priority to the room and the taut thighs I brace myself on. The thick muscles beneath my palms.

Thighs I've tattooed.

A slamming body I've inked and seen naked a few times already.

"You like that?" My breathy tone is a little bit forced, a result of doing all the damn work.

"Yeah," the man beneath me groans, his grip on my hips tightening with each wave of my ass meeting his pelvis. "I love looking at your ass when you ride me."

"Then stop talking." I grind down until he's a moaning mess and drive myself closer to the only reason I'm doing him.

Reaching between us, I tweak my clit until he's filling the condom and I reach that delicious release that's almost as good as when I do it myself.

Simple.

Easy.

The best I'm going to get.

I'm up off him once I catch my breath, handing over his shirt and pants to get his ass out of my chair and moving on to the next thing he does with his life.

"You don't always have to rush me off, baby." The lopsided grin on his face suggests otherwise as he stabs his feet into his pants and pulls them up to sit low on his waist while I yank my tank back over my braless tits and jam my feet into my cut-offs.

"I got shit I gotta do, Trey." I shake my head and do up the button on my shorts when he steps into my space to place his hands on my hips, pulling me to his sweaty chest.

"I was able to get tickets." Trey's brown eyes sparkle as he leans way too close to my face, like he might go for the kiss I've been avoiding. "So I'll see you there."

"Yeahhh," I drag out the word and spin away from his grabby hands before his lips land on mine and make him think this is more than it really is. "It's a pretty big venue. Lotsa people. I'll be pretty busy."

Shoulda never told him I was inking there. Damn tattoo talk.

I've been to the show in the past.

Actually, every year since it opened, back before it became the huge ordeal that it is now. Just never as a vendor.

And it's a madhouse at best.

Clearing my throat and busying my hands with removing the wrap from across my chair, I avoid his gaze when he leans down to meet my eyes.

"C'mon, baby." I scoff when he improvises and instead presses his hips against my ass. "Let me take you out. Dinner. Breakfast. Something."

"Nah," I spin again and break free of his hold. "I gotta get shit done for the show. Thanks though."

"Fine." I lean over my station and toss trash into the can from the tattoo I finished on Trey only a half hour ago and breathe easier when I feel his heat back away from me as I straighten. "Maybe next time."

Before I can protest, Trey leans in and smacks a dry kiss to my cheek like that will get me to change my mind next time. It's sweet and quick, but I can clearly see that it means way more to him than it does to me when my shocked eyes meet his.

Trey keeps the contact for only a beat, then spins on his heels with his shirt wringing in his hands and walks out of the parlor without a backward glance.

"Thank, Jesus." I breathe in a fresh breath now that I'm alone and finish putting shit away so that I can find it later when I need it.

The man isn't a bad guy. He's just not something I'm looking to keep around for the long haul.

Because long hauls aren't my thing.

It takes only a few minutes to right the tipped-over bottles in my box and wipe down all of the shit used to ink Trey with a cleaner strong enough to burn my nostrils.

Tying up the trash bag, I ensure the used condom made it inside and knot the thing within an inch of its life and wonder why in the hell I always end up with the clingy ones. The crazy ones.

The '*would rather see you barefoot and in my kitchen*' ones.

The '*I wanna control your every action, but I won't tell you that until you're deep in love with me*' ones.

Huffing, I snag the bag and my phone and head across the shop to the back door. I burst out into the damp, dark air and fill my lungs with fresh oxygen that doesn't reek of chemicals and body odor.

Except, this breath is filled with the scent of rotting trash and possibly a dead body thanks to the week-old dumpster sitting just outside the damn door.

Near gagging and regretting the fact that I need freaking air, I scan the alleyway out of habit for any strange people loitering where they shouldn't be, and dump the bag before the rot can transfer via air. Not that I should be worried about any bodies or bums, considering the entire shop is on full security rotation since the moment that my best friend bagged a rockstar. It's just that some habits never die when I spend so much of my time with bikers, former inmates, and just all-around odd fucking people.

Sometimes shady is too shady, even for me.

I rush back inside, where the scent sanitizes my sinuses, do a quick scrub of my hands, and peek at my phone for the time to blink back at me. I only have a few minutes to kill before I have to get my ass next door and be a part of a party that's the weirdest celebration I've ever had to assist in.

Because my best friend and sister from another mister is in need of both a bridal shower and a baby shower, while her future husband is dead set on getting the show weekend started with a fucking bang and now this is seeming more like a party for the sake of a party.

As if the number one band in the country would need a reason to celebrate.

Which really means that the band will be present, which means that Fin will be loitering around like the weird people I was concerned about in the alleyway.

And I am not looking forward to it.

I just hope that the girly shower is enough to deter someone like him from hanging around long enough for me to do my duties as the future self-proclaimed godmother, and get my ass home to sleep off the knots in my back before I tear myself apart over the next four days.

When I finally kick my ass in gear, I walk the floor to make sure all of the lights and tattoo guns are off before locking up and walking the thirty seconds down the calm street to the storefront that shares an interior wall with the parlor I've rented a chair in since I completed my apprenticeship to start inking. The boutique and studio combination that Aria and her sister moved into in order to share their art with the world, boasting both their clothing designs and photography.

Today, however, that same simple display of Aria's newest masterpiece and Aurora's photos is, instead, covered in dicks on one side and baby shit on the other. The sheer ridiculousness of it has a laugh bubbling up from my chest when I pull the door open, and more laughter spills out of the lit space.

Balloons dot the ceiling in phallic shapes while confetti litters the floor in baby bottle cutouts I know are going to stick to the soles of my boots once I step inside and shut out the warm nighttime air.

"Cedar!" Arms are around me before I can make it more than two steps into the studio, the protruding belly of my niece or nephew bumping into my hip and moving me forward another step.

"What the fuck is all this?" I snicker into Aria's hair that flings around in her excitement and snort when she jerks back to hold my biceps in her hands and keep me hostage.

"More like who ..." My best friend rolls her green eyes but yanks me back to her fuller chest for a crushing hug. "Mac was left unsupervised."

I laugh and scan the room for the drummer and future brother-in-law. "They here?"

"Oh," she says as she leans back, takes my hand in hers, and drags me around. "They're in the back doing shots." She snickers over her shoulder and stops us in front of a table loaded with enough food to feed the whole neighborhood. "I banished them when Toby lost his brain and offered me a drink. Y'know, before Rex could fucking kill him."

And that has me snorting as my bestie fills a plate of food and pushes it into my hands as I look around at some familiar faces, some new.

A few of Aria's regulars fill the space, some of the ones she's managed to hire in the last few months to help her do the designs and the heavy lifting—which has my eyes searching for the shop mascot that turned out to be a bodyguard sent on Rex's dime to watch his girl while he was away. As my eyes sweep the space in search of Jonathon, they pass over some of the road crew for As Above that I've seen around, but don't know the names of, and finally land on Aurora's shiny hair haloing around her grinning face.

To which that grin is aimed at the one I was seeking out.

She's flat-out crazy.

Shaking my head, I bring my attention back to the woman of the hour and laugh at the second plate of food piled high in her manicured hands.

"Don't you dare judge me, C. I'm eating for two."

I snort. "You know twins are hereditary, right?" Aria's knuckles land right on the ball of my shoulder as I reach to snag a jalapeno popper, and shove it into my face. "*Ow.* What the hell?"

"You're going to jinx me," Aria huffs and finally turns away from the table to find a place to sit and eat for the three humans sharing the same body. "The doctor found no such thing, now quit it. I don't even like what this one is putting me through."

I roll my eyes and stand guard over my best friend as she practically falls back into the chair instead of lowering softly simply because she's so off-center.

I also don't miss all the eyes that watch her as she moves. The inconspicuous guardian angels that keep her in their sights, even without breaking the conversations in front of them.

And I love that so many people are looking out for her. Like she deserves.

"I hear it enough from my fiancé and his *own* twin, ok?" She looks up at me with a sparkle of anger mixed with amusement in her green eyes. "So don't add to the people telling the universe I need a second one in here."

"Ari," I snicker and kneel down to speak eye to eye. "If the doc hasn't found another one in there yet, it's a little late for a second one to just show up." I pluck a fried ball of something I haven't tried yet and shove it in her face. "Now shut up and feed my nephew."

Aria rolls her eyes and nearly takes my fingers with the bite.

Hello violence.

I toss another appetizer thing at her cheek and snort when it slaps against her glowing skin and lands right on the plate held in her palm. The laugh that breaks out in response keeps a grin plastered on my face until a certain flash of orange hair floats through the archway leading from the back of the house.

My stomach drops at the knowledge of who generally follows that particular redheaded bodyguard and has my chest tightening.

"My fiancé is going to accost you about another piece." Aria's words break through my concentration as I try to both watch for the lead guitarist of As Above and attempt to avoid seeing him at all costs.

"Oh, yeah?" I mutter and nibble on a chicken tender with darting eyes and half-focus.

Because all real focus falls out the window whenever Fin enters the damn room.

And I hate it.

He's just another reminder of that night all those years ago when I should have left on my own and didn't.

Aria speaks about the design her rockstar husband is thinking of getting—like I didn't practically force the last one on him—while I pretend that my stomach isn't trying to fall out of my asshole when Finland Montgomery strides through the very same archway his bodyguard just breached with enough confidence to draw every set of eyes in the room without even trying.

Every set of freaking eyes drawn right to the strong jaw that only smiles when he's good and fucking ready. To the tattoos that pop like street art on grey-washed walls, accented with glinting piercings that scream that there is definitely more hardware beneath the clothes that meld to his sculpted body and beg to be peeled off.

To which I am certain there are plenty of willing women—and men—ready to do just that with only their teeth.

And I cannot be one of them.

I did have a crush on Fin back when he played for the Saltwater Skulls, the band he was with before As Above got ahold of him. Way back when I saw him play some of his first live shows. Before he was completely covered in ink and piercings.

And as long as I don't act on it, then Jeremy's bullshit rots along with him, and I don't have an extra voice nagging me in the back of my mind.

"C," Aria leans in until her face is kind of in my line of sight, her belly preventing her from moving much farther. "You hear me?"

No way Fin would remember that night … right?

He would have brought it up by now.

"Uh-huh." I force a breath and blink away the trance the man puts me in with a hand through my hair. "Just tell him to come over after the show."

Chapter Four

Fin

"**S**O HOW DID WE manage to both open *and* close the show?" Mac asks like he expects an answer from any one of us. Meanwhile, my eyes wander over the party thrown in Rex's baby momma's shop for the woman of the hour and try to tune out the work conversation going on right next to my head.

That's for tomorrow's band to figure out.

Tonight is to let loose.

Except the place is mostly filled with people I see on a weekly, if not a daily basis, and is not at all what I thought this pre-show party would turn out to be.

"Do you even need to ask that question?" Leo's glass smacks the surface he sits it on with an eye roll I know the band manager is throwing at the drummer without even seeing it, because these guys have lived through the fog of it all together and still irritate the fuck out of one another. Since they were kids, they've dreamt of this and now that we're all here, it's still hard as hell to believe.

"Umm, because you're not that great, pea brain. So ..." Mac's shrug bumps my shoulder and draws my attention back to the bandmates that refuse to leave each other's sides, even when not on the stage. Unless they're in love like Rex.

I guess it's hard when two of them are brothers—of the twin kind.

"Maybe it's because of the singles," Toby, the secondary guitarist slash bassist, and resident definition of intoxication for our band, as evidenced by his permanently glazed-over brown eyes, pipes up like the conversation is a real one to debate and answer as he smooths a hand down his dark beard.

"Yeah!" Mac, wide-eyed, nods in a faux enthusiasm that has his dark blond curls flipping over the top of his trademarked bandana headband and a chuckle slipping past my lips. "That's it."

"Shut up, Einstein." I witness Leo's ice blue irises flipping to the ceiling this time and lift my glass for a sip that hides my snicker. "Look at him." The manager gestures across the room with his drink hand—effectively changing the subject before anyone's feelings can get hurt—to the vocalist of our band leaning over his very pregnant and grinning fiancé. "All *gaga* and shit."

"Hey." Mac's hand snaps out, his knuckles connecting with Leo's broad chest that I know is covered in tats beneath that crisp white shirt he wears like a CEO instead of a rocker. "Don't talk about baby girl like that."

"I was pointing at your fucking brother," Leo growls.

"Jesus." It's my turn to roll my eyes as the two start trading knuckles and pull a few snickers from those close enough to watch it go down.

Leo grunts as he snags Mac's flinging hand and holds him back from making further contact. "Would you fucking quit."

"Never."

Snorting, I shake my head and step away from the chaos with drink in hand before I get sucked in and lose any chance of getting laid tonight.

Which really isn't going to happen here anyway.

Pulling out my phone as I leave Leo and Mac behind with a tipsy Toby, I search the nearest clubs and scroll through socials for where the real pre-show party is supposed to be.

Except, I come up empty.

How the fuck is that?

I scowl and widen the search, but still come up with not much of dick to do around here.

Huffing more to myself than those that filter in around me, I shove the device in my pocket and spin with the intention of heading out only to stop when another body rams into mine and nearly falls to the floor. I catch her by her outstretched wrist and probably cause more damage than if her ass would have just hit the tile, but instincts are instincts and I'm yanking the lithe body back up to her feet before she gets trampled by the onlookers that skitter out of the way.

Toe to toe, pulling the woman back to her feet puts her tits right in my sternum, her bated breath rushing so heavily against my chest that it filters through my shirt and sends a spike of confusing chills down my spine.

"You good?" I breathe in her familiar scent and that *what the fuck* feeling has the hair on the back of my neck raising with each passing second that she neither looks at me nor removes herself from my tight grip.

Her chest heaves, her face down-turned, giving me an eyeful of deep black strands piled high in a bun on her head that's almost a whole foot beneath my line of sight.

"Um," the woman clears her throat, seeming to gain some of her senses, and twists her arm out of my grasp. "Yeah, just great."

When she looks up at me, her full attention on me for the first time since the night of the awards—all ocean blue eyes and sass—I feel my breath catch just a little bit and my brow furrow a whole lot.

Okay, what in the actual fuck.

"Cedar?"

"I'm gonna just ..." Clearing her throat and taking a step back from me, she knocks into another person, plants her hands on their arm to apologize, and just ...

Takes off.

Into the crowd like she'd rather be anywhere but near me.

"What the fuck." I watch her make her way through the crowd and almost ignore the draw to follow. And I swear I try really hard not to follow her, but the woman is magnetic with her swaying hips and inked skin so smooth I can already feel it beneath my hands, as she passes people and squeezes between the other patrons to evade me.

I'm pushing through the maze of bodies before I even realize my boots have moved, and tail the woman like a predator locked onto its prey.

"Cedar," I call for her, but she ignores me and keeps on walking at a brisk pace like I'm not right behind her.

Not that I know what I'm going to do once I catch her.

And maybe, just *maybe*, she didn't hear me over the roar of the party going on around us or the music now blasting from the speakers.

I know what I *want* to do, but that's all on whether she'd let me devour that porcelain skin and pound my cock between those thick lips.

Both sets.

With my cock filling at the thought, Cedar punches the release bar on the steel door that leads to the back alley and disappears out into the darkness as if she'd rather be caught with the vagrants that hide behind the dumpsters than anywhere I happen to be, even if that means leaving her best friend's party.

And that just won't do.

I follow her earthy scent out into the nighttime air, the music cutting to a muted volume once the door slams closed behind me and my boots hit the pavement.

"Cedar," I growl when the woman practically runs down the alleyway, hellbent on making it to her side of the building and shutting me out.

"Piss off," she shouts back, her hair falling out of her messy bun and trailing behind her as my boots pound the pavement in a desperate run to catch her before she can shut me out.

Why am I doing this?

I don't chase pussy.

"Goddamnit, Fin!" The words are out of her mouth before she can reach the handle and unlock it because I'm faster than her fumbling hands and my body is now wedged between her and her escape.

"Why the rush, Cedar?" I peer down at her, the keys still held in her tight fist, with the metal prongs sticking between her fingers like a set of brass knuckles prepped and ready to defend herself.

When all she does is stare at me with hauntingly blue eyes and wild hair, her chest heaving from the run—or possibly from how close we stand—I can't help but step forward and crowd her even more, forcing her to step back or come in contact with my chest to hers.

"You hate me that much, huh." It's not a question off my lips that tip up at the corner, but a statement that has her jutting her chin up in defiance.

"Duh," she drills her point down into my growing groin with the single syllable and bounces from one foot to the other. "Now what the fuck do you want?"

I purse my lips with a noncommittal shrug as I hook my thumbs into the waistband of my torn jeans and watch her watch me loosen my stance. Cedar's eyes dance down my torso as my arms fall loose at my sides, the pressure of my thumbs pushing the pants low on my hips, drawing her attention right to where my cock hangs thick between my thighs.

"Would it be too cliché to say …" When her hot sight travels back up my body as if I'm naked in front of her, I let my lips pull up into an evil smirk. "You?"

"Oh, fuck right off." Her ocean blues roll and she steps to the side, pushing past me to stop at the door to her side of the building with keys in hand.

"Aww, C," I drawl as I spin and shove my hands into my pockets so that I know I'll keep them to myself. "C'mon."

Her back to me, Cedar's shoulders lift in a deep breath of rank-ass stale air thanks to the dumpster right next to us, her hands paused in unlocking her escape as she mutters her response.

"You are *not* invited."

And with that, Cedar pushes her way into the shop and lets the steel slam between us. *Still won't do.*

I stand there, a smirk on my face for what feels like a whole damn minute as I take in the peeling paint of the steel door and listen for the snick of the lock to engage. But it doesn't.

So I do what any sane man that was just rejected would do.

I try the handle and find that it sets itself free from the jam and grants me passage into the back of the tattoo parlor.

A weird rush of giddiness flows through my bones, twisting my stomach in that feel-good flip that I get right before I walk onstage, as I push the steel out of my way and walk right into the place like I was invited.

Semantics.

Faint light glows in the distance like a beacon calling to me as I maneuver around boxes stacked high and shelves of supplies that make my skin itch for more artwork. Padding my heavy boots across the tile, I don't try to be quiet. I don't stop the squeak of my soles or the thud of my steps when I come into the main part of the shop and find Cedar standing in the middle with a goddamn baseball bat perched on her shoulder and a wicked smirk on her lips.

Fuuuuck.

The alluring sight of Cedar before me—her tits pushed out with nipples peaked through her tank and her feet standing shoulder width apart like she's a warrior prepared to fight for her kingdom with only the weapon readied on her shoulder—has my cock filling completely and my steps bringing me closer despite the neon sight screaming I shouldn't.

She looks otherworldly with her wide shoulders and tight body, her black hair falling around her in a darkened halo that only highlights her light complexion and makes the ink pop in the faint glow.

Angelic in a way that makes you suspect she's a demon in disguise.

Stalking right into her space, when I get close enough, Cedar swings the bat. The wood lifts from her shoulder and whips around close enough that I catch the handle, my fingers wrapping around the grip over hers and I yank her whole body by the weapon set to knock me the hell out until her body is crashing into mine and I can wrap my arm around her torso.

Heaving breath scorches down my throat as I bend to look her right in her icy, murderous eyes.

"You left it unlocked."

Tightening my grip on her, and on the damn bat, I slam my lips to hers with enough force that she's nearly bent backwards, and I feel it all the way down in my toes.

My cock punches the inside of my jeans when she drops the bat, the thing clattering along the floor somewhere behind me, to push at my chest only to fist my shirt and plaster her supple body to mine.

I know she can feel the heat that races down my spine when those same hands snake up to wrap in the hair on the top of my head and pull.

Just like I know she can feel my hard cock between us, pressing into her belly and begging for attention with each strand of my hair she tugs on.

But when I open my lips, the force of my mouth against hers opens her up to me and it's like I've opened the portal to hell and been granted all my dirtiest, wildest desires.

Her tongue slides against mine with a rush of breath that she loses down my throat. I don't stop my hands from finding the backs of her thighs and lifting until Cedar's legs wrap around my waist, my cock throbbing with the closeness of her pussy.

Holding her up with one arm, I follow her lead and wrap my free hand in her dark locks and yank until her lips pop free of mine and a guttural yelp rushes out of her chest.

That sound is gonna be the soundtrack of my wet dreams.

"*Fuck,*" I growl and trail my lips down her neck to leave scorching nips and licks in my wake.

I walk, taking steps until my shins hit a surface that I lean Cedar against, pinning her hips with my rotating ones.

"Oh, fuck," Cedar moans for me, right in my ear, and has waves of tingles shooting straight to my cock in a way that says I need to back off or get her naked. "This is a terrible idea."

But pulling myself away from this woman feels impossible when she hooks her ankles above my ass and grinds herself against my achingly hard dick.

"Decide," I growl into her neck, sinking my teeth into her delicate skin to keep from groaning even as my hands grip her hips and help her move against me in that delicious friction my cock is begging for.

"So good," Cedar whimpers, her non-answer enough of one for me, and I reach between us and pop the button on her shorts free.

I'm only milliseconds away from diving a hand into her pants and feeling how wet her pussy is for me when a ring sounds in the distance and has Cedar freezing beneath me.

"Fuck," I growl and snap away from her like she's on fire, my hands going to my hair as my feet carry me in a pace away from her sexy as sin fucking body that I watch skitter off of the tattoo chair and rush over to the bleeping phone.

"H-hello?" Cedar clears her throat, her spine stretching tall as she turns her back to me and takes a goddamn call like I wasn't about to fuck her brains out.

I reach into my jeans and fist my cock with the intention of adjusting the solid length so that my head isn't cramming into my zipper but only end up groaning as I stand there and watch her back while she speaks on the phone.

Moving my hand, I pump my cock until my eyes roll back and I regret not holding her down and ignoring the damn thing she is talking into right now.

Like she senses what I'm doing, Cedar turns to me, her eyes going straight to my bulging crotch as I work myself right in front of her.

"Yeah, I'm on my way." She pulls the thing from her face and ends the call without removing her burning gaze from me. But she doesn't come to me either.

Fine.

Two can play fucking games.

I bite my lip when a ripple of pleasure rushes over me thanks to the eyes that refuse to look anywhere other than me this time, and I work my hand over my cock in the tight confines of my jeans.

I want to pull it out. Demand she come to me on her knees and suck me until I'm shooting down her throat.

I don't.

Instead, I flick my frenum piercing and work myself until my balls draw up tight and my orgasm threatens to surface.

But when Cedar's full lip pinches between her teeth, her blues shooting to my face for a split second, I blow. Cumming right in my pants where Cedar can see none of it, I let my head fall back and I groan out the waves of pleasure that rival those I get when I'm with someone else.

And when I come down, blink my sight back into focus, and bring my eyes from the ceiling, my pierced brows furrow in confusion.

Because Cedar's fucking gone.

Chapter Five

Fin

MY SCOWL HASN'T LEFT since I strolled out of the tattoo parlor last night, alone, with a load in my jeans and a fuck-all attitude.

Even now, as my boys fall in around me and the crew finishes setting up for the opening show of the biggest rock concert held on this side of the globe, I still can't find it in me to feel that normal rush of excitement.

The adrenaline has left me high and dry as I strap on my guitar and listen to the crowd filter into the now-open gates.

I looked for her. Went back to the party raging in Aria's studio, searched the shop she left me in, and came up empty.

So like a sore sack of shit, I took my ass to the nearest hotel and booked a room for the weekend to crash in even though I don't need it.

I just couldn't go back to the camp with wet pants, yet nothing to fucking show for it.

And then when I woke up in an empty bed and rubbed another one off at the thought of her sweet, *sweet* body wrapped around mine, I came to the venue and looked for her again.

Still nada.

"Yo, Fin."

She does tattoos.

That means she'd be here.

"Newb." Rex's clipped tone and snapping fingers have my sight swinging from the growing crowd to his wild curls and deep scowl at the age-old nickname I've had since I joined the band. As the '*newbie*'. "You good?"

"It's literally been a decade." I roll my eyes and tweak the tuning peg, my fingers plucking absentmindedly to check the sound before plugging in and letting my fingers flutter over the strings of my Manson guitar. "Stop calling me that."

The sound filters through the stage sound system, peaking the festival goers' interest and getting thumbs up from the audio crew.

Placing a hand over the pickup, I stop the sound and turn to Rex with a cocked head when he whistles in my direction.

"You never answered me." Rex's shoulder nudges mine as he spins, his back to the still-growing mass just a few feet below us.

"About?"

"You disappeared last night, Newb." Rex shrugs. "But then you came back. Not normal."

I return his shrug and flick my sight from him to the people packing into the venue like sardines, watching us like hawks dead set on devouring any morsel of prey they can find, and my abs finally tighten in that weird rush of excitement.

"And then I disappeared again, but you were too busy trying to put a third baby in your girl." I scoff and swing my lifted brow back to my vocalist. "So mind ya bizness."

Stepping back from the conversation with a quirk to my lips, I flip a smirking Rex Thompson the bird—which gains me a few laughs from the milling crowd—and let my fingers fly over the strings to test the shit the audio guys did to fix their problem.

With my back to everyone else, I close my eyes and let my frustration out on the axe slung against my pelvis, only to have the cheers filter through my subconscious and stop me too soon.

"You ready?" Mac's hand lands heavy on my shoulder, his other one busy with twirling both sticks between his fingers as his eyes track me from beneath his black bandana.

I jut my chin in affirmation. "Good. Toby?"

"Uhhh..." Mac looks over to the side of the stage where As Above's other guitarist is stationed, a cup in each hand and his bass dangling down his broad back. "Close enough."

I snort with a shake of the head and ready my left hand on the neck of my axe, my fingers absentmindedly stroking the smooth surface on the back I can almost feel through the callouses built up from so many years of playing. "I guess so."

"Let's do this!" Mac hops on the balls of his feet, his arms flying up around him as he practically floats over the stage, his antics amping up those filling in the not-so-open spaces right up to the barrier that keeps them from us. Rex watches his brother with a keen eye and a shake of the head, but a small grin pulls up the corner of his lips.

"Oh, Maaaac," Rex calls into the mic, the grille pressed into his pierced lips. "Your spot's back there." Hand outstretched, Rex points to the platform set up with Mac's set and garners laughter from the crowd that watches the twins.

Mac throws his arms up, his hand going to his face as he spins to Rex. "Oh, jeez," he yells over the rising volume and takes off running to the back, where he catapults himself off the platform and over the drum set.

His ability to land without racking himself or destroying his setup has me laughing and tucking my pick between my lips to clap as the crowd around us burst out into a roar that hurts my ears.

Applause drowns out any further communication with my bandmates as Mac plants his grinning ass on his stool and holds out both drumsticks.

I see the cue coming from the drummer as he holds his arms wide, absorbing the noise made for him, and shove the in-ear-monitors in before I miss my mark.

"Good morning," Rex calls out to the crowd, his voice filtering through the speaker out loud and in my ear, causing the milling patrons of the event to literally run from every entrance of the venue. Bodies flood the remaining space, the ground before us covered. "We're As Above." Rex's arm goes up, devil horns to the sky, a grin on his already sweaty face. "And welcome," he growls. "To the *Setlist Music Festival!*"

Rex's arm comes down, triggering the slam of the first note to our latest single, and sends the mass into a wicked frenzy.

Propping my foot up on the stage monitor, my fingers flitter over the fretboard as I let the vibrations take over, the muscle memory taking me down each note like a breeze over my skin, and my head bobs along to the melody.

Cameras flash, drones flying by to get the perfect shot as we play, despite the photographers creeping in the alley between the stage and the barricade that barely holds back the mob of lifted horns and screaming fans.

Out of the corner of my eye, I see Rex strutting across the stage to Toby, the two singing into the mic together as Rex slings an arm around his brother from another mother. They stay like that for the next line in the song, the vocals harmonizing together, and Rex breaks away to come back to center stage and hold the mic out to the throng of wild screaming.

But when he leans over the stage monitor and counts down with his fingers, the mass before us engages the chorus on mark and sings our song back to us.

Chills race down my spine and pull up the corner of my lips as each word echoes from the venue, louder still when Rex uses his free hand to gesture for more. He sets back on his heels, his grin unmatched as he looks from me to Toby and back again with a shake of his head. Meanwhile, the drove of patrons sing through the entire chorus and only stop when Rex motions for such and takes back over for the next verse.

"Y'all don't even need me," Rex says on a laugh into the mic between lines as he paces the front of the stage and begins the next lyric like he didn't just use his breath to speak. The crowd goes wild with applause and nooooo's as Rex smiles out at them and does what the showman does.

He conquers the fucking stage.

By the end of the third song, I'm growling into the backup mic, covered in sweat, and peeling off my shirt—much to the ladies' pleasure who scream my name in return.

I watch on as surfers make it to the front of the wave from all the way in the back, a wheelchair popping up at one point to ride along with the other bouncing bodies and arrive safely at the security that holds the barricade back.

But I don't see what I'm hoping shows up in the crowd.

Even when I stride to the other side in hopes of catching sight of long black hair and eyes that haunted my dreams last night.

"So, brother, let's hear it then." Rex juts his chin at the axe at my hips and I take the cue.

The masses roar in response, clapping and yelling shit I can't understand thanks to the IEMs, but that doesn't stop the pride I feel from broadening my chest and widening my grin.

Leaning into the guitar with downcast eyes, I let my fingers fly over the strings, my pinkie curling around the whammy bar to manipulate the pitch as I work the frets. I take the riff into the sharper beat, quickening the notes with each pass, my lip pinched between my teeth as tingles race down my spine and I'm lifting to my toes to keep the momentum.

Is Cedar here to watch?

Until I slam the rhythm in time with Mac's bass drum and we're shooting off into the next song in the smoothest transition we've had yet.

I've seen her collection of our tees. She's gotta be here.

The vibe of the set goes on just like that, jovial and hard, but much shorter than a traditional As Above show, which is what happens when fifteen other bands need the same stage we're on for their sets. So we wrap it up, avoid the hoard begging for an encore, and hand over our equipment to the road crew for safekeeping until we need it again in another four days to close this shit out.

Without the in-ear-monitors, the roar of the venue deafens me, even backstage, as me and my bandmates sweat out the post-show adrenaline.

"Holy shit," Leo greets us in the fully air-conditioned artist-only tent with a giant grin and slapping bro hugs. "That was amazing."

"Damn straight it was." Mac nods his agreement, but his eyes are not on Leo. Instead, he scans the few unfamiliar bodies around us like he's looking for someone else.

"You're already trending." Leo produces a tablet from the waistband of his pressed slacks and flashes the screen with several windows open.

All of the popular social media sites display on the device, several sets of websites, some local news and one site for the festival itself.

And every damn one of them boasts pics and headlines from our set.

"That sounds like means to celebrate." I glance around at my crew with a smirk and before I can ask, a drink is placed in my hand and we're lifting our glasses in a toast.

"As Above!"

Shots are thrown back, cups are sipped and I'm heading straight for the dedicated bar near the back for the next round.

The cool air prickles my skin as I sidle up to the bartender—a hot curvy blonde with ink and pierced nips peeking through her barely-there top—and order another round through hooded eyes.

"What name you wanna put it under, darlin'?" A faint Southern accent has me biting my lip as the blonde taps away at her tablet with long black nails and tallies up each drink she pours.

"Fin'll do, darlin'." She flutters her eyelashes at me when I pull out my wallet, a grin on her full lips that has me running my tongue over mine.

I just need to get laid.

Then I'll stop thinking about Cedar.

And when she leans into the bar, pushing her tits in my direction for the perfect place to rest my eyes, I know damn well I could have her if I just asked nicely.

"What's your name, darlin'?"

"Oh, darlin'll do." She plucks the card from my offered hand and shoves it into the reader. "You planning on venturing out there much?" Her hot gaze slides down my bare chest, pausing at the rings through my nipples and I don't miss the nibble she gives her bottom lip when she gets to the trail of tats and dark hair leading down into the pants slung low on my hips. "Getting some more ink?"

Shit.

I had planned on it.

Until a certain artist had to leave me hanging in the middle of her parlor and left a weird as fuck taste in my mouth.

And now the thought of letting anyone else put ink on my skin makes it crawl.

The cock I thought would start filling at any moment remains flaccid in my jeans, the bartender completely unaware of the train of thought I was desperately trying to avoid ruining the chances of me laying her down behind the bar.

Goddamnit.

"Thinking about it." I snag up the drinks once she hands over my card and send her a simple nodding thanks over my shoulder as I fist all five glasses between both hands.

I walk back to the gaggle of fucks I call friends and pass out the drinks to each band member. We go through another toast, but it's somehow less enthusiastic this time.

Once the liquor hits the back of my throat, I growl and shake away the remaining post-show jitters and look around at my crew.

Rex is already on his phone, no doubt calling his girl.

Leo is keeping Toby from ordering another drink.

And Mac is practically vibrating, his eyes darting all around the tent like he's seeing ghosts. Or looking for them behind the canvas walls with his non-existent X-ray vision.

Jesus, I need to get out of here.

"I'm gonna go walk."

I don't wait for a reply as I set my glass on the nearest surface and head for what looks to be the exit.

Chapter Six

Cedar

"**S**ERIOUSLY, ARIA, GET YA boy."

My best friend snorts into the receiver on the other end of the line and rustles of fabric tell me she's shaking her damn head at the predicament I'm in.

"You're the one in his sights, C. That makes him your problem." I didn't tell her quite everything about running into Fin last night and part of me really wants to get this shit off my chest.

But it becomes awkward when too many people know that the famous guitarist stood in my empty parlor and jerked off inside his jeans.

Now how am I supposed to look him in the face without getting wet?

Like I wasn't already.

"Ugh." I pinch the phone between my cheek and my shoulder with that feeling of not being good enough tightening my chest as I lean into my case and pull out supplies to clean the chair I've already had a client in despite the fact that the gates have just opened.

Thumping bass rattles the walls, making the call a little difficult to hear, but I manage because I need the voice of reason to outweigh the voice in my head, which is only giving me two options.

Baseball bat or sex.

No in-between.

Fight it or fuck it.

And both are terrible answers that complicate shit. Like what happens after when he's done with me and finds the next groupie.

Unless it's sex with the ba—And I need to stop that right there.

"C'mon, was the kiss that bad?" I huff and scrub my frustration out on the chair like it's the one that forced me to walk away or ruin this new weird group dynamic thing Aria has brought us into.

Seeing Fin again after so long has been enough of a trigger for that voice in the back of my head that likes to ruin me.

"No," I growl out and toss the towel into the bucket sitting in the corner of my little makeshift shop. "It was great—that's the damn problem."

I ignore the snicker from my best friend and the list of As Above favs that blast over the speakers in the venue, loud enough to make my ears bleed.

Even if it speaks to my soul.

"I don't know what you want from me, C." Aria's chuckle echoes over the line and has my teeth grinding. "Why don't you just try hanging around him instead of bolting? See where it goes?"

I snort at Aria's response.

Her old ways of staying the course, where boring and comfort were her go-to responses for anything difficult, are still peeking through despite sleeping with a rockstar of her own. So it doesn't surprise me that her answer is to just 'hang out'. That's progress for my bestie. It's really amazing how much she's flourished in the wake of everything that's happened to her and I'm so glad I get to witness it while she still gets to keep the pieces of herself.

Not to mention that I find myself asking for her advice more often now.

I've always loved the shit out of her. I just love her more now.

"But I'm baking a junior rock god, sooooo..." A surprised laugh pops past my lips and brings tears to my eyes. "Or just sleep with him for real. Bet he'll be great in bed."

"Oh my God." Clearing my throat when people pass and eyeball my set up through the open canvas like they might be interested, I tip the phone closer to my mouth and whisper-hiss to my bestie. "Would you fuckin' stop it?"

"Aren't you supposed to be tattooing people at this point, anyway? Not focusing on Fin?"

Another snorting laugh has me covering my mouth so I don't look crazy to the people that pass me by and I grip the phone. "You are too much. Find the receipt. I'm taking your ass back to the store."

Aria's laugh filters through the receiver and has a smile plastering on my painted lips. "I know you love me. Now stop pretending like you fucking hate the guy and just, y'know ..." I see her shrug in my head as if my best friend is right in front of me. "See what happens."

"But I do hate him," I groan at my best friend, who has no inkling of all the reasons why sleeping with Fin would not be a great idea.

Reason número uno: Jeremy's a cunt that can't be right.

"Uh-huh," she mutters, "Keep telling yourself that."

Number two being that Finland Montgomery is besties with my bestie's future husband and that just makes things weird.

Not to mention, I wasn't good enough to keep Jeremy on the right side of sanity, so what the hell would I do to a rockstar like Fin?

"Love youuuu." With an eye roll and pounding walls, I return the sentiment and end the call with my best friend, accepting the first person that inquires about my chair.

I'm set up to do small designs, pieces off of a pre-made page customers get to choose from, which means the tattoos go fast and clean and leave my back in one piece as the As Above set comes to an end.

The roar of the crowd outside makes my molars ache with jealousy because they got to see the band perform and I didn't, but the steady flow of clients help make up for it.

Several patrons take cards to do larger pieces they talk about as I ink the small designs into their skin in this blistering heat, while others admire the album of my portfolio I have set up at the entrance. Photos that highlight my larger pieces, my line work, the detail, and fine colors. The black and whites.

The ones I'm most proud of.

And with each tattoo I complete, my receptionist takes care of all payments and patching up my work so they can resume the crazy festival antics without worrying about any infections.

Thank God for Ava.

The pounding bass of the next set has my teeth chattering and Ava dashing off into the wild in search of snacks and earplugs before my brain bleeds out through my ears.

Keeping one eye on the same fucking devil tattoo everyone seems to be requesting and the other on the money box at my foot, I lean farther into the client beneath my hands and switch the angle so I can complete the line without missing the stencil and tweaking my wrist.

Because this particular patron asked for this wonderful mark on their sweaty ass cheek, and I'd rather not have to put my forearm directly in the crack.

This was a terrible idea.

Whose idea was this?

Snorting to myself, I swipe away the excess ink and clean up the piece so that the butt devil can get the fuck out of my chair.

There's a line that's formed in front of my tent—much to my hope and dismay—and when I pat the now clean chair for the next client to settle in, my breath catches in my fucking throat.

Because the client now filling my damn chair is one of the rock god variety.

A shirtless one.

Sitting taller than me even on my lifted stool, and already covered in ink with a smug as hell grin on his kissable lips, Finland Montgomery stares back at me like he's the bird and I'm the prey.

Oh shit.

"There you are, sweetness." His voice is like sin dipped in honey, his eyes dancing with mischief that has my stomach flipping and my panties wishing they didn't exist.

"*Sweetness?*" Because I can't not throw shade, a defensive snarl lifts my upper lip when that twist in my stomach cements, and he runs a hand through his already sweaty black waves that just fall back into his eyes. "Gross."

Fin shrugs and lifts a pierced brow in my direction. "You gonna ink me or just stare?"

Flashes have my attention snapping to the entrance of my little parlor and my snarl ratcheting up. "No flash photography." I snap my fingers and point at the shocked-looking man with too much skin and even more sweat than the last one. "Uh-uh."

The wannabe photographer stutters an apology as I get to my feet and usher him back out of the tent with shooing hands. "But it's the guy from As Above. That's him, right?"

"Nuh-uh," I snap and release the flap that works as a door that pushes him back farther. "And this isn't a damn signing tent. Get the fuck outta here." Gesturing to the line of people that watch, I flick my hand in the direction of the other canopies housing a multitude of other artists. "Break time, folks. Come back later."

And with that, I snap the canvas door closed and spin on a snickering guitar god.

Who's undoing his fucking pants.

"What in all that is *un*holy are you doing, Fin," I screech and slap a hand over my eyes.

"Relax." I hear the eye roll in his tone as his silky words do things to my body that I don't want to think about. Can't think about. Shouldn't think about. "I got an empty spot right here."

Except, I'm still not looking at the man that is clearly pants-less in my shop and driving my adrenaline to the brink of stopping my wildly beating heart.

"It better not be your fucking dick." His chuckle does nothing to ease my shaking hands and raggedy breaths.

He's too close.

"Nah." Large fingers wrap around my wrist, the callouses on the tips grazing over the sensitive skin that shoots electricity up my arm and pulls my hand from my eyes that I keep squeezed shut. "That's covered."

I breathe in through my nose and curse myself for the deep inhale of all that is Fin.

Sweaty. Spiced.

Man.

"I swear, if your cock is out, you're going to lose it."

Fin's hardy chuckle, but lacking an answer, has me cracking my lids open just to see anyway.

Okay, no dick.

But holy hell, the muscles that create that deliciously defined Adonis belt leading down into his *low* jeans, one side riding down farther than the other thanks to the open fly, have my mouth watering and my hands aching to touch. To ink that bare spot along his hip that leads right down that line into his groin where his trimmed hair peeks out and taunts me.

I also don't miss the lack of a secondary waistband.

Which means he's fucking commando!

"Nope." The word rushes from my lips, breathier than I intend, and I spin away from the incubus hellbent on ruining me with a hand to my damp forehead. "Won't do it."

"C'mon, C." Fin's callused fingers wrap around my free wrist and send yet another shock of electricity up my arm and down my spine.

Which is precisely why the answer has to be no.

No way I can sit through even twenty minutes of that shit. When touching him feels like licking a nine-volt battery.

I swallow when he jostles my arm and the traitor wiggles helplessly in his grip. And even harder when his hold loosens and his coarse skin trails across my palm until our fingers hook in a loose intertwine.

Which is nothing compared to how my body completely stops protesting when Fin tugs on me and I'm stepping closer as he pulls my hand down. Now I'm touching hot skin that makes my fingertips tingle and my stomach flip just like those leading ladies explain in the smut books I like to read.

Shit.

"Right here." Deep and gravelly, Fin's voice tickles down my neck and has me poking my tongue out to wet my lips.

I'm still staring at the canvas wall and pretending like this is just a dream and touching a guitar god that I've wanted since I was a teenager is just a thing I can do. Something I can get away with.

I know it's not.

And that I'm not at all on the verge of hyperventilating.

But when I turn my head and see the tanned muscle beneath my touch, the sheen of sweat built up on his skin, and the primal look darkening his eyes, I snap my hand back like he's on fire.

Cradling my wrist to my chest, I take a step back from his wicked grin and ram my lower back right into my toolbox that holds all my tattoo equipment.

"Fuck!"

Rubbing at the aching spot, I turn away from the infuriating man in my chair and let loose a growl.

Still, he doesn't give me a reprieve as I suck warm oxygen into my lungs and curse again when all I inhale is him.

Fin's heat is at my back, his scent burning in my nose, his hands on me, pushing mine aside and rubbing the aching spot for me.

It's almost tender, which seems so unlike the Fin that I know.

But do you really know him?

Nope.

Right, thanks for that.

I shrug away from his grasp and the stupid voices trying to reason in my head and dip away from his grabby hands when he reaches for me a second time.

"I'm not inking you, Fin." I shake my head, my hair falling around my face, and let my palm rest against what's sure to be a bruise forming. "So can you just go?"

"*Go.* Seriously?" When I look up, I swear I catch a flash of hurt disappearing from his face and being replaced with a scowl as he growls out the words.

Angry. That's called angry.

He's fucking mad, genius.

"What?" I snap because dealing with pissed-off dudes works best with matched enthusiasm. Any other way just ends up hurting me. Standing straight and dropping my fists to my sides with a snarl marring my face, I burn the bridge I know that Fin was trying for. "Little boy never been told no before?"

My words look like they slap him in the face when he jerks back, his wickedly sexy brows jumping so high they disappear behind the dark waves that fall from the top of his head.

"You are something the fuck else, y'know that?" Fin shakes his head and yanks the shirt hanging from his back pocket to shove his arms into the material and force his head through the top. "Just keep running away, Cedar." His furrowed brow and flaring nostrils pop through the head hole and he somehow seems sexier now than he did a second ago.

Yep, I got lots of problems.

"I'm not playing this game with you." His angry pointer finger comes out and aims in my direction. "If it's no, then fucking *mean it.*"

And with a solid few seconds of intense as shit eye contact where neither of us back down, Fin finally buttons his pants back up and strides out of my tent with tense rippling muscles and a growl.

"Guh." I let out a loud breath, the concrete walls around me beginning to pound with the next set, and I dive for my bag to retrieve the pain killers I brought as I let my hand go back to coddling my newest injury.

That is not going to feel good later.

And it's all his fault.

Chapter Seven

Fin

ANGER, RIPE AND DANGEROUS, ripples through my body like a second wave of adrenaline that needs to get out somehow before it becomes a toxic explosion of bullshit that no one else deserves.

"Is that As Above's guitarist?" I hear the question aimed somewhere nearby, but keep walking.

How in the hell one woman can infuriate me to the level that Cedar has is beyond my comprehension. Not that I'm thinking with a level head, or the right one, or a logical mindset as I stalk through the center stadium and aim right for the artist-only area where I can find someone or something to put my hands on.

"That's Fin—"

Like a drink or some willing pussy.

"No way he's out here."

But the ladder sends me into a boiling rage when even my cock remains limp at the prospect and all I hear is the crowd losing their shit as I pass and the pounding bass drum echoing the beat of my racing heart.

"Fin Montgomery?" The closer I get to the stage and the show that's going on, the less I feel like disappearing into the back with the rest of the guys, especially with the group of fans that thickens with praises of my name off of their lips.

"Oh, hey."

I'll fucking burst with all this pent-up energy.

"Fin?"

If I stop to sign one *thing, acknowledge that it's really me, I'll get swallowed up.*

Growling to myself and ignoring the calls for my attention, the noise drowned out by the massive speakers facing my direction, I pivot my heavy steps away from the path that leads to the tent, and instead head right for the mass of packed in bodies.

Goddamn woman.

She's got my head all twisted up and my balls a severe shade of blue I've never felt before.

From purple to polka dot, I see so many walks of life as I squeeze my way farther into the horde, including Rainbow Brite and blacked out aliens, effectively losing the posse I'd gained and focusing on the heavy beat of the music that has my heart rate coming down.

Why do I give a fuck about a woman that wants nothing to do with me?

"She's a runner," I say aloud, earning myself a few side-eyes, but I've learned that people don't mess with you when they think you're crazy.

Angry lyrics scream over the sound system, accompanied by screams and growls into the microphone, and I find myself bobbing my head as I finally reach the spot I knew I'd find in a crowd for music this heavy.

The pit.

Letting out a heavy breath and stopping at the edge, I watch as several shirtless guys in the spaced-out center all bounce to the beat, their sharp eyes on each other instead of the stage.

There's already bruises coloring their skin, busted lips, and brows. Hair a mess. Dirt sticking to sweaty skin.

But grins on most of their faces.

Adrenaline courses through the air, making it almost crackle as those around the pit hold the crowd safely back and prep to keep the participants not so safely in.

And it's exactly what I fucking need.

I feel the beat rising, that repeated low hum echoing through my chest, slowly coming faster with the drop that's going to blow this venue up.

Which means it's time to get in or keep them contained.

So I whip my shirt back off of my torso, letting the material fly up in the air, and step into the opened space with the rest of them.

"You know the drill." The vocalist points his horns in our direction as the pit paces, the energy rising with each passing note, despite the straightforward signs next to the stage warning against what's about to happen. "Let's light this shit up!"

And with the slam of the bass, the pit erupts. The group of rowdy guys all run right for one another—myself included. Bodies fling and elbows fly as torsos bounce off of shoulders and skin slaps against skin.

An elbow lands on my cheek as the pit fills in even more and we're quickly packed in so tight that any movement makes contact with sweat-slicked body parts.

Pushing hands and shoving chests direct the flow of the crowd and I'm quickly swallowed up in the mass as feet carry us in a giant rotation, even as more bodies pack in.

Circling, running, keeping up to not get trampled, I hear the singer call out to the pit in encouragement.

And my lungs finally loosen the tension as I let the flow carry me with a grin that almost feels right.

Almost.

"Open it the fuck up."

I feel the rumble before I see it, and I grab onto anyone within reach. Bodies slam into me and force the entire circle several yards closer to the stage, and now I know that this one is going to hurt.

It's been a while since I was inside a Wall of Death.

And still, I find myself laughing as another surge flings me forward, now only a few feet from the lead singer that motions for yet another one.

"You guys are insane!" He laughs right along and rolls his hand in the air for another surge to build as his band heats up the beat at his back. "Grab him." I see his gesture in my direction and I'm thankful for the hands that propel me forward and push me over the metal barricade into the alley that separates the mob from the artists.

With a heaving chest, I jut my chin up at the man on stage who shakes his head of frizzy faded hair.

"That's what I thought," he says to me, holding the mic away from his mouth. "It's a real honor, man."

I return the tatted fist bump he holds out as his mic holding hand comes back to his chin.

"Did y'all know you were moshing with a fucking legend?" He backs up on stage, pointing repeatedly in my direction.

And because why the fuck not, I lift my ass up until the stage hits the backs of my thighs and I look out over the crowd, the ones closest to me with wide eyes and flashing phones as I sit proper and wave like a prom queen on a float.

"Finland Montgomery!"

The crowd roars in response, claps and horns rising above the sea of heads.

"Man, would you mind?" The singer—hopeful and starry-eyed—is speaking to me again, his head nodding to the guitarist who eagerly lifts the strap of his piece up off of his shoulder. "It's a serious honor that you're out there, man. Even if you don't know who we are."

I shrug and glance over my shoulder at the banner that damn near looks homemade.

Dreadful Souls.

Aren't so dreadful.

Pushing up to my feet and dusting off my hands, the guitarist rushes over to me and offers his instrument with a bowed head like it's a sacrifice.

Snorting, I accept the axe—and it's a good one—and lift the strap over my head to settle it across my bare torso.

"You know one of ours?" I ask the singer as the guitarist skitters back and snags another bass off of the rack just off stage.

"Who doesn't?" Singer scoffs and gestures to the crowd as his drummer shifts his beat that he's held and begins the intro to an As Above song from way back.

"I know you know it," the singer says into the mic and waves at the boisterous mass at his feet. "So let's fucking hear it."

He counts us in with a tic of his fingers and I'm off like a rocket as the beat carries me through the original As Above lyrics with an added raspy tone and a growling chorus.

God, these guys are good.

So I decide to fuck with them.

Test them, if you will.

And I change the key right in the middle of the song.

I whip around and catch the drummer boy that looks like a surfer with long hair and tan skin watching me over his set.

The guitarist cocks his head at me, his wild eyes shooting to the singer, and when the third set of eyes land on me, a grin stretching his face wide, he shocks me.

Mic to his chin, the singer lifts his free hand and belts out the notes in the right pitch to match my guitar.

Dreadful Soul's audience roars in response as the singer extends the last notes, the band taking his cue to stop with the drop of his arm.

I stand there, the echo of the music ringing in my ears, and stare at the kid—well, maybe not a kid—with the frizzy hair and colored nails. In his shirt that looks too big and his height that nearly matches mine.

"Holy shit."

"Fuck yeah."

The corner of my lips lift when the band rushes in around me, hands slapping my back and fists bumping congratulatory fists.

"You got a manager?" I ask the group, who all stare at each other in return, then turn to me with lifted brows.

"You're looking at 'em."

Oh boy.

I lift the strap over my shoulder and slip my phone from my pocket, my thumbs speed dialing Leo the second the device is free from the denim and the guitar is removed from my grasp.

Phone to my ringing ear, I gesture to the singer. "We're closing out. Be there."

I don't wait for an answer from the grinning fools. I just spin and stalk off stage down the back with Leo's voice barely registering in my ear.

"Please tell me they're at least good."

"That's exactly why I'm calling." I hop down the few stairs to the trampled ground between the barricades that lead to the area meant for staff and musicians.

"Better fucking be. That shit is already blowing up."

"Have Anna share a song she likes." I pass people with badges and cameras, security clad in all black despite the scorching sun overhead, and talk into the phone about As Above's PR rep.

"Anna doesn't do that, stupid." I can hear Leo's eyes roll. "I do."

"So." I shrug my way through a conversation that's taking place right in the middle of the walkway and stomp around a woman carrying a tray of drinks—one of which I snag as I pass. "Share a fucking song *you* like then, genius." Shaking my head, I tip back the drink and growl when the bitter shit hits the back of my throat. "I have no idea what that was, but it was not good."

"Stop stealing people's shit, then, *genius.*"

I stop, right in the middle of a walking horde, and swing around in search of the wily band manager. "How'd you know?"

"I do now." Leo's chuckle filters through the phone. "Did you tell 'em to come—"

"Yeah," I cut him off and resume walking even though I have no idea where I'm going. "Dreadful Souls. Work your magic, Le." I pull the device from my head to end the call before he can give me shit for the nickname he hates and look around me.

The pathway is lined with more canopies, similar to the ones out in the venue, and boasts all kinds of shit, just like they do on the other side of the stage. Just on a smaller scale with smaller lines and fewer bodies.

And, well, better quality shit.

Like the VIP of VIP sections.

My stomach growls at me when the scent of food wafts through the air and I follow with a lifted nose to the one that subtly advertises street tacos and margaritas.

I wonder if Cedar likes margaritas...

I pause. Once again stopping in the middle of a crowd that walks around me like I'm a tree rooted in the spot and growl at myself.

Goddamn, I'm thinking about her again.

I can feel the heat rising up my chest, whether from feeling like Cedar's playing me, or because I really am fucking curious, I'm not sure. Either way, it pisses me off so much I almost forget I need a damn shirt since I lost mine in the pit.

I step to the right and snag a band tee from the table next to the tacos without a care as to who's advertised on the thing. Holding the folded fabric up, the tenant waves a dismissive hand at me.

"On the house, man." His waving hand gestures to the small tv mounted in the far corner of his tent, the screen showing the current band on stage. "Great show."

"Thanks." I jut my chin but pull out my wallet and throw a fifty on top of the pile of shirts anyway.

I step back to stand in the two-person line at the taco stand and unfold the shirt. Shoving my arms and head through, the fabric stretches tight over my chest and hangs loose around my narrow waist and I glance down as I smooth the wrinkles out of the design.

In scrolled lettering, a skull stares back at me with flames shooting from the orifices, the band name repeated throughout the design in gold lettering to make the shape.

And I snort when the name registers.

Dreadful Souls.

"Next?"

Chapter Eight

Cedar

Gᴏᴅ, I ʜᴀᴛᴇ ᴛʜᴀᴛ I want to like Fin.

That a single touch from him can make me forget all my reasons why being anywhere near him is a bad fucking call.

And I also hate that my passion and talent leave me with a sore body that just wishes it could be massaged by rough, calloused, guitarist fingers …

Hell no.

I growl my frustration out loud and sink farther down into the tub of hell hot water that's so high up, it threatens to lob over the sides with each move I make.

The sexy rockstar with a knack for showing up at the wrong place at the wrong damn time—like anytime I'm in the room—has left me feeling achy in all the wrong ways.

Like taking over my mind the second he left my tent this morning that wasn't really morning anymore. And last night.

Which left me tense over each piece I did the rest of the day and wondering if he'd show the hell back up.

Only slightly wishing he would anyway.

Bubbles float along the water's surface, catching on the edge that holds the iced margarita glass and beginning to climb up the surrounding walls that leave behind an earthy aroma I was surprised to find in the hotel toiletries.

I think it's supposed to be the men's shit, though.

Snorting, I raise my hand from the water and reach with foam-covered fingers to the glass that'll help make all the things better.

'Cause it's not sad at all to drink margs in the bath. Alone.

Not at all.

Sipping, glad that the vendors are tasked with closing down before the last show of the night starts, I was able to make it to this lake of hellfire before traffic could box me in and make the bruise blackening my skin wait.

Which fucking hurts like a bitch.

And then I add in the fact that I hunched over bodies for ten crazy hours, holding a vibrating machine, and I'm surprised I can feel my entire arm.

Six hundred and sixty-five fucking people got that same damn devil head.

The same damn one.

To which I tried to convince the last chick in my chair to get the six hundred and sixty-sixth one, but she'd already made up her mind about the flaming skull. And security was literally at my door, rushing me along to shut down.

Lames.

I stretch out my loose legs because there's enough room in this giant tub to do so and tip back the rest of my room service alcohol—both wonderful fucking amenities I've never dared to splurge on before now—as my phone rings somewhere under the layer of bubbles coating the surfaces surrounding me.

Locating the thing and silencing the noise with an answer to my best friend, I push myself up just a hair in the tub.

"Did you see it?" Aria rushes out, her question echoed somewhere in the background by a second voice I recognize.

"Did she see it?" Aurora parrots her sister and has me sitting all the way up in the tub.

"See what?" I ask, my brow furrowed as I swipe down the notifications on my phone and see the list piling up. "What the hell?"

"The video," Aria chirps into the receiver.

"Of Fin," Aurora shrieks from the back.

"Umm ..." I click on the link in our shared message thread with a furrowed brow and watch the screen populate with a pretty epic pit. "He moshed? So what."

I go to swipe away the app when Aria's voice stops me.

"No, C. He played with them."

"And it's so good."

Alright. Just kill the cat now so it can come back.

I press play on the link and watch as Fin is lifted from the rushing crowd and plants his ass on the stage like he belongs there.

Because he does belong there.

With a bleach-blonde model at his side. Not someone like me.

Ignoring that voice, and the ones that chatter over my phone speaker, my eyes refuse to move from the embodiment of legendary as he's handed a guitar and straps in to play.

As Above's first number-one hit rings through the little speaker—one I vaguely recall hearing and rolling my eyes at, because who the hell covers a band that's there—and about halfway through the song, it changes.

Like the shit was practiced, Fin leads the pitch higher than the original and the vocalist tears up the challenge like his life depends on it.

"Holy shit," I whisper into the phone, pausing on the grinning faces of Finland and some band called *Dreadful Souls.*

"There're all kinds of rumors already," Aurora pipes up from somewhere in the back of Aria's half of the phone. "Like him offering them a contract kind of thing."

"Well, I guess they technically could do that now that they're on their own label." My shrug moves enough water that I hear some splat on the floor.

Oops.

"Rex doesn't know anything. I'm the one that showed him the video."

I grunt and swipe away the video with a new band name burned into my subconscious to check out later.

"That's cool." I hear it in my voice before I can stop it. The monotone attempt at not giving a fuck about the conversation, when in reality, I want to ask Fin how cool it was to play with an up-and-comer that knew As Above enough to sell it.

And I want to know how those talented fingers would feel on my skin.

Uggghh.

"Uh-oh," Aria sighs, her tone changing as she clicks on the phone. "Why are we all *'that's cool'* and not *'holy shit, my favorite guitarist'*?"

I mumble into the phone, words that aren't words, because I really don't know what else to say.

I can't tell my best friend that I can't like Fin.

And I certainly don't plan on telling her it's all Jeremy's fault.

And Fin's fault.

Okay, goddamnit.

And mine.

"Oh, kay." Air rushes over the speaker. "I'm on my way with waffles."

"Waffles?"

"Yes," my best friend hisses as keys jingle over the line and a door closes. "Because I'm hungry, and I'm sure your ass is drinking your dinner."

"Pffft. Don't act like you know me." I scoff and cradle my empty glass to my chest.

"Right …" Aria's breathless drag of the word has my lips pulling up at the sides.

"Fine. But bring more margaritas."

"*Tequila?*" I hear Aria curse under her breath, mention something to someone else, and a door slams on her end. "I'm even more on my way now."

"Don't forget the margaritas."

It doesn't take long for my best friend to have her new bodyguard banging on my hotel door—which I can tell by the deep thudding that can only come from a fist twice my size—and me dragging my pruning ass out of the chilled water to throw on a robe and answer it.

"I grabbed the shit you use for your back, too." Aria pushes her way into my room, pregnant belly first, with her arms full of items she dumps on the desk and spins to me.

One look and she shakes her head.

Because I have another room service margarita fisted against my palm and my hair tied up in a crappy half-wet bun thanks to the bath.

There might still be bubbles in there somewhere, too.

"Oh … kay." Aria turns to the security guard, with a name I can't remember, who still stands propped in the doorway and plants her palms on his chest. "We're good in here. Need girl time."

Pushing the man big enough to snap my poor bestie in two, she manages to get him in the hallway and lets the door slam in his poor, confused face.

"Food?" The sweet scent of sugary carbs fills the air around me and has my stomach roaring in response to the minimal food I've managed to consume in the last twenty-four hours.

"Yes." Clapping her hands together, Aria rushes over to the desk and starts unpacking the bags she brought, avoiding bumping her baby belly into the desk as much as she can.

"Here." Tossing the container over her shoulder, I snag the tube before it smacks me in the face and let the sentiment put a quirk to my lips.

"Thank you." Popping off the top, I squeeze the concoction I spent weeks researching how to make because the over-the-counter shit just didn't do the job, and fish my hand into my robe without dropping the terrycloth to smear it into the skin of my lower back.

"What the hell is in that again?" Aria's nose turns up when the herbs begin to overpower the scent of breakfast food.

"Coconut oil, beeswax," I mutter as I knead the slave into the bruised spot on my back. "Ginger, jalapeno for the heat," I groan when my fingers brush over the tender skin. "Green tea, and saffron."

"Well, aren't you a walking apothecary." Aria turns to me, Styrofoam tray in hand, and shoves it into my chest.

"Gimme a damn second," I mumble and tighten the rope around my waist, the slave already working its magic on my sore muscles.

Accepting the tray with my free hand, I dump the thing onto the foot of the bed and run to the bathroom to wash my hands.

When I step back into the room, Aria is already propped up on the bed, her back against the headboard and the remote in the hand that isn't already occupied with her tray.

And a Styrofoam cup with a straw across the lid on my bedside table.

"So," my best friend starts, speaking around her mouthful of waffles and bacon as she lands on a channel and keeps the volume low. "What's going on with you."

It's not a question that comes from her lips, so I take my time settling in beside her and mimic her stance with our dinner.

"So…" I shovel a bite into my mouth, my stomach revolting at the alcohol now that I've got food in front of me. "He showed up."

"Uh-huh." Aria makes a face that screams *duh*, including a scrunched-up nose and furrowed brow. "They only kinda opened the show today. In the same place."

"Thanks, Captain Obvious." I roll my eyes and stab another bite with the plastic fork and only kind of imagine it being Fin's face instead of the syrupy almost cake.

"Okay." Aria nudges my elbow. "So he showed up where, C?"

"Guh." I let loose a heavy breath and shove the destroyed bite between my lips. "My fucking tent. Asking for a tattoo!"

"Like, oh my God," Aria mocks me, her voice high pitched and her fork hand flipping her hair. "He came for a tattoo?" She slaps my shoulder and giggles—she *giggles*—at my dilemma. "To a tattoo tent? Stop. It." Rolling her eyes, she shovels another bite into her mouth and groans at the taste. "Jesus, this is good."

Snorting, I have to shake my head and look away because my best friend and her hormones are just too much to keep from laughing at.

"Did you find the damn receipt?"

Aria's furrowed brow meets my gaze as I pinch both lips between my teeth to stop the laughter that threatens to explode.

"Oh, what*ever*, C." Realization sinks in at my earlier request to return my best-est friend back to the store I found her in because she is too damn right and I'm not ready to admit it.

Slapping my shoulder and grinning, Aria sends her last bite down the hatch since she's eating for two and sets the tray off to the side of her larger than they used to be hips. She tilts her bigger-than-it-was-yesterday ass, wobbling her torso until she's facing me and sitting with her legs only kind of tucked under her.

She stares then, her lips firmed and her forehead wrinkling with the vee popping between the perfectly shaped brows on her glowing skin.

I kinda hate that even when she's concerned, she still looks happy.

"Damn you," I say, shaking my head and dumping my dinner on the nightstand. "What do you want me to say?"

That look, the one that screams *duh* shows back up. "That you like him."

"Ugh." I roll my eyes. "He's cute, okay. Fine."

"Uh-huh. And you fucking like him." Not taking the bait, Aria's brow wings in expectation.

"I don't know him."

"And yet," she emphasizes, her hands going out to her sides. "You never shut up about him. Even before me and Rex—"

"But—"

"Nuh-uh." She wags her finger at me. "No, you totally have been obsessed with Fin since ... well ... as long as I can remember."

"Ugh," I growl at how close Aria is to me and curse myself for letting the woman past some of the walls. "Because he's a fucking legend."

"Is that what this is about?"

"Don't you dare tell him I said that. Like ever." My pointer finger comes out despite the eye roll from Aria and I pop up off the bed to pace the room.

"C, c'mon," Aria sighs as she watches me meltdown.

"I told him no, and he got mad."

"Umm." Aria's brows wing up to her hairline. "You better explain in the next five seconds before I have to call Rex."

The thought has me freezing in my trek across the room as Aria sits up on her haunches and watches me with a fire in her pretty green eyes.

"No, Ari." I hold my hands up, palms out. "Trust me, it wasn't like that."

"Oh, thank God." Letting out an audible breath, Aria settles her ass back against the mattress and holds a hand to her chest. "Now spill before I have a heart attack and the baby ends up on your sheets."

"Ew, gross."

By the time I finish telling Aria about touching Fin's hot as hell vee and then kicking him out after ramming my own self into my toolbox like a total fool, she's shooing me to the bathroom to throw on clothes so she can see the spot I can feel with every movement I make despite the magic salve.

So, I do.

Throwing on an old band tee—an As Above one from their first stateside tour, ironically—and sleep shorts, I come back to the bedroom to find her lashes fluttering closed and her hand resting on her protruding belly.

I stutter out a breathy laugh and dig in the closet for an extra blanket since my best friend decided to fall asleep on top of the damn comforter.

After snapping a pic and sending it to her rockstar fiancé, I snuggle into the mattress next to the woman I wish I could be when I grow up and flick through the channels on the TV.

Soft snores echo around the room, a buzz from my phone keeping my own eyes from drifting closed.

Rex: *That's my girl right there.*

Me: *You know I'll create a monster if I wake her up.*

I set the phone next to my head and turn back to the TV when the buzz goes off again.

Rex: *Yup. Which is why I'll bring breakfast in the am.*

It's almost as if I can hear him saying the words out loud.

Rex: *No monsters needed. My wife is baking my baby and needs the sleep.*

I snort out loud on that one and shake my head into the pillow.

Me: *Uh-huh. Cuz you totally let her get any of that.*

Rex: *Oh, she always gets it. Whenever she wants it.*

Rolling my eyes, I send a goodnight text to the man that helped make Aria a better version of herself and I ignore the ping of jealousy that knocks on my rib cage.

Because that's something I'll never have.

Chapter Nine

Fin

"**Y**OU COMING?"

Looking up from the carafe in my hands, the lid held tipped back with my thumb pressed into the little dip on the handle, I raise a brow at the long-haired lead singer that's only a little bit jealous I got on stage with another band.

It was all in fun.

"The fuck I wanna get breakfast with you for?" I snort and blow into the steaming brew before sipping a scolding hot drink that burns all the way down to my stomach. "This ain't no date shit. I'm not doing the walk of shame for you, Rex."

The man in mention snorts even though he scowls and slings his gig bag strap over his shoulder. "Not a walk of shame, Newb. An invite to come with."

"To a random hotel where your girlfriend stayed last night?" I'm already shaking my head and lifting the carafe back up in the direction of my caffeine-deficient lips.

It's too early for this shit.

"My wife—"

"She's not your wife yet, horse hoof." Mac bounds into the space from the back of the bus, his bandana wrapped around his flailing bicep instead of his head and a shit-eating grin plastered on his face. He's sweaty already and missing his shirt. "There's still time for baby girl to come to her senses."

Rex's resounding growl pulls a chuckle out of his twin, who dips just out of the vocalist's reach when he swings a fistful of knuckles. "My 'soon-to-be' *wife*."

"It's called a fiancé," I correct from behind my makeshift mug with a smirk and sip the steaming lifeforce as the twins begin to rumble around the cabin, eliciting more laughter from Mac. "At least we know she's not after your brains."

"Fuck both of you." Rex lands a thudding jab on Mac's torso, which is followed by an *oomph* from the younger of the two, if only by a minute or so, and another round of laughter is filling the air.

"No thanks," I say, but I'm drowned out by the antics of the brothers that are from the same mother who end up head-locking each other like this is some kind of grappling match.

It doesn't take long for As Above's head of security to recognize the amount of noise coming from the cabin and come stomping inside to pull the twins apart, fully prepared to whoop some asses.

And whoop ass Ian does.

At some ungodly height and muscles for days, the head of security commands your attention with just one look that has even me sitting just a little taller in my seat.

Only a little bit.

"Seriously." It's not a question off of Ian's lips, but a roll of the eyes and a snatch of both twin's scruffs.

Ian's been with the band long enough to assume the clearly unwanted role of band ref turned twin mediator only for the antics to return the moment his back is turned.

"What?" Rex huffs and steps back to cross his arms over his thick chest while his brother squirms against the hold of the man that's the closest thing to a dad I've seen these two have.

"He started it."

"Jesus," Ian sighs into the shake of his head and plants Mac on the couch beside me with enough force that the cushions puff up on my side. "Could you two for fucking once stop fighting?"

"Never," Mac declares, his middle finger raised in the direction of his twin, who fires a set right back.

"*Vida.*" The deep snap comes from the back of the bus and belongs to the one man that can get Mac to calm down.

Even if it's only for a minute.

The same man that was blamed for the leak of a video that happened to occur in Mac's hotel room and received a broken nose, curtesy of one overprotective and concerned twin.

I still don't know how the hell he got back on the job, or who was really in the video, but I guess that's not mine to know. As long as Ian's good, Rex isn't breaking noses or worse, and Mac is cool, then so the fuck am I.

Bigger fish and all.

Like making sure no one gets too close to Cedar.

"Not fair." Mac shoots up from his seat and heads after his bodyguard, who is also missing his shirt, and I try desperately to ignore the undone jeans around his trim waist.

"You're the one that said you wanted to run. Now let's go." Jordan Kauffman wraps his thick and newly tatted arm around the back of his client's neck and drags him the rest of the way down the short hall to the room in the back of the bus.

"I said *cardio*," Mac mutters as the door slams behind them and shuts them off from the rest of us before he can say any more shit I don't wanna know about.

"So?" I turn to see Rex towering over me, his hand held out in offering. "We eat and we write."

Furrowing my brow and rolling my eyes so far that they actually hurt, I sigh and slap my free hand into the lead singer's palm. "We better fuckin' write this time."

"Yep." I force the man to lift most of my weight up off of the couch until I'm the one towering over him—if only by an inch—and hold up the carafe still attached to my other hand.

"But I'm taking this." I take a sip when Rex steps back, certain that I'm not going to flop back into the comfort of my seat, and release my index finger from the handle to point it in his direction. "And you're buying me more coffee."

"Fine," Rex mutters as he rolls his eyes and adjusts the strap of his guitar bag back onto his shoulder.

Almost like it was practiced, we both turn to Ian, who stands at the ready, his eyes peeking out of the blind of the little window set in the door, then we both look at each other.

"Ian," I poke.

"There's going to be a shit ton of people," Rex adds oh so helpfully.

"Shut up," Ian mutters.

"We're camped right inside a music festival," I state.

"I can feel the fucking bass from here," Rex comments, his lips pinched between his teeth to tame his rising laughter.

"Can you two let me do my job?" Ian growls, his sight not leaving whatever target he's zeroed in on and I have to bite back the grin that threatens to break free when Rex's brow wings in my direction.

Fairly sure that was a non-verbal way of saying that we need to make Ian's life difficult. Okay.

"Or," I start and tag my knuckles against Rex's bicep when he inches closer to the irritated security guard.

"You could let us do ours," Rex finishes. I snort at that when Ian's heated gaze swings on the two of us now standing right over his shoulder in the cramped space that was not meant for one six-foot-tall guy, let alone all three of us over that.

Ian releases a growling sigh and tosses the door open, leading us out into the wild that is the backstage camp of the venue.

Cameras flash and backstage passes bob past as we make a quick escape down the side of the RV to the gap in the fence with one of our security vehicles parked just on the other side.

"They weren't supposed to let all these fuckers back here," Ian growls once we're all secured in the vehicle and the engine roars to life.

"You say that like other bands and staff can't be fans, too." I snap my seatbelt in place when Ian floors the SUV out onto the service road in the direction away from the venue.

"And like they aren't inviting fans in to 'hang out'." Rex uses air quotes to make his point, securing his guitar between his knees so he can hold on for dear life when Ian turns a corner too fast.

"Yeah, yeah," Ian huffs, his eyes darting from the windshield to the rearview. "Just makes my job harder. As if you fuckers don't do that enough as it is."

Rex snorts and slaps a heavy palm on Ian's shoulder. "You love us."

"Fuck you."

I can't help the laugh that bursts out past my lips and fogs up the windshield as I hold out my makeshift mug, maneuvering the thing in the air to make sure none of the liquid spills in my lap.

Don't want to add burned balls to the already blue ones.

"You're not the secret service, Ian." I clutch the oh-shit handle when Ian whips the SUV out onto another street with little regard for who else is around. "And that's not the endangered president in the back."

"Hey." Rex reaches between the seats and slams his raised knuckle into the ball of my already bruised shoulder. "I could fuckin' be."

"Pffft," I scoff. "In your fuckin' dreams, dillweed." I grimace and switch the carafe to my other hand so I can rub at the one now radiating tingles clear down to my elbow that may or may not have slammed into multiple humans just yesterday.

That's also bruised.

Stupid mosh pit.

I loved every minute of it.

The sloshing of the coffee in the carafe reminds me to take another long pull from the now-cooled elixir that's just the right temp to not burn, but still warm its way down.

"Did you really have to take that from the bus?" Ian shakes his head and eases the car into a parking lot at a much slower speed now that he knows we weren't followed.

"Yup."

I swear I catch him hiding a chuckle when he leans to check his blind spot on his left, but when he faces back to the front, all humor is gone from his straightened face.

"Cold, Ian."

"Again," he mutters and throws the SUV in park. "Fuck you."

The bodyguard's boots are hitting the pavement and circling the SUV before his door can even finish closing. He's got his hands to both handles for mine and Rex's doors and flings them open, only to leave us staring at his back as he just walks away from us.

"Hey," Rex calls as he unfolds himself and his instrument from the back seat. "Where the fuck you going?"

Ian's large shoulders lift and I slam my door at my back after securing my now empty carafe on the floorboard as Rex's chuckle echoes beside me.

"Looks clear as fuck to me," Ian calls, his feet carrying him closer to the entrance, which happens to be an old rusty door in the back of an establishment that looks like it could use a little TLC. His meaty fist raises, pounding on the surface that threatens to crumble under his assault. "No one said you had to get out of the fucking car."

Looking around, I note the alleyway we've parked in the middle of that's surrounded by destroyed brick walls. More pebbles and glass litter the ground than actual asphalt, with a rickety fire escape that hangs lifeless just overhead. The supports and paint long ago wiped away by the years of severe weather and serious hoodlum abuse—as if the graffiti painted onto the brick and the bars on the windows weren't enough of an indication.

I dig into my pocket, fishing out my phone and snagging Rex so that his shoulder bumps into mine. I regret the closeness when pain shoots up my arm, but raise my phone with the camera app open and snap a selfie with the grinning lead singer anyway. I snort when he raises a middle finger to the phone, and join him with one of my own.

It takes two seconds to upload the photo to socials with the single hashtag—*where are we?*—just as I have been doing since the night this tour started.

"Where the hell did you bring us, Ian?" I step closer to the bodyguard's back and tap his shoulder.

"Best breakfast in town. Again," Ian says as he throws his glacial blue, almost grey, eyes over his shoulder and tilts his head back to the car, "didn't say you had to get out."

"Right," Rex snorts and tugs to adjust the strap of the guitar he should have left in the car when the door flings open and we're rushed inside by a man clad in an already stained apron and one of those weird cook hats.

We're silently led through the kitchen, Ian taking up the back of the line like the guy in front of us is kosher, and don't stop until we're in some hallway that seems to be between where the food is prepped and where the patrons sit. The scent of bacon grease and fresh bread thickens the air in the cramped space and makes my mouth water.

The cook and our bodyguard share a single look before the apron strides away from our group and leaves us standing just down the way from the bathrooms and the milling customers taking up tables in the dining area.

Leaning around Ian to catch a glimpse of the end of the hall, the bodyguard snaps a hand out against my chest and forces me to reverse my steps until my back is against the wall and his bulky frame blocks the view of anyone that happens to get curious.

"Aw, c'mon." I roll my eyes and push his hand away, even with the icy death stare that lands on me. "What's the point of coming someplace like this if we aren't going to check it out?"

"Safety, Fin." Ian rotates his head on his neck when I can see that his rolling of the eyes is no longer conveying the true irritation tensing him up. "Fucking safety."

"I'd also love to actually get to my wife sometime today," Rex pipes up and leans his head back on the faded wallpaper holding the drywall together.

"Not your wife, yet," Ian quips.

"Fuck you, close enough." Scoffing, Rex runs a hand through his hair like his nerves are starting to get to him and props a foot up on the wall beneath him with his gig bag leaning on his raised knee. "She said she was hungry when she woke up. That was almost an hour ago."

"Shit." Ian's watchful eyes do a sweep of the hall and come back to land on Rex. "Only a few more minutes."

"Until all hell breaks loose? Yeah," I return. The down-turn of his lips and the furrow to Rex's brow almost makes me feel bad for the woman who's carrying his baking bun. Almost.

"She'll survive, Rex, Jesus." I roll my eyes but keep my ass planted against the wall when our escort shows back up from the dining end of the establishment with a damn box wider than him in his grasp.

"S'all here, man." Ian and the cook share a look over the box as it's exchanged from one set of hands to the other.

"Next time, don't come through my kitchen." We're pointed to the opposite end of the hall where an exit sign lights up the ceiling in a neon orange and we follow the direction until we're back out in the open air and nearly a block down from where we parked the car.

"It smells fucking great," Rex mutters as he accepts the box from Ian and shoves it and himself back into the back seat. "So hungry."

I snort and slam myself into the front as Ian jogs around the car and plants his big ass behind the wheel. "That's the real reason for the rush, wasn't it."

"You try to live with a pregnant woman," Rex growls as he fishes a container out and pops it open. "I give half my damn food to her."

"Then maybe don't make a baby so damn big." I chuckle and snap my seatbelt in place. "She's a grown-ass woman, Rex." I face the front when all I really want to do is snag a container for myself. My own stomach growls as the engine roars to life and we're back out in the still-early traffic. "She can feed herself just fine."

"Shut up," Rex grumbles around his mouthful. "You sound like fucking Cedar."

I feel my face fall almost as quickly as I hide it when her name rolls off his lips.

Shit, I didn't think about her being there.

"*Beeee bah bee baaah bebebe,*" Rex mocks in a high pitch. "I *know* my girl can take care of her fucking self." He reaches between the seats and smacks my cheek with a piece of bacon that leaves a streak of grease behind. "But I want to, too."

I sigh and rip the thinly sliced meat from his grasp when he smacks me with it again. "Pretty sure that makes you fucking whipped, bro." I take a vicious bite out of the strip and grind it between my teeth.

"Meh." I catch his shrug in the rearview mirror. "I call it in love, but whatever. I'm here for it."

Snorting, I force the bite down my dry throat and wipe my palms on my thighs. My shoulders are tight when Ian pulls into another parking lot, tighter than they get before my guitar strap lands across them on show nights.

Is it too late to back out?

"Get me to my wife." Rex bursts out of the car the moment it's mostly stopped and leaves Ian cursing from the driver's seat, the box of food and his instrument completely abandoned in the back.

Goddamnit.

Inhaling a deep breath that burns my nose, I sigh out the oxygen and fold my body out of the car to collect the shit Rex left behind.

There's a pregnant woman inside that needs to eat.

Or, at least, that's what I tell myself as I sling the gig bag over my back and collect the box of delicious-smelling shit instead of taking the car back to the bus.

And I completely ignore the way my stomach lifts with the possibility of seeing Cedar.

Chapter Ten

Cedar

THE HOTEL COFFEE IS subpar at best, almost burnt tasting when I leave the mug on the warmer for more than the five minutes it takes the single cup to fucking finish percolating.

"They're finally on their way," Aria says from her spot on the bed, where I left her. She hasn't moved since I came into the bathroom to start getting ready with a promise that breakfast be delivered soon.

"They better bring good coffee. This shit is gross."

"I told you to wait."

Rolling my eyes and dumping the brew straight down the sink with a scoff, I start applying my mascara when a knock at the door has me peeking out to watch my best friend trying to scoot her ass across the bed and the door opening despite the lack of invitation.

Rex is the first one through, simply because he muscles his muscle aside, and I dip back in the bathroom when he and Aria lock lips in the middle of the room like no one else is around.

I love her. And I love that she's happy.

But ew.

Swiping the black shit onto my lashes, to match the smokey black stuff that makes my blue eyes pop, I shove the applicator back into the tube and toss everything back in my little bag.

"Jesus, can you two get a different fucking room?"

The booming voice has me freezing with my hands against the collar of my very revealing, mostly sheer, top that I brought in hopes of drawing more customers. Swallowing hard, I look down at the handmade piece courtesy of my best friend's handiwork; this thing only covers my nips with black embroidered snakes that disappear down my torso and into the high waist of my black cutoffs. The rest of the top practically matches my skin in a way that makes it disappear aside from the snakes, the dark hemming around the armholes, and the high neck. It's lightweight for the unbearable heat with a side of sexy that shows off the ink I worked hard to get.

I'm not wearing a bra. My thighs are covered in fishnets. And my lips are so deep a red that there's no way I can walk out there in front of him without feeling naked.

Shit.

I snag a hotel robe from the back of the bathroom door to cover up, even though I have every intention of wearing this out in public, and wrap myself up in the terrycloth.

It's different when your bestie has had a chance to hype you up first. Which is exactly what I was going for before the texts came through that Rex was on his way with food.

"Seriously, bro." Fin's broad back is to me when I emerge from the bathroom and I am smacked with the scent of food and man that makes my stomach demanding and crampy. "I'm all for porn, but not by people I know."

"No shit." I fake a gag at the couple who get a little too handsy and walk around the group to the food. I allow it to take up more of my focus than the man I'd like to get my hands on just as much as Aria does with hers. "Fucking gross."

"Shit—"It's silent, said under Fin's breath, but I don't miss it. Even with my back to him and the tingles that threaten to undo my concentration on filling the plate in my trembling hands, I hear the surprise in his voice.

"You got her all night," Rex complains when he finally comes up for air.

"Yeah ...," I drag out the word, ignoring the heat I feel at my back. "Not to make out, though."

"Better fucking not," he says as Aria's squeal echoes through the room when Rex swoops in and hauls her up until she's half wrapped around him, half falling onto the bed.

I spin on my heels, avoiding the way I have to sidestep a way-too-quiet Fin and thrust the plate in my bestie's hands before they land in places on her rockstar lover that I'd rather not see now that he's hers. "You're going to make those babies pop out if you keep doing that." Once my hands are free, I land a solid smack on Rex's bicep, and only chuckle when the rock god practically yelps.

"Would you please stop telling the universe that I need two of them. Please."

"Damn, C." Rex lets Aria slide the rest of the way down his body as she chuckles and eyes the plate in her hands, careful not to spill any of it while her man's furrowed brow lands on me with a glint of humor in his eyes. "I thought the guys were fucking bad."

"She's worse," Aria jabs, her mouth already full of her breakfast, her fork tines pointed in my direction as she chews. "So much worse."

Snorting, I shake my head and turn back to the array of shit placed out on the desk and pick up a hashbrown for myself. One of the good ones, where it's almost the size of a piece of bread and perfectly golden brown with just a bit of crisp still clinging on despite the trip from the restaurant to here. I tear off a piece, even when I really want to just tear into the thing, and place the bite between my lips to avoid messing up the still setting lipstick.

The buttery potato goodness almost makes up for the hole that's being stared into the side of my head with each bite. Almost. But I nearly groan anyway and pop another tiny bite between my lips.

I wasn't expecting to eat for an audience.

"You would think that someone like you would know how fucking rude it is to stare." I cut my sight over to Fin, whose features are sharpened, his chest engorged, and I can't help the way my eyes harden and my pulse quickens at the sight of him.

"What the fuck are you doing?" Only his eyes move when his attention darts to the torn up hashbrown in my hands, then back to my face. "You afraid someone's going to see you eat the damn thing?"

Why does he sound so mad?

My nostrils flare at his words—because I have been criticized about eating in my lifetime, thanks to shitty people like my ex—and my stomach does a little flip, making me feel nauseous that maybe that is what he's saying.

The attention is too much.

He is too much.

"I don't wanna mess it up." The excuse comes out quiet, weak, and a whole lot not like me when I gesture to the color on my lips. I worked too damn hard on undoing all the shit I've been through.

So why does the heat in his gaze make me feel so damn small?

What I expect is a roll of the eyes, a shitty comment about not needing the lipstick, or maybe even a shrug and a dismissal.

But Fin has never been one to do what I expect.

Nope.

I subconsciously jerk when he steps forward, his scowl so deep on his face that his eyes are shrouded in a shadow that is both terrifying and intriguing. Fin wraps his large hand around my wrist in a way that's not so different from just yesterday as he leads me over to the only rollie chair in the room. The calluses on his fingers course over my skin, the feeling pulsing in my panties, and he pushes me back until my ass hits the cushion.

Taking the torn-up potato from my hands, he tosses the remnants onto a plate, along with another full hashbrown and a helping of eggs, and sets the serving in front of me with a little more force than necessary. He then snags a fork, tosses it on the plate, and repeats the process with another helping I assume is for himself.

I watch the man with a certain level of awe, confusion, and a tinge of anxiety as he piles the second plate high. Nerves battle themselves in my belly as I study the way his hands move and the tattoos that ripple along the thick muscles on every inch of exposed skin. My heart patters a little differently when my gaze comes up to his face and rests on his blue eyes set beneath an arched, pierced brow and above a pierced nose.

Eyes that dart over to me, down to my untouched plate, and then he's gone. Stalking into the bathroom and moving enough shit around that it sounds like he's practically destroying the place, he comes back out with my little makeup bag—the black one with little sparkling blue bats patterned over the surface—and slams it down next to my elbow.

"No excuses. Now fucking eat."

And then he surprises me yet again by kneeling next to me, his plate pushed up next to mine, and starts eating like this is just normal.

Like he is normal.

This is not fucking normal.

Working a swallow down my throat, I pick up the fork and stab at the eggs until the tines are full and I feel his eyes leave the side of my head.

Those eyes are back again when I gingerly place the bite between my teeth and pull the fork back clean, despite the fact that the little devil inside my head is screaming to tell him to fuck off.

If he were anyone else, I would.

I also wouldn't feel my pulse in my crotch.

What is wrong *with me?*

Clearing my throat, I repeat the process until I'm full of eggs and potatoes and Fin's piercing blue eyes have gone back to focusing on his own meal instead of mine.

"Was that so hard?" It's almost a whisper, as if a voice as deep as his could accomplish such a task without it sounding like a growl that shoots straight down my spine and settles in my core.

And still, with a full belly and a protective attitude, I shake my head but open my mouth. "No, but fuck you."

I ignore the way his words make my body react, the way his rough thoughtfulness makes me question my sanity. I definitely ignore the way Fin's eyes seem to see right through me and push up from the desk with a flip of my hair and let the robe drop to the cushion my ass just left.

I snag my makeup bag, avoiding the way his growl reverberates its way around my ribcage and use the decorative mirror hung on the wall opposite the bed to touch up the spots on my lips I wore out with eating. I straighten my spine for one last look in the reflective surface.

Tousling my hair just a little bit more and doing a quick pocket check, I spin to my bestie, grab her foot when she continues to ignore me for her vocalist, and tickle until she approves of my outfit like no one else is even in the room.

I know he is watching me. I feel the tingles all over my skin. And yet I tuck the lipstick tube in my back pocket next to my phone, check for my keycard a second time, and leave the room without another glance at the man that makes me wanna look a hundred times, not just twice.

Because that just feels dangerous.

The slam of the door at my back makes me jumpy as I shuffle across the carpet, my eyes set on making it to the elevator and getting the hell out of here as quickly as I can without breaking out in a nervous sweat that might give me away.

I hate that Fin knocks me off my game and sets me on edge any time he's near. Even more when he's so damn close that his scent is burned into my sinuses and my palms itch to touch the ropy muscles beneath his inked skin.

I know what face he makes when he cums.

The ding of the elevator jolts me like an electric shock straight to my already erratically beating heart as the doors slide open and I force a breath before stepping inside. I smash the call button for the ground floor and turn my back against the railing I cling to with another deep breath.

My eyelids lower as the box closes me in, my head resting back against the wall, and I let the perfume of the last person in the lift take over the memory of Fin's scent.

Getting my heart rate to lower is my goal, but when the hum of the slowly closing doors creak to a stop, I feel a breeze of heat rush into the space and my eyes fling open.

Oh my God.

Fin stands on the threshold, his massive shoulders squared, flexing fists down at his sides, and that hard stare directed right at me. He takes a thunderous step inside the box with a ticking jaw and flaring nostrils that turn me on and piss me off.

"What are you doing?" My eyes dart to the doors that slide closed at his back with thoughts of rushing out before they seal us in that cross my mind just a second too late.

The ding of the lift echoes through my ears and sends my heart rate into a plummet that might kill me if the look on Fin's face doesn't before we land on the ground.

The hotel is tall. Too fucking tall. And I happen to have scored a room on the top floor, which means this ride is long enough to land me in hell.

"I already asked you that." Fin's voice is rough and grating to my overstimulated mind, yet somehow makes me feel caged and horny and that is not a roller coaster I am ready to jump on.

He takes a step farther into the lift as it jolts, along with my pulse, his eyes trained low on my face. "How long does it take this shit to dry?"

I blink, my mind gone beyond blank, and pinch my lips together subconsciously testing the lack of stickiness left behind. "Few minutes. Why?"

"Mm." Fin's head lifts, his eyes not moving from what I now realize is on the color of my lips, and he takes another menacing step forward, causing me to plaster myself back into the elevator wall in some sort of desperate attempt to keep space between us. It only works because he pauses in front of me, his chest a breadth from mine, his hands going to the railing on either side of me and boxing me in.

Air catches in my lungs—the organs refusing to work with the man this goddamn close—as his darkened gaze dances all over my face, each pass pausing on my lips.

"Fin, what are you—" My breathy words stop in their tracks when he leans in, the material of his shirt grazing over my hardened nipples and his lips tauntingly close to the shell of my ear.

"Tell me you hate me and mean it." His scent, his growled words that tingle down my neck, have my eyes rolling back and my panties threatening to stop holding back the flood that ensues. "Say it, Cedar."

I moan. I can't help the helpless yet hopeful sound that escapes my throat when his tongue darts out and flips over the ring through my cartilage.

"That's what I thought." The chuckle that rushes over my ear is dark and so deep that I shudder, my core pulsing in response.

And then he's fucking gone.

Chapter Eleven

Fin

FLEXING MY TINGLING HANDS, I head out into the midmorning sun in the direction of the one thing that might be able to calm my racing pulse.

Except it's not here yet.

Leaving Cedar in that elevator, breathless and fucking hot for me, is like torture to my aching cock. I wide step to try to ease the tension in my pants.

It doesn't work.

Gripping my phone in my pocket, I slide it out and check the screen in the blinding sun, the reflection piercing my eyes and making my skull pound in time to the organ beating in my chest.

What the—

The roar of my engine coming down the block reverberates against my ear drums before I can open the screen to check for returned messages from my bodyguard, and the tension built up in my shoulders eases just enough.

Barely. But some.

I look up in time to catch Peach pulling my bike into the lot and gunning straight for me as I slide my shades onto my nose.

"You're late," I growl as he kicks the stand down without killing the engine and dismounts the powerful machine. He pulls the helmet from his head, shakes out his orange hair, and tosses the thing to me.

"Didn't give me much time, Clooney." The grin plastered to his face has me snapping my teeth at him before planting the helmet on my head and flipping him off.

I flip up the visor, raise a second middle finger to my laughing bodyguard, and straddle my bike. "Fuck you."

"The trifecta!" He chuckles, throwing up his hands and palming his face with both of them. "The height of my day has been reached."

Growling into the helmet, I slam the visor, rev the beast between my legs and burn rubber out of the lot without another glance at the asshole with orange hair.

The wind whips through my shirt, slicing through the thin jeans on my thighs, and washes away everything about the last hour of my life.

Everything except for the woodsy scent of her dark hair, and the image of those deep red lips wrapped around my cock.

Fuck.

My pulse kicks up when the light in front of me turns red and I'm forced to slow or run it. Cars line the street, both parked and waiting to get closer to the stadium where the show is starting soon. Buildings wait beyond that, with enough concrete to block out some of the sun, and bodies mill about between the two.

There's too much traffic. Too many people wearing fishnets that walk the same street that Cedar is about to walk, heading to the same event.

So much black hair, dark lips, and boots covering long legs to their knees.

Just like her.

Just. Like. Her.

My helmet feels too small on my head as I roll to a stop at the light, constrictive and claustrophobic around my skull enough that I grab at the piece that covers my mouth and tug left and right in hopes of loosening the thing. When that does nothing but increase my heart rate even more, exaggerating that trapped feeling, I yank the thing off my head and haul in a lung full of stale air.

Growling, I jerk the handlebars until I'm weaving between the cars that are practically parked on the street and maneuver next to the nearest sidewalk corner with a crowd of people waiting to cross. Feet to the pavement to keep the bike from tumbling to the asphalt, I hold up the helmet in offering.

"Who's got a marker?" I bark into the crowd, earning myself some odd glances and questionable looks before realization pulls up grins, and a Sharpie is tossed from the middle of the mass of starstruck people staring at me. I scribble my signature on the helmet as cameras and questions are aimed in my direction, the sun beating down and threatening a heat stroke if I don't start moving. "Who gave the marker?"

When the group separates instead of each claiming it as theirs, a young girl not much older than the two that found me at the café with purple streaks in her hair and an As Above tee hanging from her shoulders, steps up. I hand over the helmet with the Sharpie tossed inside to her without a word. I throw a look at those around her that admire her new possession like desperate hawks that then ease back and fist the throttle.

Hands back in control of the bike, I give it enough gas to move away from the curb and around a line of cars and hammer it when I get a clear line between the vehicles.

The freedom of the air stinging my skin eases the tension in my chest, my shoulders coming down from my jaw.

A jaw that tics with each mile, each hour, I put between me and the venue where Cedar plans to wear that fucking outfit that looked painted on and sexy as sin. The one with the snakes over her tits and not much else. Where others get to see her and not a single person that gives a fuck about her safety will be there.

"Goddamnit."

My grip tightens on the throttle for a different reason as the sun begins its descent into the afternoon, my head spinning off the rails of my mind with questions that I can't answer and a whole lot more of *what the fuck* rolling around in my thoughts.

I try to ignore the way her haunted ocean blue eyes filter into my subconscious and shake my head when the next flash is the way she jumped in the hallway, in the room, in the elevator.

Some people are just jumpy, stupid.

Except for Cedar. She's not some people.

Because not many would swing a bat at my head like she did when she felt threatened.

Growling, I slow the bike enough to yank myself into a turn without dumping it and push the throttle along the back roads in the direction that will bring me right back to the venue I was driving away from.

No one makes my dick harder than it's ever been like Cedar does.

And she's the only one that kicks my heart up just by looking at her. Smelling her scent.

Just being in the same room as her.

She's the only one that's ever made me question whether or not my feelings for her were real ones.

What the hell is wrong with me?

I eat up the distance I created, doubling my speed, and bringing me closer to the festival I was so desperate to run away from.

When I get a clear path a block over from the service road that leads into the back of the venue, the tension in my chest vanishes, my shoulders drop, and my stomach gives itself a little twist.

The closer I get, the clearer the bass vibrates with the show that's been in full swing, and that twisty feeling drops.

How many people have already been to see her?

Too fucking many.

I swear my brow has been permanently deep in a scowl since seeing her again at the party, my chest in a slowly tightening vice with each passing day that Cedar tries to avoid me and that shit just won't fucking fly with me anymore.

She can hate me while I'm right next to her.

The guarded gate comes into view, opening without pause the moment I get close enough to be recognized and I pull the bike directly into the camp where As Above's RV is set up for the weekend.

Parking the bike near our bus and killing the engine, I take the keys and dump them in my pocket.

I have to walk across the entire stadium to get to Cedar's tent, so I cut through the VIP of VIP walks I'm glad to have found last night and stop at the Mexican food place for enough tacos and margaritas to share.

Cedar's been working in this heat. The breakfast is sure to have worn off by now.

Maybe she'll consider it a peace offering of sorts.

Striding my ass the rest of the way through the throngs of people that stare and question my existence when pings of realization light up their eyes, I keep my shoulders up and a scowl on my face. They swear it's me to their friends, but there's no way I'd be out in plain sight like this without a bodyguard.

"He's gotta be a lookalike."

"A major fan."

"Just a biker with similar tats because Fin doesn't have those ones."

I hear it all as I walk in the blistering sun, swiping my sweating forehead on my bicep thanks to my full hands. Cedar's tent finally comes into view when I round the corner through the field exit to the main row of vendor canopies.

Letting my eyes scan the mass of people—some hanging out and smoking, some walking, some in lines way too long for shit that's not that good—I catch the flash of orange that has the vice in my chest relaxing and my grinding jaw loosening.

Peach's sight catches on mine with a grin when I jut my still ticking jaw in appreciation for his forethought, which he returns with a peace sign and fades into the crowd around him.

Bypassing the impressive line for Cedar's artwork, I duck straight into the tent despite the protesting groans thrown my way and come face to face with a woman's ass straight up in the air.

She's wearing pink bikini bottoms that have been pushed enough to the side that I see an ink-smeared crack I wasn't planning on witnessing as hands move over the skin and prick the permanent mark on the girl's ass.

"Hey, sweetness." I let my eyes follow the buzzing hands to the bare and inked arms of the artist. Up to the strong shoulders that hold Cedar hunched over the body at the weird angle that allows her to not put her hands in the chick's more private parts and settle on the way her nose gives a slight curve to her left I wouldn't normally be able to see.

"That better be fucking tacos I smell." The growl doesn't stop Cedar's concentration as she works the devil head into the chick's cheek with a deep brow and thinned lips.

"Sure is." I snort and step around the artist to fit myself in the corner and wait for Cedar to finish her work.

Why does it feel like days since I've seen her when it's only been hours?

"Um ..." The questioning sound has my gaze raising from Cedar's slim waist as she kneels on her stool for a better angle to the matching goth standing next to what looks like the cash register.

"Sup." I give the girl a nod when all she does is flick her eyes from Cedar to me and I let mine fall back to the muscles working in Cedar's back and her ass that pokes out just enough I wanna rub my cock on it.

That even makes me pause.

On it? Why not in it?

"Cedar?" Timid, the girl's dark-lined eyes study me cautiously from her spot across the makeshift shop.

"Ignore him. Take the tacos."

One sharp look. One raise of a pierced brow thrown in the girl's direction and she stops in her platform-clad tracks to come forward and take the shit I've set out on Cedar's toolbox.

"I think I'll step out for a bit."

"Ava, don't you dare," Cedar hisses over her client, who remains quiet under her working hands.

"Yeah, Ava. Why don't you take a walk." I jut my chin at the girl, whose pale cheeks flush, and she sends a quick nod in my direction.

"Um, that orange-haired guy is still out there, I think." And with that, the goth chick is gone and the corner of my lips tip up.

"Goddamn you."

"Don't curse me, sweetness." I don't hide the grin from my words. "I brought you tacos and alcohol."

"You'd know if I cursed you." Cedar's spine straightens with a crack that makes me cringe as she taps the chick's ass with her gloved hands and the girl flops down flat into the chair. "All done."

"Hell yes," the chick answers too loud as she reaches up and pulls an earbud from her ear.

"Just need to clean up real quick."

"Okay."

Cedar makes quick work of shining up the girl's new ass piece and cashing her out for the same devil head I saw floating around the crowd yesterday.

"How many of those have you done?"

"Today?" Cedar shrugs and douses her hands in cleaner, so strong it burns my nose hair. "Over one-fifty."

My brow shoots up, my finger tapping the phone on top of the toolbox to double-check the time. "Just since the gates opened?"

"Yes." She wipes her hands dry on a towel she tosses to a bucket in the corner as she steps close enough that her scent finally overtakes whatever paint-thinner-cleaner shit she just used and rips open the Styrofoam container filled with foil-wrapped tacos. "Goes faster when you don't chase off the help."

Her gorgeous yet scowling blues snap to me in a way that has my lips pulling up at the corner and that vice easing another notch in my chest.

"Sorry, not sorry." I lift the less achy shoulder in a shrug, snag the unwrapped taco she's yet to taste right from her hands, and shove half the thing in my mouth.

"Fucking savage," Cedar grunts, snatching another foil-packed taco and spins on her heels away from me so fast that her hair floats out around her and smacks me in the damn face.

My dick immediately inflates as her scent burrows in my nose and the feel of her silky hair against my skin fades away too fucking quick.

Goddamn.

I'm stepping after her before I realize my booted feet have moved, and I catch myself mid-stride when she flops onto the chair and takes a tiny bite of the filled tortilla with hands that tremble.

From work or nerves?

Finishing the first helping still pinched between my fingers, I grab the tray and dump my ass right onto Cedar's wheely stool next to the chair she occupies and steady the Styrofoam on my angled knee.

My legs are too damn long to sit any other way, so I end up with my knees jutting up nearly to my chest, but it doesn't matter much when I feel Cedar's heat lean closer to pick up another foil pack to dump in her lap and she doesn't skitter right back to the furthest side of the seat.

It matters even less when I notice the shake of her hands ease with each small bite.

And all of it means absolutely nothing when her ocean blues focus on me for what feels like the first time with a severity to her softened brow and tipped lips.

Chest vice?

Gone.

In its place, a warmth that burns me from the inside out.

Oh, shit.

Chapter Twelve

Cedar

"Thank you."

Fin's eyes lock on mine for what feels like a lifetime before I can work my throat enough to get out the words and I immediately want to catch them in the air and shove them back in my face.

I feel heat rise on my face even when I don't do that. My voice that trembles, comes out breathy and quiet on a tongue that tingles thanks to that battery I decided to lick anyway.

Definitely don't do that.

Letting out a sigh, I break away from his hypnotizing stare and let my eyes fall back down to the food in my lap.

The taco is no longer appetizing, my stomach turning in knots, and that margarita I bypassed seems increasingly appealing the longer Fin bores a hole in the side of my hanging head.

This is why I don't do nice things.

"Cedar." My name is soft off his lips but rides rough down my spine and settles into my already aching lower back.

He says it again when I don't move or answer, stronger this time, and even easier to ignore because I'm just an asshole who doesn't like to be bossed around or told what to do.

"Look at me." The demand is deep, gravelly in a way that my core pulses, and has my sight snapping to Fin's strong brow like I might actually like being told what to do despite the shit I just told myself.

"What?" I growl back. "I was trying to be nice, goddamnit."

His chuckle sends shocks straight down between my legs as his eyes roam over me, but then he pushes to his feet and walks the tray of food back over to my toolbox, severing any attempt at a connection I thought I might be going for.

The view of his back sends a wave of nausea through my stomach and I wad up the foil in my hands to toss in the trash with pent-up frustration that the packaging did nothing to deserve, along with wasting the second taco I thought was a promising idea.

I don't like eating in front of others anyway.

"Cedar." Fin leans into my toolbox as he growls, massive hands braced on the stepped-out second level, his head tipped back on his tatted neck in a way that I know he's staring at the ceiling and it's like I can feel the rejection already coming off of him in waves.

I didn't even try this time.

"Whatever." I hop up from the chair and brush the crumbs from my lap when I feel the rush of heat adding to the already hot space. Fin's boots fill my downcast gaze as I brush away more from my torso even though I don't see anymore because I'd rather watch his feet disappear than his back and that's when his hand reaches into view.

I flinch. It's a subtle twitch of the eye and tension flooding into my shoulders, but it's there when Fin's hand comes closer.

I can't help it.

"I want you to look at me."

Just as I can't help the way I sink my teeth into the inside of my lip when his calluses caress the underside of my chin and I fight the way he tilts my head almost all the way back to meet his eyes.

Because while I hate physical touch, I also want him to touch me.

"Why?"

The look I see, the severity darkening his blue eyes, makes me cringe and nearly rip my own head off of my neck twisting away from it.

"Cedar," he starts in that stupid deep tone that does shit to me I don't fucking like as I step away from him and start to round the chair in the middle of my setup, like having something between us will stop him.

It doesn't.

Fin's fingers pinch my elbow and spin me around until my hands are slamming into his solid chest and I can't help the way my brain registers the rings beneath his shirt.

His heavy gaze is locked on mine, his free hand easing its way beneath the hair that curtains my face to cup the nape of my neck as his thumb plays gently over my tingling jaw.

"Tell me who did this to you."

Being wrapped up in him like this ... his focus on me, and only me ... has my heart racing out of my chest and my stomach flipping with want.

Except, that voice in the back of my head is screaming to run.

To panic, or to melt.

These are the real questions.

"Sweetness."

Instead of either, all I do is stare at his handsome fucking face with enough piercings that should've hurt to stop at the last one and a yellowish tinge to his right cheek.

My chest contracts, releases, tensing back up again like I'm on the most dangerous roller coaster of my life and while there's so much of me that's better than I used to be, all I hear is the sound of my ex's voice echoing in the back of my head the longer that Fin stands here and touches me.

So he's coming to rescue you now?

I trusted that boy that I'd thought was a man to hold my young, naïve heart. To be my first damn near everything. I trusted him not to break my spirit when I showed him those intimate parts of myself, and that's exactly what he did.

"I can't." The words are off my parting lips as my breath rushes out of me and I push Fin away so hard I end up spinning myself. "I have ... I have clients waiting."

Sucking in a breath, I square my shoulders and rush to my toolbox to fiddle with shit that doesn't really need fiddling with. My hands begin to twitch. My heart contracts with the dismissal, the knowledge that Fin is going to walk out of here again with an attitude that I don't know I'll ever be able to face. All of it has my stomach twisting all over itself.

I can't. Not again.

"Yo. She's ready for the next one." I whip around with a deep set to my brow and waves in my gut to see Fin standing with the makeshift door flap held back and nodding to a guy half his size that walks in.

What the fuck is he doing?

I just stare for a moment, somewhat in shock, before I snag gloves from the box to busy my trembling hands and try to focus on the grinning dude that settles in my chair.

Anything except the second elephant that just entered the room.

"I'll take the demon head, please."

"Pants stay on, bro," Fin half growls as he lets the canvas fall back to shut out the rest of the pulsing venue and stalks over to the corner he took station in when he first showed up.

"No worries." The guy nods, way too enthusiastically as he pulls up the sleeve of his tee and points to the underside of his arm. "I was thinking right here."

I tightly nod and get to work prepping the area and my equipment as the guy settles all the way back in the chair with a raised arm I'm glad to be able to focus on.

Instead of whatever the hell is going on behind my ribcage.

Meanwhile, the sound of a straw forcing its way through a plastic lid has me glancing over my shoulder and finding Fin standing with the Styrofoam cup dwarfed by his hand and the plastic tube pinched between his lips.

He would look almost innocent, like a child with a fresh Slurpee on a sizzling summer day, if it weren't for the ink coloring his tanned skin clear up to his chin and the rings through various parts of his face.

But those eyes. So intense and focused directly on me.

"Wha?" he asks around the straw with a tip to the corner of his lips.

Some people would call that a smirk, stupid.

So why do I wanna smack it off of his face?

But also kiss it to make sure it stays there?

Sighing when Fin holds out the cup in offering, I shake my head and turn back to the client in my chair. "Can't drink and ink."

"Sure you could." Hands to the tattoo gun, foot to the pedal, I dip the needle end in the little cup of ink and roll my eyes. "I'm sure dude wouldn't mind."

"I wouldn't mind," Dude affirms when I raise my gaze to meet his. I'm trying to ask if he's ready, but instead I'm met with humor glinting back at me. So I look over my shoulder and scrunch up my face at Fin.

"You would want a drunk bitch tattooing you?" Fin's heavy shoulders lift in a shrug that elicits another creak of the straw moving inside the lid as he sips.

"If it's you? Fuck yes."

"I'll agree to that." Dude nods when my gaze swings back to him, but then his smile falls right off his face as his eyes go over my shoulder and a growl that makes my hair stand up reverberates from behind me. "I mean ... uh ... if it was someone like you."

"Stop talking," Fin deadpans.

"Yep."

I snort when my client averts his eyes but keeps his ass in my chair and his arm out, ready for the same tattoo that so many other people have gotten that I've lost count.

The silence of the tent that isn't really all that silent with a rock concert going on around us is a level of awkwardness that it actually puts a hidden smile on my face while I freehand the line work into Dude's skin. He keeps still, his skin the perfect combo of elasticity over the somewhat firm muscle, that the tattoo is one of the smoothest ones I've done yet.

Once I get him cleaned up and cashed out, he disappears with a simple thanks that has my scowl snapping to Fin who still stands in the corner, the second drink in his hands and a quirk to his brow.

"Are you going to continue harassing my clients?" My hands go to my hips as my shoulders square and my stance widens, but that only tweaks Fin's smirk farther up on his face.

"Hm," he grunts, pulling his phone from his pocket to glance at the screen that lights up. "Yep." He juts his chin and tucks the thing back in his too-sexy jeans. "All day."

I balk at him. "Fuck you mean all day?"

"All." He waves his hand out, a finger loose from the cup in his fist. "Day. Now go get the next one."

Growling, I spin on my heel and do exactly as he suggests.

Because I don't want to keep my clients waiting.

And not because he told me to.

The rest of the afternoon flies by in a haze of devil heads and ink mixed with the scent of a man that somehow irritates me with his existence, yet manages to be soothing with his looming presence. My clients throw glances his way when they walk in, but dismiss the possibility that a rockstar—the same one that was on stage just yesterday and is scheduled to be back on stage as the headliner closing the festival out—is really standing inside a tattoo tent like mine.

The canvas enclosure isn't in the best shape, having been gently used in its past life and thrifted to me via my savvy-as-hell bestie for cheap. There are a few holes all over, mostly pinpricks that let in extra light and put my portable air to the ultimate test in this heat, but it's doing exactly what I needed when I signed up for this gig.

What's not doing well, though, is the pain in my lower back from leaning over so many damn bodies with what feels like a bruised kidney testing my patience more than the man that refuses to leave. Even when the clients ask for ink in more … private areas and remove their pants or shirts despite Fin's demands not to.

And I admit, I almost encouraged a few, just to piss him off. But all that accomplished was Fin needing something to do which led to him taking cash and pulling the next ones in like he was my receptionist instead of the woman that only returned long enough to be dismissed again.

I hope she *enjoys the fucking show.*

Asshole.

"Clooney!" I look up from cleaning my equipment and fixing a tick in the hammer that has grated my last nerve for more than a few hours before I accept the next human canvas to see Fin's orange-haired bodyguard stepping into my workspace in search of his client.

"Fuck you," Fin growls and slams the cash drawer closed. "Will you go grab food? I'm fucking starving."

Peach's deeply furrowed brow swings on me. "Who's this? What did you do with Fin?"

I snort and shake my head. "Ate all his tacos and demand he leave. Possibly threatened his life, but only a few times." I shrug when Peach's grin breaks out, bright and mischievous.

"But he asked nicely. Now I have to. *Ow—*"

"I also said fuck you," Fin cuts in, his fist retracting from his swing on the bodyguard's bicep. "Food. Now. Before your client dies of starvation and you're out of a job."

A laugh that brings a smile to my face bursts out from between Peach's lips as I piece my tattoo gun back together and test it with the foot pedal and bring the buzz to life.

"Pretty sure I gotta just walk around and I'll find another few hundred clients to not protect."

The incessant hammering is gone, thank God, and I tap the pedal again just to hear the easy hum that makes my own skin itch for another piece.

"Cedar," Fin growls into the tent, his head hung back on his neck. "I want those fucking hands on me every time you do that."

I don't have time to react to the way his words raise a flush on my face because his bodyguard's ass slams into the chair. "Me first!"

Chuckling, I look from the muscular man in my chair that's supposed to be protecting, to the way Fin glares a hole right through Peach's chest.

"Not a fucking chance, Peach."

"Nah, I made it first. My turn." Grinning, Peach leans up enough to whip his shirt off and greet me with a chest piece on fair skin over washboard abs that should make my mouth water.

It does a little bit, not gonna lie.

Which is not what I expected. Peach is slim instead of bulky, narrow instead of wide. But the definition is there, and it's nice to look at.

"Goddamnit, Peach."

"I'll take the devil head."

"No." I shake my head and feel the relief sigh out of Fin behind me, even if it's misunderstood. "I'm not doing that generic shit anywhere near a piece like this. Do you trust me?"

"Oh, for fuck's sake."

"Shhhh, I need to be attentive to my client," I speak to Fin but don't take my sight from the pale man in my chair who's nodding despite his client's clear aversion to the situation he's put himself in.

"Absolutely." Peach's unwavering grin sticks to his flushed face as he leans back and rests his arms behind his head. "Do your worst, chick."

"Fuck you, Peach."

Chapter Thirteen

Fin

I CAN'T BELIEVE MY *asshole bodyguard.*

Who does that?

Peach is supposed to be out here watching my ass, but he's back at the tent, getting ink from my—

Goddamnit.

Grumbling under my breath, I shake the thoughts from my head and inch up in the line to the infamous noodle place while the smell of Caribbean seasoning threatens to have my stomach eat itself if I don't get to the sustenance soon. The crowd steps in closer with each passing minute that I stand out in the open, all alone, and completely myself in my faded black holey jeans and Dreadful Souls tee that I swear I washed.

That fucker really let me come out here all by myself.

All so he could get inked by the one person I want ink from.

Fucker.

Glancing left, and then to my right to make sure that no one is paying too much attention to me, I finally step up to the truck and growl my order through the little window.

Another step down to pay, and another past that to wait some more for the containers to be handed out, I stack the shit in my arms in a way that maneuvering around the crowd won't force me to drop them.

I hope his ink is ugly.

And stupid.

As I walk what feels like a mile on the surface of the sun back to Cedar's setup, I know my face is screaming what I'm feeling in my gut when the crowd parts for me without requiring pointed looks and pretending to throw daggers their way. They just move, and they watch, until I'm too far out of sight to keep an eye on.

Normally, I'd be having a heyday. Snapping pictures and posting online just for the kicks of those potential people to look back and realize they were so fucking close to someone from As Above, they could have licked me.

Which is a comment I've actually gotten.

And I fucking laughed.

But Peach and his bullshit. And Cedar and her twitching bullshit that has me on a much higher alert than I was when I jerked off in her parlor.

Probably shouldn't have done that.

I can't take it back now, though.

The thought of what could make a woman like Cedar jumpy and distant has my palms itching to hurt and my blood boiling through my veins.

Her ability to threaten me with the bat that night, and practically lob it at my head, means that she's had to protect herself from someone in the past, doesn't it?

Someone like me?

Pausing at the threshold between the stadium that pulses and the main vendor row, I force a breath as I glance up at the fading sun with a clenched jaw and a racing heart.

And that sends me right back to one of the last nights I played with the Saltwater Skulls, where some chick's boyfriend got taught a valuable lesson about treating women poorly while I signed her shirt.

Not someone like me.

I leave women twitchy for a different reason.

I puff out my cheeks with the force of the breath I release and compel my feet to move me forward. It's not a difficult feat knowing that I'll have Cedar back in my sights soon, but I'm more concerned with how hard it was to leave her there to begin with, even with Peach.

And how difficult she'll make it later when the show closes.

Still, I shake those thoughts from my mind. That's a problem for me to figure out later because not having her in my sights is no longer an option.

I shoulder my way into Cedar's worn-ass tent with every intention of making her eat, even if that means Peach's ink is incomplete.

"What the—" Freezing in place, my face falls when I find Peach leaning over Cedar's curled-up body. She's in the chair, her face hidden from me, her feet kicking in little pedaling motions that make the heat rise up my chest and my words growl out past my lips. "You have three goddamn seconds to step the fuck back."

"Not so hard!" Cedar throws her head back, her mouth wide, her blue eyes scrunched up and hidden from me.

My hands are already clearing to wrap around my bodyguard's neck when the sound that ratchets its way past Cedar's red-stained lips registers in my foggy brain.

"If I lighten up at all, you do this shit."

"Because it tickles—"

Cackling.

She's fucking laughing?

"Who the fuck thinks a tattoo tickles?"

My lungs heave. My fists clench. And my boots stop right behind the man with orange hair and a death wish.

"I do. Because it does!"

Breathe. Don't kill him.

Don't. Kill. Him.

The hum of the tattoo gun leaks into my ears as the show outside of the tent comes down. But that doesn't do much to bring me down from the adrenaline spike set to murder.

Because that means he's inking my—

"Fin. Tell him this shit tickles."

"I have ink, too," Peach protests on a chuckle that makes my skin prickle with sweat. "And that shit did not tickle. No more peach trees from you, Ma'am."

I try to stop my heavy hand from landing on Peach's shoulder. I really do.

But when he glances over at me and his face drops, I know I'm still not hiding my cards very well.

"Hey, Clooney," Peach tries, the corner of his lips tipping up and a devilish glint shining in his light eyes. "She said she wanted my name, so I signed it."

"Oh, shit." I hear Cedar snort as I wrap my fist up in Peach's shirt and haul him up from the stool to bring his nose to mine.

"I certainly hope you didn't." I stalk us back until Peach is clear from my girl and his back is ramming into the very toolbox that knocked out Cedar's back. Except he's tall enough that I would bet it buries itself in his ass.

Hopefully painfully.

"Oh." Peach's grin notches up, his breath washing over my face in a laugh that he refuses to contain despite the noticeably clear danger in front of him. "I just gave her what she asked for, Clooney."

Growling, I arch my head back and slam it right into Peach's nose so fast he doesn't have time to react.

"Jesus. Fin—" Small hands crowd my shoulders and tug at me as I watch Peach's nose leak like a faucet and a bloody grin spread across his face.

"I fucking knew it." His words are a deep whispered chuckle as the hands continue to tug at me and Cedar cusses at my back that refuses to move.

"Fin, c'mon. What the hell?"

"Hands to yourself," I snarl with a wing to my brow aimed at my too-giddy body-guard's knowing look. "Feel me?"

"Yup," he snickers and wraps his fingers around the wrist that still holds him hostage. "I heard you loud and clear, Clooney."

Slowly, I let Peach unravel his shirt from my grip until he's loose and I take a step back.

Finally taking my sight off of my bodyguard, I swing my ticking jaw on the woman that pushes between us with towels wadded in her lifting hand. Snatching the wad from her, I toss the paper at Peach and grab her wrist to spin her. She whips around, her hair flinging out and smacking me in the chest as I tug her arm in my direction to examine the shit he put on her skin.

And what I see there pulls a laugh from deep in my chest.

Because on her wrist is a simple yellow smiley face with oval eyes and a thick grinning mouth.

The man has always been an artist, doodling in his sketchpad or the little notebook he keeps in his pocket that he almost never shows to anyone. But inking is different.

The line work is decent with only a few jagged spots from where she more than likely moved, the color is solid throughout, and only a few pinpricks' worth of blood sitting on the surface.

"Are you fucking done?" Yanking her arm from my grip with a scowl, I let my laugh die, but not my grin as Cedar spins back around and snags more towels to hold against Peach's still leaking nose. "Fucking ridiculous—"

"Meh." I shrug as I step back to the entrance and find that I somehow managed to stack the food containers in a leaning tower on top of the cash register in my haze of pissed off and didn't dump them on the floor. "Who's hungry?"

"Me." Peach's exclamation comes out nasally as he shrugs out of Cedar's reach with a paper towel pinched to his nose and accepts the container I offer.

"Seriously?" Cedar looks between us, a pinched look etched into her pretty face. "You two just ... but then you just ...?" Her hand wings out, gesturing between Peach and me as her words fail her and she just stares at the two of us. "What the fuck?"

Shrugging, I look over to Peach who already has chopsticks to his full mouth before he can finish settling his ass back into the chair, and bring my lifted brow back to Cedar. "We came to an understanding. Now," I say and thrust a container in her hands when I want to thrust something else. "Eat."

The need to pull her aside when all she does is stare at me, smack her ass, and make sure she knows not to let anyone else touch her ever again is hard to resist the longer I hold my arm out with her dinner in my grasp that she refuses to take.

"What is wrong with you?"

Peach snorts at her question. "A lot. You have no idea."

"Nobody asked you, Red," I growl.

"It's literally orange, dipshit." I can hear the eye roll in his tone more than I see it because my gaze refuses to leave Cedar until she cracks and takes the food. "Orange. *Oh-rah-nge.*"

Except all she does is scoff and twirl on her platformed heels until she's facing away from me and snagging cleaning supplies. "You turned my shop into a fucking crime scene!"

I let my arm drop and dump her container back on top of the register, along with mine. "It's not that bad, sweet."

"Oh, shut up," Cedar snaps when I approach her and take a bottle of cleaner to drown out the few blood drops that made their way to the pavement beneath us. She viciously wipes away at the toolbox, clearly convinced the thing is contaminated, until I'm certain I see her scrub off some of the paint. "Guys always think they can just—*Ugh.*"

"Hey." With a furrowed brow and a knot in my stomach, I let my fingers brush over Cedar's bare shoulder where her top leaves the skin exposed.

She jumps.

I grind my teeth.

Dipping out from beneath my hand, she turns farther away from me and starts scrubbing another surface like the secret to all her problems lie just underneath.

Or maybe the cure to her panic.

I shoot a look over to Peach, who pretends not to watch, but I know he sees because he gets the unspoken message written in my ticking jaw and vacates the tent with not much sound.

Turning back to the woman who's trying to sanitize the damn concrete, I pause.

I never pause.

Fuck, why does my stomach roll with an ache for revenge?

"Cedar," I bark from my stance only a foot or so away because touching her seems like a terrible idea, even though that's all I want to do.

She jumps again, and my chest tightens in a vice so gripping, it's hard to breathe.

Words leave her painted lips, but they're so quiet I don't hear what she says.

"Sweetness, c'mon," I try, softer this time, and gesture despite the fact that she's still refusing to look at me. "Get off the floor."

Like a switch is flipped, Cedar hauls up from her crouch, dropping the supplies in her hands, and swings her body in my direction with a snarl marring her once soft features. "Fuck. You. "

Her hands are on me, pushing at my chest, and when I don't move, her hands ball into fists that smash into the muscle on my pecs.

"Get. Out."

"No."

Standing tall, I let Cedar hit me. I let her take out her frustration and anger on me in a way that I would never let anyone else as I watch the top of her head and her powerful swings fly from her muscular shoulders.

If she hit me in the face, she'd knock me out.

It's not until her arms fall limp at her sides that I step into her, her heaving chest meeting mine and the heat pouring off of her exposed skin.

"Don't." It's a quiet, weak threat off of lips that I ignore when I wrap my arms around Cedar and pull her all the way into my chest.

Tucking her head beneath my chin, I wrap my body around her and inhale the woodsy scent of her silky, straight hair with a hole in my chest and an ache I can't explain in my heart.

Words stick to the tip of my tongue. Reassurances that I feel like she needs, yet none of it feels right to say out loud. So I keep my breathing as even as I can and tighten my grip on the woman that drives me mad with lust and worry.

Even now, my cock takes notice of her closeness, of her scent filling my nose, and threatens to start poking her if I don't back up.

But I don't.

Because having her this close feels too good to be true.

Which, it is.

I know it is when the next audible words off her lips leave that ache in my chest feeling a little wider, more painful.

"Please just go, Fin."

The desperation in her tone, the ease of her pulling her body back from mine and leaving a gaping chill in her wake despite the heat, almost knocks the breath out of me.

"No—"

Her eyes meet mine for what feels like the first time in hours, and I don't like the determination I see cementing her blues in a way that cuts her off from the outside world. Hardened and defensive. Too wise for too many reasons I wish I knew.

The walls go up and she cuts herself off from me.

"Just go."

With a grinding jaw and a weight caving my chest in, I jut my chin and do as she asks. I leave.

Chapter Fourteen

Cedar

I F THIS WERE ANY other time, day, or fucking year …

I'd be drowning my woes in a pint of ice cream with my besties, then heading off into the world to find someone else to get under so that I could get over someone I wasn't even involved with. Someone I didn't sleep with, or feel like I was in a relationship with, or spent much time with.

Because I just don't know how to not push people away.

I'd rather steer clear than put myself back in the same old situation with the same old people over and over again. Where someone gets the idea that they have more say in my life than they really do.

Better to cut it off now, before anyone gets sticky ideas and complicates the group dynamic we've got going here.

That still doesn't stop the aches that make my hands tremble and the bags that have worsened under my eyes to the point where even my concealer doesn't conceal the shit.

I didn't sleep last night. Which isn't uncommon for me, but normally, I can bag at least a couple of hours before I'm back up again drawing my nightmares or heading to the parlor for opening time.

Or inking myself.

It's one of the few things that brings me peace when my mind is chaotic.

Which is why I'm currently circling the shading needle around the fresh smiley face on my wrist, adding a hint of smoke swirls with twinkling stars that make the yellow pop like a full harvest moon in the darkened night sky.

Leaning back, I twist my arm in the dim glow coming off the single lamp on my hotel room's desk and it's not lost on me how I've managed to add darkness to yet another piece of light that has been given to me.

Guess it's just my thing.

I glance at the clock glowing on the nightstand that screams back at me about my lack of sleep and the late as hell hour which only makes me scoff and turn back to the piece on my wrist.

Adding another layer of smoke, I kill the machine and clean up the work. It shines when I rub the salve over it, fresh and crisp with the lines I fixed, as I wrap the protective thin plastic around my forearm and hope that maybe I can fall face first into the bed to pass out for the next hour or so before my alarms taunt me.

Why do I do this to myself?

Doing exactly as I'd hoped, I fall straight into the fluffy mattress with my head buried in the pillow and pretend to rest my anxious mind until the chirping from my phone sends me into a panic.

I shoot up in bed, scrambling to get to the thing as it rings a sound that isn't my alarm, and slam it to my ear before I even look at the caller ID to verify it's not what my heart is hoping it's not.

It's too soon for the baby.

Right?

"Hello?" My voice is croaky and dry. "Aria? What's wrong?"

My heart beating in my throat, I fall back on the mattress when my knees are too weak to hold me up and listen desperately to the all too quiet line.

Click.

The line goes dead.

I pull the device from my head and stare at the black screen with my breath stuck in my throat and a twist to my stomach. It lights up when I settle it against my thigh, the notification trying desperately to worm its way into my foggy brain and sleep-deprived eyes.

No way.

It's almost five in the morning, which is what sinks in first, and my phone highlights in a fancy white box that the number I have programmed as '*Do Not Answer*' is the one I just did, in fact, answer.

Oh, no.

My stomach drops as bile rises in the back of my throat.

So he's coming to save you, now?

With shaking hands, I toss the device across the room and shoot to my feet as if that will get the memories of the nightmare on the other side of that call as far away from me as possible.

Do you think he'd give it to you better than me?

Huh, Cedar?

I jab my twitching limbs into the nearest pair of shorts, desperately trying to beat back the tears that prick the backs of my eyes, and jet out of the room with rapidly pumping lungs.

I leave behind the phone that taunts me with memories I'd rather burn than keep, my heart threatening to beat right through my ribcage.

I don't bother checking for my keycard or my credit cards as my feet carry me down the hall and my fingertips go numb.

Heading straight to the elevator, I slam the call button with a fist I don't feel and bounce on the balls of my feet.

Panic, raw, and angry crawls its way up my spine when the ding echoes through the hall like a hammer to metal and the doors slide open with grinding whirrs that pierce my eardrums.

Practically diving into the metal box, I nearly scream when I crash into a hard chest.

"Oh my God."

"Morning—"

Hands wrap around my biceps and pull me into the lift with a gentleness that allows the doors to close and my eyes to trail up the As Above tee across his chest.

"Peach?"

"What's going on, C?"

I grit my jaw to keep it from wobbling at the familiar sight of Peach's face, except his brow is set in an uncharacteristically firm line that broadcasts his concern.

"Um, I," I say, my voice clogging in my throat with all the words I don't want to share. All the things I don't want to talk about, because talking about them brings them back to life.

Like a phone call when I haven't heard from him in years.

And I need that part of my life to die.

"Is it Fin?" Peach's light eyes search mine, his hands still holding me up by my upper arms when my jelly legs refuse to.

"No." I shake my head even though it feels like it weighs a hundred pounds. "I just … Can I use your phone?"

"Yeah, yeah." He nods and smashes the call button for the paused elevator and fishes out his phone while one hand still clings to me as if I'll fall over if he doesn't.

I might.

Dialing the number I know by heart with quivering fingers, I put the device to my ear and wait.

And wait.

And wait.

"Hello?" Gruff as ever and full of sleep, the voice on the other side has my wobbling legs steadying and my torso strengthening against Peach's steadying grip. "Can I help you?"

I sigh into the phone, my heart rate slowing. "It's me."

"Cedar?" The voice on the other end shoots up an octave, audible with worry. "Princess, what's wrong?"

"He …" I work a swallow down my dry throat and turn my upper body away from Peach to whisper into the receiver. "He called."

Silence greets me at the admission, and it's like I can feel the heat of anger rising through the phone.

"Why are you whispering? Is he there?"

"No." I shake my head, even though I know he can't see me. "He just … hung up."

Breathing a lift back into my shoulders, I step to the opposite side of the cube from Fin's bodyguard and do my best to have a private conversation with the one man that knows more than most.

Peach and Fin are together a lot, but I don't know how close the two really are considering the dark-rimmed eyes that watch me.

And I don't need another man involved.

"I'm coming to get you."

"No, wait." I glance over to meet Peach's curious but soft gaze. "I'll come to you."

"Alright." A sigh makes its way over the line, along with rustling and beeping that sounds an awful lot like a coffee pot. "If you're not here in twenty, I'm coming for you."

"How do you know I'm that close?" A small smile creeps its way onto my face as the elevator dings open on the main floor of the hotel and a grunt responds to my question.

"Twenty minutes or I'm coming. That's a promise, Princess."

I grunt back and pull the phone from my face to kill the call.

Slapping the phone against Peach's chest, I meet his eyes with a levity I didn't feel when he first saw me.

"Can I get a ride?"

His grin notches up as he tips his chin and leads me out of the lift. "As long as you're good on a bike."

"Fuck yes."

Stepping out into the damp morning air, I force a breath to keep my nerves down and follow Peach to the motorcycle that's parked in the fire lane.

"You like her?" Peach's pride shines in his smile as he hands over the helmet and straddles the beast when I accept.

"She's beautiful." Planting the protective gear on my head that smells of fresh mint like he brushed his teeth right before he put it on last, I nestle my body in behind Peach and hook my arms under his biceps and around his shoulders. "Why did you come?"

His shrug is the only answer I get as he starts up the machine beneath us and is pulling out into the nonexistent traffic.

The wind slices through my thin tee shirt, the dampness leaving a chill on my exposed skin as Peach speeds and weaves around the city streets until we're hitting the outskirts of town where fog claims the fielded hills.

Sunlight breaks through the mist on the horizon when we slow, baiting back the low-hanging clouds and releasing the ominous feeling left in their wake.

Peach pulls into the treelined driveway lit with inground lights that guide the bike along the curves of the path up to the only building on the property.

The porch light is on, illuminating the single wooden rocking chair and the worn decking that could use a fresh layer of paint and it would look as good as new. The rest of the house is in immaculate condition with its brand-new siding, recently replaced windows, and meticulously kept lawn.

My eyes wander over the porch when Peach pulls the bike off to the side of the two-car garage, and I chuckle at the single cushion that sits in the rocker as I pop off the helmet.

Dismounting the machine, Peach kills the engine and accepts the helmet back from me.

"How'd you know where to go?"

"I do my homework." He tilts his head in the direction of the screen door. "Better hurry, you might turn into a punkin'."

Snorting, I shake my head and turn away from Peach's grin to find the very door he referenced darkened with a heavy frame that would have made me gulp to find standing there if this were over a decade ago.

Pulling up on a bike?

With a stranger?

In the dead of the morning?

Instead, I jog up the steps with a lightness I'm glad to feel as the screen creaks open, and I all but throw myself into the safety of thick tattooed arms that smell of fake citrus soap that never really cleans away the grease stains left behind, mixed in with the scent of clean clothes.

My hands have steadied as the warmth settles in around me. My chest releases the tension I've been holding since the call despite the tight arms locking around my shoulders. My lungs take in the first full breath in what feels like weeks, but it's only been a day since I felt safe in the arms of someone.

Arms that belonged to Fin.

When my chest lifts, I catch the matched movement like maybe it's the first full breath for us both in too long.

"Hey, Princess." The grumble ruffles the top of my head when lips make contact with my hair and vibrates through the chest I still hold tight. "Who the fuck is that?"

"A friend," I answer easily and snicker when I lean back and I'm met with a thick-cocked brow and sharp blue eyes that only show some aging around the edges.

"He can stay outside." Nodding, I throw an apologetic look over my shoulder to a shrugging Peach, as my wrist is wrapped up in a heavily callused hand and I'm tugged inside the dimly lit house to the kitchen. "Tell me why I can't bury him, Princess."

Once we're inside the safety of the house, away from prying ears, with fresh coffee to palms, I shrug and sip the burning brew as I prop my hip into the counter and watch my dad settle at the worn table in the same seat he's taken up for the last twenty or so years. "I don't want you going to prison."

"Princess." I hide my smile behind the ceramic when he lowers the mug, and resolve stares back at me. "You know I know things. And people. I've seen action. That little fucking twerp is nothing but a blip on the radar if he disappears."

Rolling my eyes, I ditch the mug on the counter and pull out the remaining chair across the small table. "I know you were in combat, smartass." I shake my head. "But that was forever ago."

A deep scoff rings out, echoing off of the wallpapered drywall. "As good as I once was."

"You have the shop. I don't want you in trouble. There's a thing called aiding, or involuntary, that can accompany shit like manslaughter or homicide."

A grunt and an interest in the coffee in my dad's palms are all I'm met with.

"But you came to me." Setting the mug to the old wooden surface, eyes the same as mine crash to my stare with an intensity I haven't seen in years. "I'm calling Alex."

"No!" I grab his massive forearm when he stands from the table, only to stop when those same intense eyes beam down at me with a grinding jaw.

"You're gonna live your life. And I'm gonna make sure you can without scum dimming that pretty smile." I watch him straighten, his height looming over me. "Alex can watch the shop for the day. I know you have to be at the festival, so I'm coming with."

I shake my head and stand along with the man I've adored my entire life. "You can't end up in jail."

"You know I don't make promises I can't keep, Princess." I let out a heavy breath as he speaks because I know where this is going, even as he shakes his head. We've been here before, except it was easier then, when taking care of a minor was his number one priority. But I'm grown now, out of the house, and have been off on my own for almost a decade.

"But—"

"Nuh-uh. Not when it comes to you. Now let's go."

Chapter Fifteen

Peach

"So ...?"

"So, what?"

"How was she?"

"You've been dying to ask me that, haven't you?" The growling scoff that greets me from my client's crouch plants a grin right on my bruising face. My eyes are showing color, my nose painful to touch after meeting with Fin's misplaced protectiveness and big ass head.

"Fuck you," Fin growls and straightens to his full height from adjusting whatever cord that leads into the speaker and spit out a sound he didn't like.

I couldn't hear a damn thing, but whatever.

I'm not that kind of artist.

Pushing off from my lean on the thing I've come to know as a stack—which is really just a tower of speakers and shit—I follow my client as he stalks across the open space back to his notes and his extension.

The extension being his guitar, or what I call it, because the man rarely leaves home without it. Not that it's a terrible thing when he also happens to be a huge part of the songwriting process for the band I love to hear on the radio. Or see the shows of. And hang out with.

It was never a phase.

I grin knowingly when he snatches the thing with less care than normal and shrugs the strap over his barely-covered torso before the intensity in his eyes meets mine. "So?"

Fin stands in front of his setup, his hopeful attention completely on me instead of the reason we came here, in a shirt that shows practically all of his inked chest, including the rings through his nipples, and jeans that let the colors peak through, too.

Subconsciously, I tap on the itchy peach tree now inked into the left side of my ribs, courtesy of the same woman Fin's asking me about.

"Pfft." Laughing into a shrug, I glance around to find a new place out of arm's reach to perch and harass my client from afar since he has no problem throwing hands when he gets aggravated. *Hello two almost black eyes.* And possibly to avoid his burning gaze. "Alive."

"That's it?" Another scoff and a shake of the head translates into Fin strumming across the strings of his guitar without thought. The sound is melodic, one that you would hear in a song without Fin even trying. "That's all you fucking got?"

The music, the notes flowing effortlessly, it's just natural for him.

"I'm sworn, Clooney." I shrug and make sure the wheellocks are engaged on a giant case that normally holds a rack of string instruments before hopping up to sit on top of it. "She had a pretty convincing argument."

Like a nearly seven-foot-tall former soldier with a rap sheet there's no way she knows about and lots of connections that I would want nothing to do with.

"About what?"

Add in the silent communication via the death glares from piercing eyes that made even me pause, and now I can't wait until the two of them are in the same room together. It's going to be fireworks all over.

The thought alone makes the black eyes worth it.

Landing with an *umpf,* I dust my hands off on my pants and answer my client with a noncommittal shrug as I let my eyes roam over the place.

Racks line the walls, some of the shelves filled with pallets or cases like the ones around us. It's mostly empty though, wide open space for storage, but the dropped electric is set up for exactly what Fin's doing—practice.

Another perk to being a rockstar, invited to the biggest festival held to date, by some of the biggest names in rock—you get access to shit like their very own practice studio while you're here.

And I get a front-row seat, again, to witness the magic that is As Above. The sorcery that occurs when Fin is deep in songwriting.

And I'm so glad I took this job.

"That's all you're going to say."

"Yup." Snickering when I'm met with another death glare for what feels like the hundredth time today, Fin growls and curls around his guitar.

The sound that comes from his frustration burst forth from the amplifiers and pulls my already grinning lips up.

What can I say? Pain and lust make good music.

"I knew I shouldn't have sent you."

"*Moi?*" Hand to my chest and wide-eyed, I draw in a sharp breath. "I was the perfect man for the job, Clooney."

"God, I hate you." Shaking his head, Fin bites at his lip and picks at the strings.

"No, you don't."

He grunts and scribbles something on the page open next to his thigh and plays a strand of cords put together in a heavy pulse he cuts off too soon with a growl of frustration that echoes off the empty walls.

Pacing, he yanks the strap over his shoulder and holds the instrument by the neck as his boots thump over the cement beneath us.

"Maybe you just need some ... inspiration."

"Shut up, Peach."

"I mean." I shrug off the words and lift my hand to stare at my nails. "You haven't gotten laid in like a week."

"I said shut *up*." He points at me menacingly but whips his head back toward the hole he's trying to wear into the flooring.

"I'm just sayin', Clooney." I keep my snicker low when he shakes his head and growls. "She's dicking with your mojo."

I swear I don't have a death wish. I really don't.

But when Fin's sharpened blues wing back to me with a darkness I've not seen in him before, I begin to rethink my taunting methods that would normally bring levity to the tension in my client.

The man stalks to me with a deep scowl and a ticking jaw set into a ropy neck that doesn't normally look that fucking defined and I'll admit my asshole puckers.

I'm his bodyguard.

Yet when it comes to that chick—who is pretty cool—his demons let loose enough to make me question his necessity for someone like me.

I'd hate to have to put him on his ass because his head is too far up it to see the truth.

Which is ... drumroll, please ... that he's got it bad for the tattooist.

But how bad is bad?

"Just speaking what I see, Fin." I square my shoulders when he stops at my feet because it's too late to take it back now and meet his hard glare with one of my own.

"You don't know what you're talking about." Fin spins from me with lifted shoulders and back muscles that ripple a little too hard for just a little guitar session.

Hopping down from the case, my combat boots smash into the concrete with an echoing thud as he jams that axe into a nearby holder. "You mean I didn't see you look right by the bartender to go find her?"

Okay, I guess I do have a death wish.

"And I completely missed how you spent the entire day being her bitch?" He freezes at my words, his shoulders filling with pumping heat that radiates off of him like a haze in the chilled warehouse-esque space. "Oh, and I totally misunderstood the headbutt I got for goofing around."

He whips around so fast, I barely register the snarl on his face before he opens his mouth. "Goofing around with my—"

"Your what?" I push when he cuts himself off, stepping right up into his face until his labored chest meets mine. "Time to wake the fuck up, Fin."

"Fuck you." Fin's palms land on my pecs in a bruising push that sends me back a step. "You didn't see the way she shook," he spits, his face contorted in what I now recognize as defensiveness ... and, though he'd never admit to it, fear. "You didn't see the way her fucking hands ..." He lifts his and shows the vibration to his limbs as his breath rushes out of him in puffs similar to that of a bull readying to charge. "And you didn't see the shit in her eyes when she asked me to leave."

Nodding, I purse my lips and step back up to Fin until we're only about a foot apart. "And when have you ever let the past stop you?"

Growling, Fin's hands both go to his hair. "Peach, I don't know how to be that."

"Be what?"

"*Soft,*" he growls.

"Clearly." I scoff and roll my eyes that still ache. "You don't know how to share either."

The sound that comes from him is feral and threatening. "Peach."

"Oh, shut up before I fucking hit your ass back." I pin him with a glare and point. "That's two I owe you. Two. And you called me 'Red'." Shaking my head, my very clearly orange hair falls into my eyes. "That counts as a third all on its own."

Fin stands there, his arms up and fingers laced behind his head with a laboring chest and that caged yet feral look in his eyes.

"Peach, I'm fucked," he breathes through flared nostrils and licks his dried lips.

"Oh, Clooney." I shake my head and try, but fail, to hide my chuckle. "You have no idea."

Fucked on so many levels.

Just wait until he sees the barricade he's gotta get through before he can get to the girl he really wants as his, but refuses to see how deep that shit really goes.

The knowledge of who is between Fin and Cedar should give me pause. It should concern me as his bodyguard. And I probably should warn him about the man I met in the wee hours of the misting morning with fists bigger than my head.

But honestly?

It's payback for the headbutt.

"Now pack it up." I nod to the guitar still sitting in the holder when his brow furrows at me and he picks it up.

"Why?"

"Just," I sigh and shake my head. "Can you listen for once in your life?"

"Nope." Somehow, he crosses his arms over his large chest, even with the instrument still in his grip.

"Jesus." Reaching forward, I snatch the thing from him, which he releases easily enough, and walk it back to the case I was using as a seat.

"You need a fucking drink." I place the axe inside, lock the shit up and toss him the keys.

"Damn, that sounds like a great idea."

What bad could possibly come from drowning your issues in alcohol?

Stepping out into the blinding and blistering sunlight, Fin and I mount the bikes we rode in on and I follow his lead back to the camp set up just outside of the venue. I stomp down the kickstand that likes to stick, tug off the helmet, and shake out my hair.

"Of course, you'd pick the Setlist." With an eye roll and a chuckle when Fin flips me off, I dismount the bike and hang the protective gear on the handlebars.

"Don't have to drive anywhere else if I get plastered here." Fin shrugs tightly and clips his helmet to his bars like I did.

His lifted brow meets mine and I don't miss that flash of hope sparkling in his eyes that fades fast when he turns to start walking.

Hope that he can run into Cedar.

"This is a terrible idea," I mutter to myself because my client is damn near gone, washed away in the crowd of rockers and staff. "Fucking terrible idea. Fin—"

"Hurry up, Scarecrow." My feet are already carrying me at a jog in the direction of my client's fading back.

"Oh, fuck you."

"Drinks first." My laugh bursts out when people's gazes swing to watch me chase his ass down, our traded comments lacking any kind of quietness.

"No thanks."

Jesus, this is a terrible idea.

So terrible.

I love it.

Chapter Sixteen

Cedar

WITH MY BRAND-NEW GARGOYLE planted at the entrance to my tent, the clients have been flowing since we opened up this morning and haven't stopped.

The whole page of samples that included the devil head has been completely ripped out of the book when it was the first thing requested this morning and it's been smooth sailing since.

"How the hell did you get him in here?" Ava asks me for the sixteenth time over the top of the woman that leans back in my chair.

I've been answering with grunts because she tends to ask when my brain is too full of the line work I'm doing, but this time, I swipe away the excess ink and lean back. "Said he was staff."

"And no one questioned it?" Her voice comes out on a higher octave, as if that is such an unbelievable feat that I got another body in the venue when the rest of us basically went through clearance checks so thorough I'm surprised they forgot the body cavity search.

I shrug, knowing the answer is because my dad's not one you question, but keeping that part to myself. He's gained enough attention today that my line is wrapped around the main row and back again and my back aches just thinking about how many more people are out there.

"Next," I call when the lady in my chair accepts her completion and heads over to Ava for cover-up and payment.

"Coming up, Princess."

The canvas that comes in next is a shadow I barely register as I do a quick wipe down and prep around the millions of water bottles that keep showing up, mostly unopened because I just don't drink that much, but were refused removal when I knocked ten of them over in my reach to tattoo at a weird angle.

Much like the food that was thrust at me over an hour ago that sits in the corner of my toolbox and stinks up my tent.

It sounded like a good idea—even smelled good then—when the offer was extended and the line seemed shorter. Until it wasn't and I couldn't stop long enough to eat.

The catering and errand running between my actual and my not actual employees are enough to make me wish Fin was here.

At least he knew when to leave me the hell alone.

This morning's event has left a bad taste in my mouth, simply because of the questions that keep rolling through my brain. Ones that I know I'll never get the answers to, considering the last thing I wanna do is talk to the boy and find out.

Ain't happening.

But with my belongings retrieved, the guard at my door, and the shitty words I spewed at Fin yesterday, I would say that I'm set to make it through the day without incident pertaining to the male suitors I've had, or wished I had in my life.

Thank God.

So why do I wonder what Fin would do if he knew?

"Hey, baby." Freezing with one gloved hand trying to cover the second one, I close my eyes and take a deep breath.

Spoke too soon.

"You have two options," I growl as I lean my head back and have to stretch out the growing tension in my neck from one side to the other. "Either walk out right now or shut your mouth and pay double."

"Wow, good to see you, too." Trey's words fall off his thick lips with a chuckle I've heard and send a chill—not the good kind—down my spine.

The air shifts when he settles into the chair behind me and I run a quick pass of my tongue over my lips before I spin to face him.

Ava's apologetic and knowing gaze meets mine over the top of Trey's stretched-out frame.

'Charge double,' I mouth to my receptionist, who tips her chin and I roll my eyes.

Because the last thing I need is to toss him out and gain myself more attention about the guys I've slept with.

The world doesn't need to know about this one.

"I've stood in your line for three damn days, baby. I'm ready."

Pulling in a deep as hell breath, I let the oxygen lift my shoulders and expand my chest before puffing out my cheeks and shaking my head.

"I am so going to make this one hurt."

Trey's deep chuckle insults my eardrums, and he stretches farther back in my chair and grins. "Do your worst."

So I fucking do.

Trey picks the biggest piece I have in the sample book, and when I lean in with the heavy hand and the deep needle strokes so I don't have to use my own strength to hold myself up, he squirms.

The shading to this one takes almost an hour of working the ink into the taut skin of his ribs, which only makes me grin the more he hisses and taps his leg as a distraction to keep the rest of him still.

He was warned.

"Good God, I need a drink," he mumbles through clenched teeth that make me giddy as I pass over the sensitive skin for another layer of shading. "You're killin' me, woman."

"Huh." I shrug and swirl the tattoo gun over the flesh that pricks with blood, only to hear Ava try her best to stifle her giggle.

Incoherent arguing perks my ears up as the hum from the tattoo gun pauses and words I don't understand begin to filter through the noise of the show going on around us.

Intrigued by the possibility of a fight—probably because I'm a little messed up in the head—I lay off the pedal controlling the device in my hand and cock my head in the direction I think the argument is coming from.

"Who the fuck are you?"

My spine snaps straight as the deep growl penetrates the canvas of my tent, the voice clear, the rage clearer still.

"Depends on who the fuck you think you are to ask."

Wide eyes meet Ava's over the top of the human canvas in my chair as the second growl responds, and the hair raises on the back of my neck.

"I'm her—just move!"

"Shit." I thrust to my feet, swipe away the last bit of ink on Trey's rib with the towel already in my hand and tear off the gloves. I'm moving before I can toss them in the trash, heading to the voices that are escalating and certainly going to get into a much bigger fight than just the drunk tussle I was hoping for only a second ago.

God, please tell me it's not what I think it is.

Yanking back the door flaps, I'm first met with the blistering heat that makes me feel like the little portable AC unit is doing its job and the blinding sun that takes a moment of rapid blinking to focus in.

"Her, what?"

Oh, God.

I blink back the focus, hoping that the sun has burned a vision into my eyes that isn't real because the one in front of me makes me question my sanity and my bravery all in one.

Wrapped up before me like rivals before a cage match, with fists tangled in shirts and muscles pumped full of adrenaline, is the protector I called for reassurance that refused to let me come alone to the one place I knew I'd be fine.

Aka Jaxon "Atlas" Jones, with a salt and pepper beard trimmed close and hair long enough to run his grease-stained hands through.

A combat veteran of Desert Storm.

Mechanic.

Owner of *Jones Auto.*

Facing off against a rockstar that I kicked out of my tent yesterday for trying damn near the very same thing.

Except he was trying to protect me from myself.

Finland Montgomery.

"Nope." Dashing over the pavement, I shout over the top of them and wiggle my way between their bodies with my back pressed up against my unofficial bodyguard and my hands pushing into Fin's pecs, who does take a step back, but doesn't remove his anger-filled gaze from the man behind me.

And the fire I see when his gaze flashes to mine for a split second sets my blood to boil.

I see rage. Hunger. And the last one that makes my chest hurt.

Betrayal.

An arm I've needled ink into wraps around my waist and hauls me back a step, angling so that I'm almost behind a wall of muscle. "You know him, Princess?"

"*Princess?*" Veins. So many veins popping out of Fin's neck and forehead are all the warning I catch before his big body is moving and he lunges.

"Shit."

Pushing me aside with a large hand to my bicep, the tussle knocks me back in time for a fist to fly and connect with flesh in a sickening crack that would normally make me snicker.

What? I said I was fucked up.

But this time ... it just makes my stomach roll and my teeth clench as a flash of orange joins in the mix of flinging arms and bruising knuckles.

Make those bloodying knuckles.

Red spray flies when one of the two—or maybe all damn three—get smashed in the nose with an elbow that makes my own nose ache and my instincts have me jumping back when I should be running forward.

The crowd thickens in a large circle around us the longer the three grapple, and blood dribbles.

My feet frozen, I stand there unable to see a way in to stop the carnage, when two very brave attendees of the concert decide to step in.

With wrapped-up arms, they haul back men twice their size while Peach stands in the middle and keeps each of them back with punishing hands to their chests.

"What the fuck is wrong with you two?" Peach exclaims with a heaving chest and blood draining from his now crooked nose. "Since when do you fight over women who can fight for themselves?" His hard gaze swings from one participant to the other, his brow deep and cut, as his words growl out. "Get your heads out of your fucking asses."

I chuckle. I can't stop the bubble that works its way past my throat and draws the attention of each man standing around me.

Because how fucking apropos is it that these two would meet this way?

The rockstar crush and the overprotective asshole I've had to deal with my entire life.

"Care to enlighten the room, Princess?"

The growl that emanates from Fin's chest at the nickname I've had since before I was born pulls another laugh up from the depths of my belly.

Because if I don't, then I'd have to acknowledge that Fin's growl actually turns me on.

"Nah, I think I'll hang on for a little while longer." With a grin I shouldn't have and a tremor to my hands, I gesture to my tent. "If you two promise not to destroy anything …"

"Yeah …," Peach drawls, his sight trained on something in the distance. "We need to step inside before we have a bigger problem."

"What's that?"

"Oh, I don't know." Peach shrugs, nonchalant despite the crimson draining down his reddened and sweaty face. "Maybe the horde led by security that's heading this way?"

"Oh, fuck."

Like a teenager caught doing what they aren't supposed to, Peach snatches Fin's bicep and all but tosses his ass into the confines of the canvas tent, then comes out and does the same with me.

"Sit tight, I got this."

"Umm," I hum with a smirk when Peach pauses in his step to head back outside. "You might wanna," I gesture to my face, "get that."

Peach curses and wheels around in circles, looking for something to wipe away the evidence on his face.

"Here, kid." Accepting the offered roll of paper towels, Peach nods a thanks to the man that raised me and steps back out into the heat of the afternoon.

"What the hell, Cedar." It's not a question that comes from the steaming rockstar in the corner, who I'd swear has slurs on his words and sits a little sideways on my stool.

"Watch your mouth." With a growl, Jax swipes the back of his hand across his red-stained chin and doesn't hide the snarl on his weathered face.

"Baby?" Trey says.

Almost timid, almost quiet, the little voice from the third man still in my space has my head falling back and my lungs catching in my chest.

Oh, hell.

Fin jets to his feet so fast I'm surprised he doesn't shoot through the roof at the same damn time Jax wheels around. Both with hard sets to their jaws and growls off their lips.

Oh, God, what have I done?

"Leave." I spin on my heeled feet to Trey—who can never take a hint—and throw my arm out in the direction of the exit. "I'm not your fucking baby."

"But—" Trey steps closer to me but freezes when I feel the shadows heat at my back.

"Pretty sure leave means just that," my dad huffs.

"Don't make me show you," Fin growls.

"Oh ... k-k-kay," Trey stammers with impossibly wide eyes, his hands held up in surrender to the men that are his complete opposite as he sidesteps closer to the exit.

"Find a new artist, Trey. I'm good."

Once his tucked tail disappears, I spin on the remaining two jerkoffs standing over me like pillars erected to protect the little artist that is me and place my hands on my hips.

"Story time, Princess."

Again, Fin's growl cuts through the space before I have a chance to answer, reverberating from his chest so hard I swear I see his ribs vibrate through his torn shirt.

Not that it looks like there was much shirt there to begin with, considering the proud pierced nipples and even prouder ink begging for my attention.

"Jax," I start with a sigh and a shake of my head. "Meet Fin."

"Great," Fin spits, his gaze flipping to the man that named me after his favorite tree, with an intensity I don't quite understand shining in his brilliantly blue eyes and flexing fists.

"Fin." I let my eyes float over the man that makes me look a fucking lot and push out another sigh with the knowledge that shit is about to get weird considering the last person to meet the man at my elbow is the damn reason he's here today. "Meet my dad."

Chapter Seventeen

Fin

Now I know I'm still drunk.

I gotta be.

Because the tree of a man in front of me, with his roughened sausage fingers pinching Cedar's elbow and barely enough grey in his head to be this woman's father—considering I feel like I've sprouted a head full just in the last few days of getting a little more personal—is nothing like I'd envisioned for a parent to Cedar.

Is he the reason she shakes?

"I'm sorry." I scoff and shake my head, my hands refusing to stop curling into fists. "Your *what*?"

"My daddy." The way she leans into him innocently makes my skin prickle. The way her hand goes to his chest and she puts her head against his pec ...

Makes my fucking blood boil.

And when his hand goes to her shoulder instead of her waist, it's almost—*almost*—enough to make me believe her.

Except he could still be the reason she jumps.

"Is he—" I bite off my own words with a curse, afraid that the thoughts rolling around in my head won't be too far removed from the truth she'd never admit in front of him and rub my aching hands over my face. A face that bears cuts and what's surely purpling skin.

"Spit it out, kid."

"Don't—" Growling, I twist my neck one way and then the other. "I'm not a fucking kid."

"Uh-huh." *Jax* tips his bearded chin at me, his eyes a striking resemblance to the ones in Cedar's head that stare at me with a little too much enthusiasm.

"What the fuck is he doing here, Cedar?" Sighing, she rolls her eyes and steps back from the man that makes me question things I shouldn't be questioning, but I am.

"He's overbearing." Shaking her head, Cedar cracks the door flap for a peek and lets it fall closed.

"I don't think you mean that nice." My gaze swings from Cedar and the nerves she settles into my gut, because deep down, I know eventually she's going to run and meet the humor laced in ocean blues that match hers.

"Not one single bit," she grunts, and walks between our bodies to plop her ass in the tattoo chair.

It's easy. Calm, almost.

And when she settles back into the cushion and allows her feet to swing where they don't touch the ground, I feel that tension in my chest begin to ease.

Her gaze swings between me and the man she claims is her father with such nonchalance that my lungs allow a full, chest-expanding breath.

"But ..." I dip my tongue out to wet my cracked lips and furrow my brow when my confusion refuses to let go of me. "Why's he here?"

"You don't know when to let shit go, do you, Kid?" Jax's heavy hand lands on my shoulder in an unexpectedly punishing pat that knocks me forward a step. "I'm gonna go case the scene. Be good, Princess."

"Me?" Cedar scoffs. "I wasn't the one grappling strangers."

"Right," Jax snaps on a chuckle and spins on his boots. "Gotta go clean up my mess."

"Dad," Cedar calls to his disappearing back, but growls when his trek doesn't stop.

Silence stretches over the space except for the small AC unit blubbering in the incessant heat in a desperate attempt to keep up.

"I'm gonna give you two a minute." The little goth receptionist disappears after Cedar's *dad* and leaves us all alone.

I stand there, with cracked open knuckles and half my shirt, staring at Cedar while she sinks her teeth into that plump bottom lip and pretends not to stare right back.

She thinks I don't see it.

She thinks I miss the way her eyes travel over my exposed chest, leaving hot trails in her wake only to dart away long enough to make me question my sanity.

Then back again, higher this time, like her gaze is stroking its soft touch down the ink on my neck.

The air ... it fucking crackles like a venue pumped to see As Above play for the first—or the hundredth—time with each pass of her sight over my skin.

Cedar is the only woman who has made me stop and look more than once. The only woman to make my skin both hot and chilled at once, while also making my heart both race and settle into a rhythm. The only fucking woman to have me unloading in my fucking pants in the middle of an empty tattoo parlor all on my own.

So when I stalk forward with a filling cock and pinch her chin to tilt her head back, I meet a set of eyes so blue I'd swear they captured the depths of the ocean in the sunlight from beneath the surface.

And a twitch.

It's subtle. Barely there.

But one of those beautiful, lined eyes gives a jerk that has my heart pounding for a different reason, and my hands itching all over again.

"Cedar," I start, leaning in close enough that I taste her breath on my tongue. "Tell me why he's here."

She forces a hard swallow down her extended throat, her tongue darting out to wet her lips in a way that catches my cautious, yet turned on eye.

Raising a hand, Cedar wraps her slender fingers around my wrist, the heat from her touch like a caress down my spine, and her lips part on a breath I'd rather catch than let loose.

I don't. But I really fucking want to.

"He's, um ..." Clearing the lower octave from her throat, she shakes her head.

"Don't." I hold her gaze, and her chin when she goes to pull away from me. "Don't you dare shut me out. Not again."

"Why not?" Her words challenge me, but her tone is breathy and all kinds of sexy, that sends my head into another tailspin.

I could go with the façade Cedar's put up. Dismiss the shit like she does and pretend that it doesn't exist. Just go on about the night with a smile and ignore the way she tries to hide her flinches. Focus on how hot she is with the red lips and how feisty she is with everyone else.

But I can't.

I won't.

"Because I need to know why you jerk every time I get close to you." I hear the change in my own voice when her eyes widen at my words and her nostrils flare with a deep breath.

Her dismissive scoff that follows makes my jaw firm, and my grip on her chin slips right into cupping her jaw to hold her close without forcing her. She's soft in my grip, but lightning against my palm that shoots straight to my aching and confused cock.

"So?" Pressing our foreheads together, I let my gaze float between hers.

"Soooo?" She drags out with a winging brow that I feel against my own forehead. "Some people at least try to kiss when they're this close."

I snort, the corner of my lips tipping up.

"Is that what you want?"

"Huh," Cedar half grunts. "I never took you as the asking type."

"No?" It's my turn to wing my brow at her. "Then what did you peg me as?"

"Take now, ask never." It comes off breathily, borderline whispered as her blues shine at me in a way that has my cock responding and my gut twisting.

"I'll cave." I give a gentle nudge of my head against hers as affirmation. "I'll give in. Once you tell me why you called in the papa bear."

"Um," Cedar licks her lips, her downcast gaze searching for mine that part and release my panting breath. "My ... ex calle—"

Slamming my lips to Cedar's, I don't wait for the words to finish leaving her throat.

Instead, I claim them with my tongue when she opens for me and pull them from the depths of her mouth as I cup her face in both hands and bend my body in half just to stay close to her.

She groans into me, her hands finding my hair and tugging in all the right ways that I feel it in the base of my spine and my throbbing cock.

My toes threaten to go numb when her tongue slides over mine and my cock promises to punish—me, or her—when Cedar leans back enough to angle farther into me.

The heat of her supple body against me, the ease of her cropped top riding up just enough to tease when her chest meets mine, has my cock solid and my head tilting to deepen the kiss that makes me question everything I've ever known.

Everything.

"Sweetness," I growl when I come up for the air my lungs beg me for. "Tell me."

With a heaving chest, Cedar reaches up to swipe her thumb beneath her lower lip. "No."

My jaw clenches, and my adrenaline runs hot in too many directions at her bat down. "No to what?"

"I don't have to tell you shit, Fin." If she wasn't so close, if her breath wasn't rushing down my throat, I'd bet that she would have growled the words, backed away, maybe even ran.

"Stubborn ass." It comes out gravelly, deepened with the desire I feel coursing through my veins with her so close, so soft and warm in my hands.

"Uh-huh," Cedar breathes, but her eyes are all for what I'm certain is a red stain now transferred onto on my lips from hers and thoughts of repeating that kiss that lit my nerve endings on fire.

Like I am.

"But you want to." I slam my lips to hers for the second time today and relish in the way she groans into me, her hands finding my shoulders to latch on.

Nails digging into my skin, I pry her lips apart with mine and return her groan when Cedar's tongue dances against mine.

My hips work themselves between her legs, my cock aching to get close to the warmth she radiates from her core.

She gasps when I pull back enough to trail my tongue down her jaw and nip between the rings in her ear.

"Tell me, Cedar," I growl, with a pulsing cock and a grip on her hair. "Tell me who did this to you."

"Jeremy."

Like a slap straight to my subconscious, my stomach drops out of my body and my cock rages harder with the possibilities of undoing all the things that'd been done to her.

How I can show Cedar the way a real man treats a goddess like her.

I'm going to fuck his memory right out of her.

But what I don't expect when I fill my lungs with the scent of the soft flesh of her neck is a memory to flood me.

A memory of a girl that looks an awful lot like a young Cedar with a pep to her step and a determination to get an autograph from one particular person.

Only for that hopefulness in her eye to be crushed by bruising hands and hate filled words.

"Cedar," I growl into her neck with that familiar vice back around my chest and a grip on her thighs that's probably a little too tight as I drag her closer. "You deserve better than that."

"Just shut up, Fin." She gasps when my jean clad cock rams into her core and makes both of us groan.

"Fuck," I breathe into her neck when even the friction of her hips against my covered cock threatens to have me too close to the edge. "Tell me to stop, Cedar."

"Guh," she groans, her arms around my neck, holding me close. "Why the hell would I do that?"

I release a chuckle and let my hips fall forward into her one more time, retracting completely from her warmth and snagging her hand before she can think too much of it.

Tugging her along, she hops off the tattoo chair on her platformed feet and follows me easily until we reach the door that her dad stands on the other side of. "Nuh-uh."

"Too late, now, sweetness." I shake my head and peek out of the small crack I make in the fabric with a single callused finger. "*Run.*"

Darting out into the scorching sunlight with Cedar's wrist wrapped up in my hand, I yank her left when her dad looks right and snicker when her squeals follow me.

It's lighthearted and exhilarating when we round the corner to the main part of the venue that blocks out the sun with a concrete throughway that bounces the echoes of her cackles right back into my ears.

Keeping up the pace, we rush through crowds, pass lines way too long for shitty food and merch and somewhere through it all, Cedar's fingers interlock around mine.

She holds on for dear life when her legs don't keep up with mine, allowing me to tug her along through the passages and manned gates that are up to keep the riffraff like us out.

But it doesn't and they don't.

As we pass the taco stand, I glance back over my shoulder at her and see the grin lighting up her face. The light shining in her gorgeous blue eyes. And the childlike laughter falling from her plump lips I can't wait to get another taste of.

My chest constricts at the sight of her, so wild and carefree and so close to being in my arms that the tension building behind my ribcage actually puts a smile on my face.

Good God, I am so fucked.

Chapter Eighteen

Fin

THE DOOR TO THE RV my band has kept on site since we got here days ago slams against the side wall of the vehicle with a loud bang that draws attention and elicits a snorting laugh from the woman following my lead.

It's that laugh that has me tugging Cedar into my arms by our intertwined fingers before we even make it up the few steps, and fills my stomach with a lightness I don't think I've ever felt when she comes to me easily.

I seal my lips to hers as I blindly reach for the handle to shut us in and the rest of the world out while my other wraps around her waist, hauling her in as close as I can get her.

The heat of her body against me, her tits pressing into my side, has my cock filling and my tongue diving in to claim her mouth once again.

She tastes divine and feels even better when her arms hook around my neck, tentatively at first, as if she's testing the waters and my feet stumble over each other as I move us farther into the bus in the direction of the bedroom I'm praying is empty in the back.

Growling when she lifts a leg and wraps a tight thigh around my hip, I grip the back of her knee and raise it higher. The angle, the openness of her, has me finding the nearest surface to pin her against and my aching cock grinding in search of friction.

Cedar's lips pop free on a gasp as I press harder into her covered core. I curse at the way my zipper digs into my swollen head and the way the smooth skin of her throat feels against my traveling tongue.

"We need a bed," she breathes, her words whispering over the shell of my ear and sending chills right down my heated spine.

Chuckling, I reach between us and pop free the button on her shorts. "Says you, sweetness."

She groans in a way that I feel the vibrations of her throat against my lips as I lower myself slowly, licking and nipping at each bit of exposed, creamy flesh. From the hollow of her throat, I dip to breathe warmth over her peeked nipples through the top she wears, while my fingers curl into the waistband of her shorts and drag them down with me.

On my knees at her feet, with her shorts bunched at her ankles, I take in the sight of her smooth stomach, exposed beneath the too-short shirt and showing off the ink I would bet money she managed to do herself. It's somehow her, her fiery style, accentuated by a simple curved barbell through her navel that begs for me to taste.

So I do.

"Fin." Leaning in, I flick at the jewelry with the tip of my tongue as I slide my fingertips back up the outside of her calves and I can't help how the sound she emits edges me closer, makes my cock harder.

Lower still, I trail my licks from the barbell to the waistband of her pretty little panties as Cedar buries her hands in my hair, tugging and pushing me like a war wages inside her.

Go lower, she presses down.

Come higher, she yanks up.

"Tell me, sweetness," I growl against her creamy skin and hook my hands in the thin elastic at her hips. "Am I going to find you wet for me?"

I look up in time to catch her head falling back and a full on groan escaping her lips swollen from my kisses.

"Sounds like a yes if I've heard one." I chuckle. Slowly, so achingly slow, I guide down the one thing keeping me from diving into her face first. The lace glides down her colorful thighs and when the material finally frees itself from between her legs, I see the result of my words, of my actions. "Fuuuuuck."

I'm panting along with her by the time her pussy is set free, my cock so painfully hard in my jeans, I have to pause and pop my own button for some relief. It doesn't do shit to relieve anything, so I shove my hand in and adjust.

Just the friction of denim on my sensitive cock has me rolling my eyes back and practically begging to get inside her.

I've never been so damn hard in my life.

"Fin," Cedar breathes, her hands tugging my hair and demanding my attention.

What is this woman doing to me?

"Yeah?" I let my sight trail up her body, slow and hot, until her eyes meet mine over top of her perfect tits and it's like I've gazed into the portal straight to hell.

The one where all the temptations are kept.

Desire, thick and so fucking sweet, flushes her cheeks and parts those thick lips. "Before I change my mind."

It's what she doesn't say, but instead does, that has my groan catching in the back of my throat.

Cedar leans back, bracing her hands on the surface of the counter I've had her up against, and hops up onto the marble surface. She lets her legs fall open, demanding my sight, and when I follow the lead and look at her exposed pink pussy, my breath stops in my chest like a full on tackle made contact to my torso and stole every bit of oxygen left in my cells.

Because what stares back at me is another little gem of adornment to the temple that is Cedar's body.

A fucking hood piercing.

Smirking, I let out a breath before flicking my eyes up to hers for one last confirmation. One last out. One last attempt for her to make her move and run.

She doesn't do anything of the sort, though. Instead, she catches that thick bottom lip between her pearly whites and forever etches herself in the back of my eyelids as *the* hottest woman I've ever had my hands on.

And hopefully my dick in, soon.

Gripping her hips to hold her up, I spread her knees with my elbows as wide as the shorts around her ankles will allow, and lean in.

First, I trail the tip of my nose over her from one side of the apex of her thighs to the other, just short of where she's glistening and so fucking wet for me.

Then, when she tugs at my hair and demands contact with a growl, I lengthen my tongue until just the very tip flicks the ring and her gasp fills the cabin around us.

"Shit," she groans from above me, her thighs trembling beneath my grasp as she leans back farther onto the counter and braces against the surface.

"Ah." Smirking, I curl my tongue back to run over the roof of my mouth, savoring the taste of her lingering there as my hands go to her thighs to keep her open for me. "She likes the tip."

"Shut up and eat me, Fin."

Chuckling, I release air through my nose and watch as goosebumps rise all over her exposed skin. The reaction is visceral, immediate, and my restraint snaps.

Deep from the depths of my gut, a growl erupts, and I bury my face between Cedar's legs.

The rush of her taste on my tongue has my cock punching the zipper of my jeans and threatening to tear through the denim, if it means some kind of friction.

But the taste.

Goddamn.

Her sweet wetness coating my lips and chin has my head spinning and ignoring anything that doesn't involve her clit in my mouth, because that would mean acknowledging anything other than the woman in my grasp exists.

And right now, nothing else does.

She moans when I flick my tongue over her pierced hood, licking and lapping at her slick pussy until she's tugging my hair and gasping for air.

"Fin," she moans, almost in warning, as she yanks my head back by the strands wrapped around her knuckles and meets my hungry gaze with one so dark I question what she's about to do.

Is she going ... or cumming?

When all she does is stare at me with a heaving chest and trembling thighs beneath my hands, I dart my tongue out and lick every bit of her arousal from my lips. "You need somethin', sweetness?"

"Fuck," she whimpers, her eyes rolling and her head falling back.

"That's the plan."

I dive back in, flicking the ring as I suck on her clit and when I pinch the silver between my teeth and give it a gentle tug, she creams on my tongue.

"That's it, sweet," I say between laps of my tongue on her pussy.

"*Oh, fuck,*" Cedar moans for me, burying both hands in my hair. "I'm gonna—"

I groan into her heat when her hips jam up into my face and a scream rips from her throat as she's cumming down mine.

My cock pulses with each clench of her pussy on my tongue, and each tug of my hair to keep me close as she rocks her orgasm out on my chin.

"Yes," Cedar chokes out when my tongue refuses to let any bit of her orgasm go untouched and she's spasming under the assault of the aftershocks.

Drawing back and licking her taste from my lips, I watch her watch me with a heated gaze as I stretch to my full height and hold out a hand in offering. "Can you walk?"

"Um," she half groans, her brow furrowing in confusion. "Duh."

"Then we aren't done yet." Grabbing her hand and yanking her to her feet, I stomp on the shorts that make it hard for her to walk until she fights her ankles free and the fabric is left discarded on the floor. She reaches down as she moves and manages to get the panties back up her thighs with the one free hand she has, and now I know that I'm going to shred those things just so she can't wear them out of here.

Breaching the bedroom in the back, I'm grateful to find the room clean and the bed made with fresh sheets I fully intend to dirty up.

I catapult Cedar forward until she's falling to the mattress and bouncing back up with a laugh that makes my chest swell with warmth.

She settles into the fluffed pillows with a grin as I rake my gaze over her almost naked body and commit the sight of her spread out for me to my memory.

A band tee cut short exposes her belly and still hides her tits I can't wait to get my mouth on, while only the thin, lacy, black panties cover that pussy I can't wait to dive into. Platformed combat boots cover her feet in a shade that's as dark as her long hair, and while I'd normally go for the heels on my shoulders, I'm hungry to have those resting behind my head.

"You on the pill, sweetness?" My words come out deep and darkened with desire. I kneel on the bed at her feet when she shakes her head no, crawling closer and closer until I'm between her spread legs. Her body vibrates—the good kind—with anticipation and need as I lean back on my haunches and fish my wallet from the back pocket of my jeans.

Inside the bifold leather is a foil pack I replaced just last night and a travel packet of lube because one can never be too prepared.

Fingering the one I need, I toss the wallet to the floor and rip the foil open with my teeth.

"Touch yourself," I demand, groaning when she complies and runs her fingers over her slickness beneath the lacy shit covering her. "That's it, sweet. Make sure you leave some for me."

Unzipping my jeans, I use my free hand to push the denim halfway down my thighs and fist my stiff cock. I pump myself in time to her strokes, my eyes nearly rolling when she says my name, and I release a groan of my own.

"You ready?" Gripping my length at the base, I pinch the tip of the rubber and start to roll the condom down to the root of my shaft.

When she nods on a groan, I lean over her and brace myself with one hand on the mattress next to her head.

And because I can't get enough of her, I plant my lips to hers in a scorching kiss that I feel straight down to my balls. Her hands go up the mattress, her breath scorching down my throat.

I am fucked.

"Last chance, Cedar." I pull back just enough to see her darkened gaze and wrap my fingers around the lacy panties.

"Goddamn, just shut up and do it."

Hovering over her entrance, I rip the lace to shreds and tap the head of my cock against her clit. The contact of her heat against me sends chills that race over my heated skin and all of my blood rushing south.

God, yes.

Lining up at her slick entrance, I thrust forward until I'm seated completely inside her pussy in one hard stroke.

Fuckfuckfuck.

She lets out a choked squeal when her body moves up the bed from the force, her limbs going taut and her mouth stuck open in a silent scream.

So tight yet so wet, she takes every inch of me in and steals every bit of the breath from my lungs.

Frozen, with sweat beading on my skin despite the AC the bus pumps through the system, I beg my heart not to stop from how hard my cock pulses and how still Cedar goes.

"Talk to me." The words are barely a choke out of my throat that's desperate to drag in air.

"Fuuuck," she finally releases, the tension easing, and arches her back.

"Yeah, sweet. That's fucking it." I steal the moan from her lips and snake my bracing arm beneath the arch of her spine to wrap her hair around my fist and keep her curved up.

Hooking my other arm around the back of her knee, I grit my teeth when the zipper on her boot grazes over my bicep and I sink deeper into her heat.

"Fuck," I groan, my hips retreating on their own, only to sink back inside her tight pussy.

"God, yes," Cedar wails as her nails find purchase in my shoulders and dig in deep.

"That's right." I lean down and nuzzle my nose across her covered tits that are still pushed up into the air. "Lift up your shirt. Show me." Clenching my jaw to keep myself together long enough, I groan from behind my teeth when I pull back and the ridges of her tight pussy tug on my piercing. "Fuck."

Shivers run down my spine as she releases my shoulders and drags her top up to show me those delicious pale tits with pebbled pink nipples she latches onto. Twisting and pulling, she teases herself while I move my cock inside her and her swollen lips fall open with a groan.

"Yes, that's it, sweetness. Tease yourself for me."

"Fin," she moans, her back arching up painfully farther into my hips as I grind my cock into her.

My balls draw up tight when Cedar clenches around me, tight on my cock like she's close to cumming, and a flood of her arousal slicks over me.

"Oh, fuck," I pant, sweat slicking my skin and hers, and harden my thrusts. "I wanna feel that pussy clench. Cum on my cock, sweetness."

"Oh, God." Cedar's body tightens beneath me, her muscles tensing as her nails find my shoulders again and send shock waves through my system.

The sight of her, the taste of her still lingering on my tongue, burns into my subconscious as she spasms and does exactly what I asked.

Cedar comes on my cock.

Quickening my pace, I dive as deep into her hot pussy as I can and I watch as she comes undone beneath me with gasping breath and a roll to her eyes.

I ride it out with a jaw so tight I might need dental work when we're done and I don't stop the way my spine tingles or my toes actually fucking curl when she moans my name.

"*Fin.*"

With her body beneath me, perfect and vibrating with a second orgasm that crashes into her, I arch my hips back and slam home.

The roar that rips from my throat would scare even me if I wasn't instead worried about keeping consciousness and not crushing her as my orgasm wrecks my body. I'm filling the condom, my hips grinding so every last drop is pulled from me.

"Fuck."

Panting and sweaty, I groan when my hips jut forward a final time and my body threatens to crash down over Cedar's heaving chest.

I peel my fingers from her dark hair and bite inside my lip when the movement sends shock waves straight to my still hard cock that would rather not leave her warmth.

I could stay inside her forever.

Unhooking my arm from her knee, I let it glide gently back to the bed when she groans and flexes her foot.

I force my body over her leg with a push off of the mattress and allow myself to crash into the comforter I didn't even bother to pull down.

"Think you can walk, sweetness?" I grumble into the pillow my face is smushed into with muffled words.

"Uh, duh," Cedar says, but she's still panting, breathy, and unconvincing.

"Gimme five and I'll fix that."

Chapter Nineteen

Cedar

I LIED.

I can't fucking walk.

And I liked it.

My legs shake like a brand new doe and now I hate the man that's passed out beside me even more for being the best lay I've ever had.

Clenching my jaw, I fight off the aftershocks that threaten to keep me in this bed when I know damn well I shouldn't have followed him here to begin with.

Reality slams into me, what I've done, and my stomach clenches with each passing second I'm on my back next to him.

I left my post to get fucked.

How ridiculous is that?

That's beyond desperate.

I snuck around my own dad, Peach, and a whole line of people waiting for my work to be inked into their bodies to get laid by a devilishly handsome Rock god.

To get fucked.

My actions are what make me a whore.

Unworthy.

Jeremy just happened to be the one to call me out on it, and I've been a fool to ignore that part of myself this whole time. Just blaming him for his bullshit.

He was right all along.

Raw and unchained panic settles into my bones as Fin lies beside me, unmoving, and unknowing of my rising dread. He's so out of it from the encounter that was the two of us finally crashing together that he has no clue.

I can't stay here.

My chest heaves, my breath rushing faster than when he was fucking me and I hate the way my pussy clenches at just the thought of Finland Montgomery inside of me.

I hate the way my pussy slicks when I sit up, wetting the bedding beneath me and leaving evidence behind of my wrongdoing.

I shouldn't have caved.

I should have never come here.

Pinching my lips between my teeth with too much force, I hold back the sob that demands release.

Jeremy was right.

I did fuck him. I did make fuck-me eyes and got Fin to sleep with me.

I did want it all along.

Pushing up on shaking legs and numb feet, I push back the stars that line my vision and all but rip the remaining waistband of my already shredded underwear from my hips when the damp cloth hits my too-sensitive skin.

Another reminder of what I did.

Making it to the doorway with watery vision, I pause to try and catch my breath when I make a mistake and look over my shoulder.

On the bed, Fin lies face down where he collapsed with his jeans still around his thighs and his gloriously inked ass on full display. Red streaks deface the ink of his back where his torn shirt barely hangs onto his frame—marks I put there—and his hair is mussed from my hands.

He made me cum, without my assistance, for the first time ever.

And all the things he said while we fucked ...

Oh, God.

My hand shoots up to cover the first muffled squeak of a sob that escapes my lips.

I just need to get to the bathroom. Clean up.

But my feet don't stop until my shorts are in my hands and I'm desperately trying to rub out the boot print that stands out on the ass.

Growling, hot tears streaking down my cheeks, I give up trying to get rid of the print no one will actually see and jam my booted feet into the cut-off denim.

We're at a rock concert. No one is going to know.

But they are *going to know.*

I secure the shorts on my waist and dash to the door as I do my best to swipe away the raccoon eyes forming under my heavily lined, and still leaking, lids.

My hands shake when I grasp the handle to let me outside into the freedom I need from the situation I've put myself in.

Jeremy was right.

I don't deserve someone like Fin.

Dragging in a ragged breath, I take another look over my shoulder into the dark cabin of As Above's RV. There's a light on above the sink, but the rest of the hallway leading back to where I left the one man that made me feel alive for the first time since I was a teenager is so black that I can't tell if my eyes betray me, or if it's really a tall as hell silhouette I see standing in the doorway.

I blink, and I squint, and when the air remains tense from the dismay I bleed out into the space, I rachet the handle and release myself out into the wild of the music festival.

The ultimate walk of shame.

I'm vibrating with nerves, my limbs trembling with the shakes, when I make it back to my tent to find Ava on the inside, alone, and dry inking into her own thigh.

"Oh, hey, C." She jumps when I slam in and scrambles to put the tattoo gun back where she found it. "I didn't realize you were coming back."

"I—um." Clearing my shaking voice, I avoid looking her in the eye as I head to my toolbox where I know I left my phone. "Just clean it when you're done, Ava."

"Your dad saw you left your phone and said to tell you he saw you leaving. Call him."

"Yeah, okay." Snagging the device, I'm dialing and dashing back out of the tent before she can say anything else.

The main show is already over for the night and the moon has taken its place in the dark sky. I maneuver around lingering sweaty bodies that smell like the dumpster outside of my tattoo shop in the humid nighttime air as I slam the phone to my ear and a sense of relief washes over me when the line clicks.

"I know it's late, Sara," I say into the receiver before she can even get a greeting out as the exit to the venue comes into view. "But I need to talk."

"Yeah, Cedar." I freeze when the voice on the other side is not the woman that has helped me through some of the shit my brain has put me through, but instead has an inky oil slicking over my stomach and makes me more nauseous. "We need to talk."

No, no, no, no.

I freeze and yank the phone from my head and kill the call with a tremor in my unsteady hands as a group of exiting concert goers bump into me. They smash into my arms and elbows, and the phone goes skittering across the pavement.

Watching in shock as the thing gets kicked around and all but glides over the cement walkway, I flip my loose hair out of my face and chase off after it.

My heart stuttering in my chest and my words stuck in my throat, I force my heavy feet to the device as I bump into bodies and get tousled around by those I'm being equally as rude to.

I need to call for a ride and get my therapist on the line instead of the man that made me crazy and a sense of relief almost washes over me when the phone finally stops beneath the flat sole of a skater shoe.

Forcing a breath, I watch as hands come down to pick up the device from beneath their feet. Long hair falls around the face as the person bends and I work my dry throat to use my words and tell them it belongs to me so they don't take off with it.

"Hey, man." It's not as loud as I'd hoped with the crowd chatter picking up around me, the last ones of the night set on being the loudest ones yet as they all head to their after parties. "Hey!"

Stumbling through the dark as the crowd thins, and the person straightens with my phone in their grasp and it's not until a slender arm comes up and swipes the hair out of his face that I'm stuck motionless like I've sunk into the concrete.

"When I said we needed to talk ..." Jeremy's muddled hazel eyes, rimmed with a darkened red and sunken into his once handsome face, meet mine over the few people that meander around on quick feet in the distance between us. "I didn't think it'd be so soon, baby."

Bile, hot and acidic, rushes up the back of my throat. "What do you want, Jeremy?"

"Well baby," he chuckles a sickening sound from the base of his throat as he cups his junk. "You. I want you and that whore's pussy you like to dish out."

I bite back the dry heave that threatens me and eye my phone pinched loosely between his fingers and thumb.

He looks so sick. In the head.

Like me.

Gritting my jaw when I know there's no way I could outrun him then, and there's next to no chance I could now, I bow my shoulders in and take a tentative step forward.

I need my phone.

"Jeremy," I try, with an outstretched hand and another step closer to the man that fuels my nightmares.

"Oh, baby," he chides with a tsk and takes a step back and it's then that I realize he's just outside of the gate of the venue. Where security is less than and the cameras are non-existent. "I *just* want to talk."

Do I really need the phone?

Shit, how else do I get home?

Biting the inside of my lip to keep from screaming, it's moments like these that I really wish I just carried my bat with me. I doubt he could outrun the Slugger.

"Quit fucking around and give me my phone, Jeremy." I take another step forward, a little more menacingly this time, which only earns me a sickening laugh and him retreating another step. Closer to the bag set up by the tree and a mound of cigarette butts sitting next to it.

Like he'd been sitting here waiting for me.

Sick to my stomach, I wrap an arm around my torso and drop the arm I had outstretched to the man I once thought I'd loved. "Rot in hell, Jeremy."

Heat rushes against my shoulders when I take a step back from the abusive fuck, convinced that my phone can die along with him, and it's not until I turn to escape that I slam into a wall of muscle.

"I believe the lady asked for her phone back."

Massive hands keep me steady as I trail my gaze up the hard chest covered in the curly hair falling from his head and land on a darkened blue-green stare down.

"So you're fucking him now?" Jeremy sneers with a level of disgust I'll never understand. "*He's* saving you?"

"Cedar." Deep and downright dangerous, Rex Thompson's gaze flicks to mine, his hands still holding me close, before settling his death stare back on the man across from us. "You good?"

"Um." *No.* "Yeah."

"You know him?"

Pausing, I let my sight wander over the small grass patch now between us and take in the state of Jeremy and his tattered clothes, his greasy hair I once loved to play with and the snarl marring his sunken face.

"No. I don't." *Because I never really did.*

"Cedar, baby, c'mon." It's Jeremy's turn to become pleading when Rex pushes me to his side and takes a menacing step forward.

In front of me.

My stomach rolls, threatening to evacuate when Rex takes another step closer to the man that ruined my life and my mental stability. "I said," Rex growls into the damp night air. "The lady wants her phone back."

"Fine." Jeremy shrugs like this whole thing is no big deal to him, a smiling sneer planted on his pitted face. "But it's going to cost you."

Rex's shoulders square, making him seem bigger, more menacing.

He's downright terrifying.

"Rex, don't," I whisper-hiss at his back when his arm comes up and his hand flicks in the *gimme* motion.

"You've got three fucking second to hand it over."

"Touch me, and I'll sue your ass off." Jeremy chuckles, a dark and dangerous sound echoing off of the short trees around us.

"Go ahead." Rex shrugs with a tightness to his upper back. "Pretty sure what you're doing is harassment to begin with."

"Oh?" Jeremy takes another step back, edging closer and closer to the bag left against the tree. "And you aren't, Rex Thompson?" He shakes his head, his oily hair falling around his face. "Harassing a fan, that is? Someone who's just trying to hear your music?"

"Listen, you fucking rat," Rex growls and stomps forward as he fingers his wallet from his back pocket. Fisting two fifties, he tosses them to the ground at Jeremy's feet and snatches the phone when the excuse of a man dives for the money and ditches the device in the process. "Now get the fuck out of here."

Jeremy looks up from his crouch with a maniacal grin and shoves the bills into his torn clothes. "Pleasure doing business with you. I'll be back."

"I said *now*." Rex flexes at the man who took my virginity—and then some—and has him scurrying off into the night with his snatched bag and fresh cash.

"Rex." Finding my voice and my feet, I launch myself at the man that just saved my life and pound my fists against his hard chest. "Why did you *do that?*"

"Cedar," he scoffs as he grabs for my hands and wraps my wrists up in one of his. "Stop hitting me. I'm fucking mad."

"*Mad?*" I struggle against his hold when he drags me to his side. "I'm mad!"

"What the fuck do you have to be mad about?" Rex nearly yells, his adrenaline evident in the way his chest heaves with his panting breath. "You're lucky it was me that fucking found you."

"I was handling it just fine," I shoot back.

Growling, Rex's jaw snaps shut as he moves me to stand right in front of him. "Where the fuck did you find this guy?"

I growl right back when his eyes shimmer with the result of his anger. "I don't have to explain shit to anyone, Rex." Jerking my hands from his grasp, I spin, fully prepared to stomp away from his overbearing bullshit and come face to face with Rex's bodyguard jogging our way. "Just fucking great. It's a whole family affair. You gonna call Ari, too?"

I sneer when I know I shouldn't. I argue and yell that it's none of his damn business. Flail my arms around and make a crazy woman scene like a total tool.

But the last—and I mean the *last*—thing I need is another man thinking that I owe him something. That I need protecting. That I need a fucking savior.

I don't.

"Cedar." I yank my shoulder away when Rex grabs it, but that doesn't stop the man from trying again and succeeding in spinning me back to face his grave features. "You are family."

"Oh, shut. Up," I spit and deflect his warming gaze and his hand on me.

"Cedar, I'm glad I got to you."

Chapter Twenty

Cedar

"I **WAS FUCKING FINE.**"

"Don't care," Rex deflects. "Ian, check this, please."

We're back at my tent when I refused Rex's invite to the bus where my best friend waits for her man, along with the man I slept with only an hour or so ago, probably still fucking napping.

I stare over my crossed arms at the lead singer of As Above and his damn bodyguard as they trade my phone between them and Ian works his super-secret security guard magic.

"I literally watched him the whole time. There's nothing on my phone except missed calls from my dad." I hold my hand out, expecting Ian to cave and just give the thing over.

He doesn't.

"You have no clue what he's been up to, Cedar," Ian growls and props his tablet up on the top of my toolbox, attaching a cord from it to the phone.

"And you fucking do?"

The skeptically winged brow I get from the man that kind of reminds me of my own father has me throwing my hands up and scoffing. "Seriously."

"Dead," Ian deadpans.

"C, listen." Rex pushes to his feet and steps closer to me with his hands held innocently out in front of him. "I just want to make sure he didn't do anything weird. Guys like that are fucking crazy."

Ian's scoff echoes over the dead space between us and draws my attention. "Like she doesn't know."

"Ian."

But it's too late to put the words back in his mouth.

I told Rex I didn't know Jeremy.

The lead singer spins on his booted feet to his bodyguard with a cocked head. "What's that supposed to mean?"

I shake my head behind Rex's back when Ian looks over the man's shoulder at me and I see the tick in his jaw start. "I think that's on Ms. Jones to tell you. Not me."

No way he knows.

He couldn't.

Growling at Ian, I run my hands through my hair and avoid Rex's pinning stare when he rotates back to me. "No."

Could he?

"Cedar," Rex says firmly with those caring, yet deadly, eyes that have my stomach twisting at the idea that Rex would know the truth.

"Don't, Rex."

"Someone better fucking tell me something," he growls out, "before I get pissed."

When the tent remains silent and Ian distracts himself with whatever he's doing to check my phone, I swallow the lump that builds in the back of my throat and fight off the tears that prick the backs of my eyes.

"Fine," Rex growls and pulls his phone from his pocket. "My wife will know."

"*Still* not married yet, Rex."

"Shut up, Ian."

The longer his thumbs work over the device, the more my eyes itch and my hands shake.

"Stop." Shaking my head when he looks up at me with a lifted brow. "You can't."

Sighing, Rex slips the phone back into his pocket and crosses his arms over his thick chest. "Can't what, C?"

I drag in a shaky breath, my eyes misting over and my jaw working to form the words.

Which ones?

How much do I tell him when even my best friend doesn't know?

None. The answer is tell him nothing.

"I, um ..." I clear the emotion that builds in my throat and stare at the ground. "That was ..."

"Cedar." Rex's heavy hand lands on my shoulder and makes my skin crawl—not because the rockstar repulses me, but because it takes me a minute of preparation to be okay with physical touch from the people I give a shit about. "Sit down, sis. Jesus, you're making my chest hurt."

I snicker, but it comes out watery and weak when Rex leads me to my chair. With my hands limp in my lap and tears building on my lashes, I eye my tattoo gun, the one thing that has always brought me peace, and reach for it.

"Here," Rex says as he pulls my stool over and sits with wide knees over the cushion, his arm outstretched in my direction. Pointing directly beneath the lyrics that area already scripted into his skin, he continues. "*Wipe away the decay and sing me your songs of praise.*"

"What's that from?" My voice sounds too small, too weak, and it makes me mad at myself.

"The new song we've been working on." He nods to the thin strip with minimal shading already present on his forearm that he props across my thighs. "Go ahead."

I draw in a deep breath and snag the cleaning solution on the tray next to us. Wiping away at his skin, I kick the pedal around to reach from where I sit and begin to freehand the letters into his arm—not so different from the last time I inked the lead singer.

This time definitely is different, though.

This time, I'm not trying to get the man to cave and admit he's no good for my best friend.

With teeth sunk into the inside of my lip to force the concentration on the ink instead of the ache in my chest, the tears begin to build for another reason as realization settles in.

Fin.

"He wrote these, didn't he?" I ask.

"Yes."

My stomach flips.

He deserves so much better than me.

"When?" I sniffle.

"Last night." Rex's words are softened, his eyes glued to the way my hand still moves over his skin.

After I sent him away.

Before we slept together and I left him.

I withdraw my trembling hands and lay the equipment on the table to bury my face in my hands.

"Talk to me, Cedar," Rex begs and pulls his arm back, his grip attaching to my knee in a reassuring gesture I hate that I want. "Tell me what happened."

"Why?" I cry with a pathetic sniffle and a watering chuckle. "Why does everyone keep asking me to fucking talk?"

"Maybe because we want to help."

"*No one can*," I bellow in shame as I meet the gaze of my best friend's future husband with leaking eyes and an unbearable ache clawing in my chest.

"If you'd just get out of your fucking head, you'd see that some of us can."

My spine snaps straight at the growled words that come from behind me and my pussy betrays me with a clench at the sound of the guitarist's voice interjecting into the conversation.

Rex's eyes trail over my shoulder to the source and regret leaks out of me.

"Shit." I roughly swipe away at my leaking eyes to hide the shame the tears betray and follow Rex's stare.

Eyes darkened and shoulders that seem twice their size, I suck in a breath at the sight of Fin standing behind me and stop myself from reaching out to him.

I want to.

Biting the inside of my lip until I taste blood, I face front and lean to pick the tattoo gun back up.

I can't.

"You ready?" Tipping the machine to Rex in question, whose gaze flips between me and the guitar legend at my back, I dip to take his wrist in my grasp anyway.

"That's it?" It's quiet. Too quiet. "You're just going to ignore it?"

Ignore, ignore, ignore.

Shivers run down my spine at Fin's words that I refuse to acknowledge as I turn Rex's arm in my grip and assess the work I've done, giving it another swipe of cleaner.

"Can't," I bite. "Busy."

Deflect, deflect, deflect.

At least I'm self-aware enough to recognize it. That's a step.

Tapping the pedal, I trigger the tattoo gun to buzz to life and lean over Rex's forearm to finish the piece I started. It only takes a few more minutes of awkward tension to complete the small piece of intricate font, but when it's done, I clean Rex up and cover the fresh ink.

And as I take my time cleaning up the rest of the mess created with down-turned eyes and a tightness in my shoulders, I try desperately to will the lot of them to leave me with my thoughts.

Telepathy, please be real.

It's not. And they don't.

Instead, Ian hands over my phone with a stiff nod and the three of them circle around me.

"Stop," I beg.

"Tell them who Jeremy is, Cedar," Fin growls. "Tell them why your dad's hanging around."

"No, I—"

"You mean the one that was just outside?" Ian asks with a firm brow and a floating gaze.

"Which one?" Fin's attention snaps to the bodyguard with a feral growl that makes me grimace.

"The crack-headed gutter rat?" Rex asks and my head begins to spin with the conversation that's going on over my head.

The voices filter in around me and jumble together into incoherent sentences I can't even begin to understand, though I know they're asking me questions and expecting answers.

"Please stop." My voice is barely a whisper as my heart races, my breath running right along with it.

"Cedar, tell me what the hell happened." Rex's desperation leaks out of his words.

"C'mon," Fin pushes.

"C, please."

"*Stop,*" I roar with a heaving chest and push up from the chair they crowd to plant my ass right on the concrete and throw my legs up the length of my toolbox. It's steady enough to hold my heavy boots up in the air as I flatten my spine to the cool ground.

On your back again, I hear Jeremy's sneer in my head as the tears break free and roll down the side of my face. Pushing my palms into the sockets, I can't hold back the sob that rakes from my stuttering chest.

Because of course I'd have a panic attack. In front of everyone.

It feels like chaos erupts around me, the chattering and static of noise that my brain refuses to register assaulting my ears and assisting in the flow of tears from my eyes.

"*I fucking lied, okay?*" I'm blubbering, a hot fucking mess on the floor of what was supposed to be the best weekend I've ever had.

Poetic, I guess.

Certainly, heavy therapy material.

"I lied and said I could walk. I lied about knowing Jeremy. I *lied*."

The moment the words are off my lips, I'm ripped from the floor with such force that the air whooshes from my lungs and the stuck sobs intensify. Shaking and numb, and so fucking angry, I barely feel the warmth wrap around me as my ass is settled against muscular legs. My hair fills my mouth, wet from the shit that leaks from my face, and leaves me with a level of shame I've never felt before.

They all deserve better.

"Sweetness." Fin's voice fills my ear and adds to the tension built up in my chest, enough that I feel like it might actually snap. "You're okay."

It feels like I shake my head, but I'm so fucked that I can't tell.

"You're okay," Fin almost coos—if an angry man can—and cradles my head to his hard chest. "You're safe, I promise."

He cups my jaw gently, his callused fingertips grazing my skin and pulling another incontrollable sob from deep in my gut.

I cling to his shirt—different that the one he wore earlier—with tight fists and cry into his pec as he holds me close and speaks softly in my ear.

"You're safe, Cedar. I've got you." His voice is deep and scratchy and easy to focus on when it's whispering over the shell of my ear in repeated affirmations. "No one's gonna hurt you."

My breath stutters in my throat, catching up on the emotions that spill out of me like a cathartic purge and I suck in the first breath in what feels like hours.

Pulling back just enough to breathe fresh air, Fin tilts my face up with a thumb under my chin and his fingers curled into the back of my neck.

"Sweet, you're safe with me. Always," he whispers with shining eyes and a firmed jaw. A jaw that reminds me that there's other people around me and another level of panic arises.

With wide eyes, I glance around my setup, only to find it empty.

"It's just you and me." Fin's grasp brings me back to him and his stupidly pretty blue eyes. "It's just me."

"I—" Poking out my tongue to gather moisture for my dried lips and froggy throat, I bite the inside of my lip when I find there are no words that can make the last few minutes disappear. "I'm sorry."

"Nuh-uh." Fin shakes his head, a subtle tip to the corner of his thinned lips. "No, you're not. You shouldn't be."

"But I—"

"Nope."

"Fin," I growl, which only earns me a ghost of a smile on his thick lips.

"Go ahead. Say my name."

"*Ugggghhh.*" Fist to his chest, I go to push him but don't get very far when I'm the one on top of him.

Snickering, Fin cups my face and guides my chin to face him. His free hand swipes tacky hair from my forehead, the rough pad of his finger smoothing down the side of my face to slide behind my ear and press his palm to my jaw.

The things I see flash in his eyes as he moves over my face should terrify me.

Actually, they do.

But it's a different kind of fear that takes a back seat to the curiosity of the warmth it brings me. The calmness it allows me.

He just held me while I freaked. While I bawled my eyes out and screamed.

And he still doesn't know why.

Yet he's not running for the hills.

"Even if you hate me, sweet, you'll always be safe with me."

And somehow, I believe him.

"Fuckin' always."

Chapter Twenty-One

Fin

GOOD GOD, THIS WOMAN *brings so many emotions out in me. Shit I can't even begin to describe.*

Staring into red-rimmed eyes that are too puffy and sad, I cradle the woman I'm fucked over and hope I can muster the restraint not to find the rat that put her here.

Crying on the floor.

No, fuck that.

The motherfucker that put her here better hope I find my restraint somewhere along the way because he is not going to live much longer.

With her hand in my vice grip, I drag her across the long ago emptied venue in the dark to the main stage As Above is going to play on in less than twenty-four hours.

It's almost the size of our touring stage, filled with all kinds of special effects for tomorrow's show, and meant to withstand even Rex Thompson's wild antics.

Like falling off the damn thing.

Except for now, it's littered with equipment and cases that create the perfect nooks to hide in.

"What the fuck are we doing, Fin?"

Shrugging, I use my free hand to lift my weight up onto the abandoned stage but stay crouched when she stays several feet below me.

"C'mon. I'll give you a private show."

Cedar plants a booted foot on the floor of the stage and lets me lift her the rest of the way up onto the platform by our hands that I've managed to keep intertwined.

I can't lie to myself, though. I keep my grip on her because I like the way she feels in it. Like the way she gives me little tingles that feed up my arm and fuck me right in the heart.

And then I catch her eyes on me?

Hot damn, I am done for.

"Seriously, Fin, I gotta get back."

"To where?" I shrug and tug her across the platform to stage left where the drawn curtain creates the perfect hiding spot I found earlier. "You got a curfew or somethin', princess?"

"Oh, fuck you, Fin." Cedar rolls her bloodshot eyes, but puts up no resistance to my lead.

"Um, yeah, that'd be nice."

"No."

"Maybe later then." I smirk at the woman. "Before you turn into a punkin'."

"Shut up." She slaps my bicep, but grins softly—which was the whole damn point—as I reach back behind the heavy fabric of the unused stage curtain and wrap my fingers around the neck of the guitar I stashed there during Rex's writing session early this morning.

Jesus, it feels like it's been a week since then.

With both hands occupied, I use the fingers wrapped around Cedar's grip to pull her close enough that I smell that woodsy scent fresh from her instead of what still clings to my skin. The heat of her penetrates the shirt I wear as she easily steps into me, then stands still against my chest. Her normally vicious eyes are set to intrigued, and I don't miss the way her breath catches when I dip closer.

Her forehead reaches my chin when she leans in, releasing our hands so that she can wrap an arm around my waist and tuck her head into my chest.

What the ... fuck ...?

I sigh at her warmth there in my side, from my toes up to my damn nose that I rest against the top of her head and inhale deep. She smells of the forest on a damp morning, just before the sun rises and breaks up the dewy fog the night has left behind.

Fresh, crisp, and on the horizon of something that I hope isn't going to hurt.

Pressing my lips to her hair, I feel the way she melts into me with tightened arms and releases a breath when I wrap an arm around her ribs.

"Cedar," I whisper as best as my deep voice will allow. "You trust me, yeah?"

Sighing, she gives a slight shrug that moves her body against my torso and stirs my cock. "Not one single bit."

Stilled, I let her rest against me knowing that she's full of shit or else I would've lost an eye by now.

Seeing how that fucker made her twitchy makes me even angrier.

"If this is you putting on a show, it's the worst one yet." Momentarily stunned, stuck in the way this woman drives me mad in all the ways, it takes a moment for her humor and slight shifting shoulders to sink in.

She's fucking chuckling at herself.

Shaking my head and hiding the way she plants a smirk on my lips, I spin away and release her for the first time in over an hour to fist my guitar. I feed my torso through the strap, tweaking the tuning pegs as I give soft plucks over each string to make sure the pitch is right. I keep the volume low, just for us.

Once the instrument is ready, I pull over a stool left abandoned on its side and plant the wood right in front of the woman I'm pretty sure I'm falling in love with.

"Let's play a game, sweetness." I strum as I talk, creating a soft melody without taking my eyes off the goddess in front of me. She pokes her tongue out and licks her lip as her eyes dart down to where my fingers work the strings and back up to the grin stretching across my face. "For each groove you don't recognize, you have to take something off."

She's shaking her head before the words are off my lips, but her grin is telling another story. "You want me to strip to you playing."

"Uh, duh," I snicker and strum into the darkness enveloping us, thankful to not be a part of the after-the-party parties that are keeping the attention of anyone still hanging out at the venue. It's late as hell, but as long as my girl's smiling, I'm staying. "Won't take much."

Cedar lets out a growly scoff. "I know a lot of songs."

"I said grooves," I correct. "As in riffs. Guitar parts. I'll start easy." She rolls her eyes and shifts her weight onto her back foot so that she can pop her hip and place her hands against her waist.

"Try me, smartass."

Smirking, I tip my chin to the melody I'm already playing in question and let my eyes do a quick sweep to ensure that we're still alone in the maze of equipment. "Then what's this one?"

"Oh, fuck you." Cedar's hands drop, one coming up to her face to place a finger across those thick lips I'd rather be kissing—*don't push it, asshole.* "It's As Above."

"Uh-huh," I say with a quick nod. "Which one?"

Frozen in place like the thinking wheel is turning, Cedar's smile drops when the song I play doesn't sound the same without all the other shit behind it. Without the drums pounding the beat, or the rhythm guitar accenting the melody. Or Rex's voice serenading a crowd of thousands.

Or played in the right pitch.

Because I'd rather see the sexy goddess naked on this empty stage than play clean.

Sue me.

"Dammit," Cedar huffs, her hands going to the hem of her shirt before I can replay the riff and she's ripping the short top over her head, letting it flitter to the floor.

"Fuck," I growl at the sight of her not wearing any damn thing underneath, and my eyes settle right on her creamy and fully exposed tits.

I miss the mark, fumble the notes, and nearly haul my ass out of the stool.

"Well?" she pushes, with a hand gesture to the guitar. "What is it?"

Chuckling, I let my sight wander up her torso like a slow caress. "Next one."

I change the melody, play a different riff, and grin when she growls.

"Fuck you." Cedar pops the button on her shorts and lets the fuckers drop to her feet, stepping out of them without pause.

How my fingers keep working the strings, I don't understand, because all blood rushes south at the sight of her naked in front of me.

Unwavering and panty-less.

Because she left the remnants of the ripped thong on my floor and it is now burning a hole in my pocket.

Sucking in a breath, I rake my gaze down her body in a hot once over that makes my cock throb and her hands go back to her bare hips.

"You got me, hotshot. Now what?"

Slamming my hand to the bridge, I stop all sound coming from the guitar and push to my feet. I stalk to her with thunderous steps, Cedar's gaze tracking my every move as I slip the guitar behind me and rush her.

My hands are on her skin the second she's within reach, tugging her against me as the body of the axe slaps against my ass at my sudden stop.

"Now." I pause and tilt her chin up to look at me. "*This.*"

I slam my lips to hers and swallow the surprised squeak she lets loose. I see her eyes flash wide before closing mine and tilting my head. I swipe my tongue out and run it across her lower lip, silently begging for her to open those thick lips and let me in for a taste I don't think I'll ever get enough of.

God, yes.

She parts for me as her slender arms trail up my chest to wrap around my neck to pull me closer.

Diving in, our tongues clashing in the perfect battle for dominance, I slip an arm around her waist and haul her close enough to feel my cock against her belly as I step backwards.

I take another step backwards, and then another without breaking the connection until the extended heel of my boot taps against the tall stack I spin us to. With her back against the surface, our lips part for a breath as I dip to run the tip of my tongue down her neck and inhale the earthy scent of her like my life might depend on remembering it.

"Sweet," I groan out when her hands feed into my hair and tug. "When I asked about the pill ...?"

"IUD," she pants as I nip at her creamy flesh. "You didn't ask about control, just the pill."

Rolling my eyes to myself, I sink my teeth into the tight muscle of her shoulder. "Smartass."

"Fin," she breathes into the pain, moaning into the pleasure when I run my tongue over to soothe the bite.

"Mm," I grunt and lean down to hook a hand around the back of her knee. "I should make you pay for that." Lifting Cedar, I hook my other hand around her loose thigh and straighten until her back slams into the stack and another delicious sound escapes her throat. "But I'm a little impatient right now."

She groans in response to my lips trailing back up her neck and sealing to hers in a way that lets me swallow the rest of the sounds she makes when I press my hips between her spread thighs.

Having her like this, open for me with her legs draped over my forearms and trapped against my body, has my cock throbbing and the jeans threatening to do harm with the zipper if I don't get them open.

"Sweetness," I growl into her before sinking my teeth into her lower lip and earning myself a mewl from the goddess. "Get my cock out."

The breath rushes out of Cedar at my demand, and her fumbling hands squeeze between us to work down the zipper.

"*Fuck,*" I bite off when the metal does in fact catch on the head of my pulsing cock before releasing and lowering for the freedom I sigh at. "Shit, sweet."

Snickering, Cedar wraps a fist around the base and short pumps until my eyes are rolling back and my chest caves with a groan.

"Enough of that," I breathe and jerk my cock from her grip.

"Why's that?" She asks with feigned innocent, fluttering eyelashes and all, and reaches for me again.

Chuckling, I pin her hand between us with my chest and lean in to run my tongue over the shell of her ear. The move lines my cock right against her heat that feels like it pulses against me and drives me insane with an insatiable desire.

"Because," I whisper, my voice all gravel in her ear. "I'm gonna cum in you. Not on you."

Cedar's shuddering frame in my hands is all the permission I need to slam my hips forward and bury my cock inside her.

"Fin!" Her gasp flies over my ear and sends chills straight down to my drawn up balls.

"Tell me you're good," I breathe into her hair, the strands sticking to my lips and inhaling into my mouth, but I don't give a shit. The warmth of her pussy wrapped around my cock has me ready to fucking cum faster than I've ever known. "Need to hear it."

"Good," she squeaks out, gasping again when I withdraw my hips and slam into her heat again. "*God, yes, Fin.*"

Her words spur me on, my motion picking up speed almost as much as the breath rushing out of her. Motion that has the guitar at my back reminding me it's still there with every slap to my ass.

"That's it. Fuck," I groan into her neck, my own lungs racing with each thrust that drives me closer to that edge I'm so ready to fling myself off of as long as it's with her.

Only her.

"Fin," Cedar moans into my ear as her pussy tightens around me, telling me she's as close as I am.

"Wait for me, sweet." I drive my hips into her, rotating so that the zipper brushes over her clit with each intake of my cock.

"Oh, God," she mewls and clings to me with sweat slicked limbs. "I can't wait, Fin."

"Yes," I pant. "You will."

"Can't," she growls out with a clench to the heat wrapped around me and threads her fingers into my hair with a pull so hard that wrenches my head back and throbs down to my cock.

Slamming her lips to mine, Cedar works to grind against me with a moan I catch on my tongue and an even tighter pussy.

"Shit," I groan when her lips pop free and she stretches to sink her teeth into my neck. "That's it. God, you take my cock so well." My shaft pulses, my impending orgasm building harder and higher.

"Need to cum." It's like I can hear the roll of her eyes in her breathy words as her lips find mine again and her tongue slips between my panting lips.

Thrusting harder into her, I grind us close to oblivion until my balls draw completely up and Cedar throws her head back.

"Now, Cedar," I growl when her mouth falls open and her eyes roll back. "Cum. Now."

"Fuck," she gasps as her pussy clenches around me tight enough that it throws me into my own raging orgasm. "FIN. "

"Yes," I growl as my cock shoots deep inside her with every grip of her hot pussy. "That's it, sweet. Take every bit of me."

Groaning and sweaty, I thrust with each wave that crashes into us until she's wet and limp in my arms.

"Fuck," Cedar finally whispers as her chest heaves against me and I feel our arousal leaking down my shaft.

"That we did." Snickering when her head rolls and her brow wings in my direction, I plant a quick kiss on her lips. "You ready for me to put you down?"

"You already did." A lighthearted laugh expands my chest when her head falls back and a sated sigh escapes her lips. "Fuckin' twice."

"Mm," I grunt and lean in to run my nose along the column of her throat. "Sure did." My tongue retraces the trail back up to the underside of her chin and I suck in a sharp breath at the salty taste of her skin. "Now tell me you hate me again."

"Pfft," Cedar scoffs. "Not even close."

Chapter Twenty-Two

Cedar

*H*OW IS IT THAT *this time with Fin feels so much different?*

Him resting his head against my cheek moments before he pulls out of me, his cock still ragingly hard, feels so ... saccharine.

Slowly, he lowers my legs until I'm no longer practically bent in half and keeps me steady with my back still against the stack and his arms wrapped around me.

Fin's warmth, and intimate lips against my forehead, feels like my heart is wrapped in a fuzzy blanket in front of the fire with the hottest smutty book I can find.

I want to slap him away, but I don't.

It feels nice.

My pussy still throbs as he ensures I won't fall over and steps away, my body an aching mess of muscle spasms and relieved tension that makes no sense to my foggy sex brain.

And neither does the fact that we just fucked on an empty stage.

On stage!

"Here, sweet." Clearing my throat and blinking away the replay of his cock slamming inside me for the second time tonight from my exhausted brain, I come back in focus to see Fin holding out my shorts along with my shirt and missing the guitar he was wearing.

I look down, see my wholly nakedness and—even though there's a small part of me that instinctively wants to cover myself—I chuckle.

"Cover up." Fin grabs my hand when I just stare at his offering because I'm too blissed out to do much else, and plants the fabric in my grip. "The after-the-party parties will be over soon. We're lucky we got this long."

"Mm," I grunt and watch as Fin walks away again with only a faint pinch in my chest.

Is he leaving me?

He reappears within seconds, a roll of paper towels in his hands and a sly smirk tipping his lips.

Instead of shoving it in my hands, along with the rest of the shit I'm still holding—like I half expect him to—Finland Montgomery drops to his knees at my feet and tears a piece off of the roll with a snap.

Blinking when he grips my thigh, half prepared to pinch myself to make sure this is real life when he spreads my legs wider, and sighing when he takes a moment to stare at me, Fin then runs the almost clothlike material up the inside of my leg to swipe away the mess left behind.

Finland. Montgomery.

Is cleaning up his mess.

He tosses the paper aside and rips off another section to repeat it on the other leg, both times stopping just short of the apex between my thighs.

"Fin," I sigh more than I intend to, drawing his sparkling eyes up to me.

"Yeah?" he asks as he tears off a third section.

"You missed a spot."

Fin scoffs, his head falling but his shoulders bouncing in a muted laugh that brings my own snicker bubbling up my throat.

"Show—" He clears his throat when his words betray his humor and lets the gravel filter back into his sexy tone. "Show me where."

I point directly at my crotch with pursed lips and a caged laugh. "Right there."

"Goddamn, sweet." Fin chuckles at my antics and raises his towel wielding hands. "Can you give a man a second?"

"Nope," I rush out on a snicker that dies down the second his hands are spreading my thighs and coming between to swipe away at my soaking pussy.

Fin tosses the towel and reaches for another to repeat the torture that has soft mewls and little gasps chasing his actions.

"All better?" He asks as he looks up at me, that earlier sparkle replaced with a heated and dark look that makes me almost ask for another to sop up the new mess I'm making.

"Better," I breathe because I don't want to seem needy, but I can't look away from him as he straightens.

"Now put your clothes on." Fin leans down to press a tender kiss to my lips and pinches my chin. He tilts my head to the side, bringing his lips to my ear. "So I can peel them back off of you later."

Chills. Shivers. Goosebumps.

They all run down my spine and across my body.

Because Fin Montgomery wants to peel my clothes off.

Again.

And I'm not freaking out about it.

Again.

"Can't." *Babe, honey, dear?* He keeps calling me sweet and I feel like I should say something back, even though I hate that I love the endearment. "I gotta head back."

"To where?" His snapped frame stands tall as shit against me when his spine straightens and his deep brow stares down at me.

I swallow when the man feels slightly intimidating and square my shoulders against the changed aura. "To places."

Fin growls. "So you're just going to *dine and dash*?" Rolling his eyes, he pushes away from me and shoves a hand through his hair.

Wait ...

He's, what ... worried? Feeling used?

A humorless laugh nearly busts from my lips, but even it is too exhausted to make its way up my throat.

How many times has he made women feel like that?

Stupid rockstar.

He's had his fill of me. Now he can move on.

I furrow my brow as I watch the man pace across the stage, then back again. Each time he faces me, his mouth opens then snaps shut as if there are words ready to tumble off of his tongue, but he holds them back and spins away for another lap.

Scoffing to myself, I jab my limbs through the clothes I should have never taken off and shake my head with a level of adrenaline slamming into my system.

And I thought Fin might be different.

Look who was wrong again.

"Cedar." Fin steps up to me when I approach the edge of the stage, preparing myself to jump down and beat feet so that I can avoid this weird as hell interaction. "Let me come with you."

What?

"Why in the hell would I do that?"

Fin shoves that hand through his sexy as hell waves again and stares at the floor with a tick in his jaw. "Because I don't want that fucker finding you."

"Riiiight," I drag out with a roll to my eyes and dip down to plant a steadying hand on the stage. "Catch ya later, Fin."

"Cedar, wait," Fin calls when I jump down from the platform and start walking.

I hear the boots smash into the heavy mats at my back and I ignore the sound following me, even when every fiber of me wants to turn around and hear him out.

It's time for the guitar god to just move on with his life.

"Sweet." Fin's gravelly whisper is closer than I expected, making my shoulders jerk unconsciously. "Goddamnit, Cedar."

"Fuck. Off," I growl when I feel the heat of him sidle closer with each step.

"Cedar," Fin growls as he steps in front of me, rotating with surrendering hands held between us, his gaze set alight. "Sweet," he breathes in that deep baritone that vibrates down my spine. "You can invite me along, or I can follow you from a distance."

"And that doesn't sound stalkerish at all." I roll my eyes and continue walking, forcing him to move backwards or get ran over.

"You're about to leave here alone. And he was just out there. I can't in good conscious leave you."

"Just shut up." I scoff and flutter my hand between us in the *go away* motion. "I've been doing this whole life thing for a while now."

"Cedar." Fin halts dead in his tracks, and forces me to skid to a stop or ram into him.

I considered the latter.

"I don't want to leave you alone."

Yep, should have run him over.

Shaking my head and sidestepping the infuriating man that fucks just as good, if not better, than I'd ever hoped, I walk straight for the exit on weakened knees with no plan of how to get from here to my dad's place.

I know I could call him.

Have him at the gate by the time I make it there.

But my dad instilled in my head at an early as hell age that independence is necessary and that I have to live my life without relying on others.

I learned that the hard way anyway.

Stupid teenage heart.

And I've subconsciously been trying to prove it ever since Jeremy removed himself from my life.

Just up and left without another word after that night at the Saltwater Skulls show, to follow a different band for years despite my devastated, naïve heart, only to show back up again and treat my heart—my body—even worse.

Not even my dad knows the whole truth.

Or Aria.

No one does.

Except the therapist my dad made me see.

So why does each step away from Fin, where he trails farther and farther behind, feel like I'm walking through solidifying concrete? Concrete that makes me wanna turn around and tell him the truth of it all. Like maybe breathing the words will take this ache from my chest.

He'd never look at me the same.

My boots get heavier to move with each pass of my feet and my chest caves with the weight of the truth that I know will send any rational man packing. Running for the hills. Screaming and yelling for anyone in the vicinity to stay far away from Cedar Jones.

Damaged goods.

Incapable of healing.

Broken.

Unworthy of anyone.

Finland Montgomery is legendary.

I am just ordinary.

All of the things I've already been called by the one I thought I loved. Thought I trusted.

Disgusting.

A freak.

All because I asked to try something … different.

None of the other guys I've slept with since have had an issue with … different-ish. Not that I really gave any of them those parts of me, the ones that Jeremy soiled.

God, my brains are fucking scrambled.

So scrambled that I go against my instincts that have managed to keep me alive so far with everyone at a distance and halt at the threshold between the main entry and the venue. I spin to find Fin standing several feet back, granting me the space I was all but demanding, his jaw ticking and his hands shoved in his pockets.

His gaze is darkened by the night, with anger I can feel radiating off of him despite the distance, though I still want to run to him.

I don't.

Because cement shoes.

But I want to. Straight into his arms where I can pretend like the rest of it doesn't exist. Make believe that I'm normal and this is possible.

Would he even accept me? If he knew the truth?

"What did you mean when you said, 'you don't want to'?" I call across the distance as my feet decide they aren't so heavy after all, and I take a tentative step in Fin's direction.

"I don't wanna leave you alone, Cedar," he returns strongly.

"Yeah, you said that." I take another step. "But what does it mean?"

"It means that you're a pain in my ass."

I don't know why that makes me chuckle, but it does.

Yet another thing I've been called my entire life.

Another step.

This one I don't mind, though. Not when it's coming from him.

Another step closer and he's matching my advances.

"I know that," I say as the space between us dwindles.

Maybe … maybe he means it.

Like, the normal joking way and not in the controlling way.

"At least you acknowledge that part," Fin almost growls, his boots carrying him forward. "I'm serious, Cedar. I don't want to leave you alone."

"You said that."

"Not what I meant." Shaking his head, I see Fin's smirk stretch his lips as his pace quickens and he's coming closer. "Sweet, you have two seconds." His features are dark, his voice guttural, as his gait turns into a stalk right in my direction.

"Before what?"

Fin jogs the remaining distance until his breath is washing over my face and his feet stop with his toes touching mine.

"This." Bending, Fin wraps up my thighs and lifts me into the air until I'm forced to double over his shoulder or be impaled with his tense as hell muscles.

"Fin," I squeal as I bounce with each of his steps, my fists planting in his ass and hammering away at the tight muscles in my face. Growling when my assault gains me nothing but a quick swat to my own ass that sends another squeal bounding from between my lips, I grip the waistband of his pants and almost hope that I can tug them down enough to embarrass him with a full moon to the world. "Put me down!"

"I'm taking you home with me. End of discussion."

"No." I squirm against the forearm he has hooked around the backs of my knees. "I gotta get back to my dad."

"Ohhh-ho-ho." Fin's deep chuckle reverberates from his thick muscles and lands along the parts of my torso that connect with his. "Daddy needs his princess back now, huh?"

I knew not to say that.

"You gonna turn into a punkin' after all?" Another swat lands on my ass cheek and warms my face more than the blood rushing to it. "Daddy dearest is so going to ground you for being out past curfew."

"Stop calling him that. It's fucking weird," I grunt and push at his pants, unsuccessful in my attempt to de-pants the asshole caveman. "Put me down, Fin."

"Nah," he responds as he bounces down a step onto pavement, that I watch pass and my guts scramble a little more with the contact. "I think I'll hand you right off to your *daddy*."

Torture. This is torture.

"Guhhh." I push up from his torso when he comes to a stop and plants another quick slap to my ass that sets my blood on fire.

In the good way.

The freaky way.

Lowering me slowly, Fin slides my body down his in a way that I feel every ridge of tight muscle, every tensed ab, until my feet hit the ground and I'm panting all over again.

Shit.

"Put the fucking helmet on, Cedar." His demand makes my skin tingle and my pussy clench and my palms sweat.

This is a terrible idea.

Swinging my gaze, I see the As Above RV lit up on the inside, two bikes parked up close and the helmet that Fin snags to shove in my direction.

This is such a bad idea.

I accept the helmet, plant the thing on my head, and watch as Fin's powerful thighs mount the blacked out bike I've only seen in his online pictures.

The air charges when he looks over at me, that mischievous look back in his eyes. "C'mon, sweet," Fin says in the voice that feels like the crunch of a gravel driveway running straight up to my missing panties. "Spread those thighs for me."

Yep, that's fucking hot.

The engine roars to life between us, accenting his words with such power that I would have soaked the panties anyway.

If I were wearing any.

"Oh, goddamnit."

Chapter Twenty-Three

Fin

T HE HEAT OF CEDAR wrapped around me has my cock hardening in my jeans again and my grip tight on the clutch.

I don't weave as hard or drive as fast with Cedar on the back, but I do enjoy the whip of wind that rushes past me and sends chills over her clammy skin.

It feels ... freeing.

Like walking up on stage for the first hundred times to find the crowd just a little bit bigger than last time.

Like nailing that solo that drives the masses wild.

Or being nominated for all the years and hard work of playing the best goddamn guitar this generation has seen. And then winning.

Only to come back to the table where my brothers sat to see Cedar there among them with her eyes glued to me.

Those haunted blue eyes smiling at me, clapping for me and my band, even after her best friend announced her pregnancy.

She's been in the background ever since, a faint reminder, a distant desire that never felt unobtainable until her ass decided to crash into me at the party.

And I've been chasing her ever since.

Shit.

Leaning back, I pull on the throttle and ease us into a slower pace along the dark country roads illuminated by the single headlight that leads back to her daddy's place.

Jesus Christ, I met her father today.

I might get my ass hit a second time, but it doesn't matter that my knuckles still ache or my jaw is going to show some bruising tomorrow. Or that she might lose her shit at both of us for acting like cavemen over her when she clearly doesn't want or need it.

But she deserves it. The respect, the protection.

The backup.

None of it matters because it's led me right to this moment. This rush of being wrapped up in the only one I've ever given more than a flying fuck about. The one woman I want to see tomorrow instead of running her off before she can pass out in my bed like every other broad that's darkened my doorstep.

Everyone that came before her was just practice.

Slowing the bike, I pull off into the gravel skirt of someone's long as shit driveway and run my hand along the chilled forearms wrapped around my torso.

"What are you doing, Fin?"

I shrug and shoot a grin over my shoulder as I fish my phone out with my free hand. Holding the device up, I lift my middle finger from the skin of Cedar's arm without removing my grip and snap a picture that includes her helmeted head behind my shoulder and her arms wrapping me up.

"Wait, no—" Cedar moves behind me, the bike bouncing on its shocks when she damn near climbs over my shoulder with her grabby hands aimed right for the phone. "You did not just take a *where am I* picture?"

Snickering, I extend my reach past hers, even when she ditches the helmet and climbs up my shoulders with her hips leaning into my neck.

"Gimme that!"

"Hell no." I shake my head and grab her wrist to hold her back, but also keep her from falling on her damn head when her heels plant in the seat her ass should be in. "I got dick pics on here."

"I've already seen that."

I grunt when she unintentionally pumps her pelvis into the back of my head in an attempt to reach farther. "Technically, you haven't seen it." I tuck my torso and yank her arm around until she's wrapped around the opposite side of my body from the phone. "I might have a monster cock, you don't know."

"Pffft," she scoffs into a laugh. "No way." Anchoring herself with claws to my bicep, she gains leverage and throws an arm out. "I bet it's pretty and tan," she grunts. "All smooth skin from all that lotion."

"Wow, burn." Rolling my eyes, I hold my arm straight up in the air and away from her advances as her warm body clings to my left side and slowly works her way to straddling me and my hardening cock.

"Fin," Cedar snaps when she finally lands directly in my lap, her thighs spread on either side of me and her breath coming in fast pants. "You can't post that."

Narrowing my gaze on her and all the sexiness she exudes, I bite the inside of my lip to hold back my grin. "Why's that?"

Her blue eyes sparkle even though her brow furrows. "Someone's gonna know it's me." She holds up her arm, the one that has the snake that wraps around her entire forearm and the head that rests on the back of her hand. "Ink they're gonna recognize." Then she flashes the wrist that Peach inked and my held-back grin drops.

"When did he do that?" It comes out as a growl when I didn't intend for it to be, but for once, Cedar shrugs instead of jumping or snapping at me.

"I filled it in when I couldn't sleep."

Gripping her wrist, I rotate it in the faint light coming from the very same moon the once-was emoji now resembles and admire the way she captured the night sky surrounding it with smokey clouds and glistening stars. The cheeky grin is still there, but now it blends into craters and shadows on the bright surface.

"Jesus," I breathe and bring her arm closer to my face. "You turned Peach's whack job into this?"

Cedar snickers, but nods. "His wasn't bad. But I'm not a smiley kinda gal."

"Mm," I half grunt and raise her wrist to press my lips against the heel of her palm, just below the fresh ink, as my other shoves my phone into the safety of my pocket. "It's beautiful, sweet."

And I don't know how the hell I missed it.

Somewhere between the compliment and lifting my gaze to hers, the air between us changes. Charges. Feels, some-fucking-how, both heated and heavy.

Darting my tongue out to wet my lips, I hold her gaze as the next words tumble off of my lips. "But not as beautiful as the woman who carries it."

I would swear I see a rush of red flush over her face, but this damn lack of light and the distance between us plays me.

Which only makes me wonder if she's ever been called that before.

I want to ask her, simply because I'm finding that I want to know everything there is to know about Cedar Jones, but I don't. Instead, I plant another kiss to the palm I still hold and watch her as she watches me with parted lips and a chest that picks up with each quickening breath.

"Shut up," Cedar breathes, almost silently.

"Why would I do that?" I whisper and yank her close by the hand I hold to wrap an arm around her back when her small frame flies forward. She yelps as her tits crash into my chest and her hips slide up close and personal with mine, her warmth feeding straight to my stiff cock.

"I don't know," Cedar half sighs when my free hand lands on her bare thigh and the tip of my thumb finds the edge of her shorts. "Maybe don't then."

"Mm," I sigh as Cedar wraps her arms around my neck and brings her lips dangerously close to mine. "I'm definitely not gonna."

Cedar Jones is full of surprises. One minute we're arguing, the next we're almost making out. One second we're fucking and the next she's hightailing it out of the RV like I didn't watch her ass go. One moment she looks at me like she hates my guts, then she looks at me like maybe she doesn't.

Like right now, with her warm body against me, straddling me on my bike like the sexiest pinup I've ever seen when she was just ready to walk away from me again.

And I almost let her.

But instead, she's here, with that *I might not hate you* look in her eye feeding hope into the beating organ in my chest.

Hope for what, I've yet to figure out, but that sounds like a problem for tomorrow's Fin to work through. Right now, I just want my hands on my girl.

"Cedar," I half whisper as I trail my wandering thumb over the smooth skin of her leg, a smidge higher with each pass until the digit disappears beneath the stretchy denim.

"Fin," she mocks with a deepened voice and a smirk. "Make your move, hotshot."

Chuckling, I purse my lips. "Remember that you asked for it."

I don't wait for the rebuttal I see forming in that pretty little head to come out before I yank her body forward until there's no space left between us and slam my lips to hers.

The motion jams my thumb farther up her shorts, the material cutting into the web between and instead of removing it, I feed my whole hand up the denim until the pad of my thumb strokes the space where her bare pussy meets her thigh in time to my tongue against hers.

I swallow down her groans when I edge closer to the place I know she wants me to touch, her skin like lava beneath my fingers.

Too hot to touch. Too pretty to look away.

I'm the dumb kid that always touched the stove anyway.

But none of that heat even comes close to Cedar's when I slip the pad of my thumb between her slick pussy lips and her moan shoots down my throat.

She draws back on a gasp when I rotate over her clit, her head falling back and exposing that deliciously inked throat of hers that I don't wait to dive in and taste.

Nips and licks up from the hollow of her throat to the base of her chin, her groans and whimpers fuel me to press harder on her clit, flipping the ring with each pass.

I know the metal tugs, possibly even stings if it's anything like the one through my frenum.

But that's part of the pleasure of having it.

Smirking when her back arches, I guide her back until Cedar is laid out across my bike with her head hanging over the handlebars and her back lands on the hand I use to cover the gas cap. "That's it, sweet."

"Mm," Cedar moans into the night air, her dark hair spread all over as her hands find my knees and dig in. "Feels so good."

"Fuck yes, you do, Cedar." My jaw clenches when her throbbing clit feeds all the way back to my pulsing cock and sends waves of heated chills down my spine.

Cedar's lips part on a gasp, her nails sinking into my skin through my pants when she arches up again, her hips moving in sync with my hand.

"Fin," she whimpers.

"Right here, sweetness." It comes out half growl and all gravel when I feel her tighten beneath my grip. "I know you're close."

"Yeah," Cedar sighs up into the darkness, her chest heaving with each pass of my thumb over her. "Gonna."

"Then cum, sweet. This one's all for you."

Like I pressed the button, flipped the switch, and plugged in the tree, Cedar's arched back lifts up off the gas tank and she shatters in my grip with a cry of my name off of her thick lips. My cock pulses at the sight of her cumming on my bike with me between her legs and a sheen of sweat built up on her glowing skin. Her mouth is propped open with an almost silent groan and her grip flexes against my knee with each wave that slams her.

The only thing that would have made it better is if I'd been inside her to feel it.

"That's it," I soothe as she comes down to my slowing strokes over her slick clit. "Fucking beautiful."

She groans when she finally goes limp beneath me, her orgasm running out until nothing but the aftershocks are left.

"Bet it tastes better than it did to watch." Withdrawing my hand from her shorts, I raise the slicked calluses of my thumb to my lips and dart my tongue out when she lifts her head.

The taste, when it hits my tongue, is like a battery straight to my tastebuds, electric and tingly enough to have me shoving the digit between my lips to suck it clean.

"God," Cedar groans. "You are ridiculous."

"Why's that?" I ask around my thumb as my tongue works to catch every bit of her—us—from my skin.

"You came in there," she half squeals, shooting straight up and grinding her hot as fuck pussy against my throbbing cock.

I groan, even as she moves back and grips my wrist, yanking my thumb from between my lips.

"Oh, c'mon." She rolls her eyes. "No one likes the fucking taste of that."

"*Oh, sweetness,*" I chide and rotate our hands so that I'm the one doing the holding. "If you honestly believe that, then I have a lot of work to do."

Cedar scoffs, her armor of attitude sliding right back in place. "Bullshit, Fin. That's gross."

"Gross?" Shaking my head, I let go of her hand to cup her face in both of mine and bring her so close that I feel her breath on my tongue. "Sweetness, I could *live* off of your pussy for the rest of my life."

Cedar blinks.

And blinks.

Her throat bobs with a swallow before her lips part and her heated exhale flows over my chin. "Um," she half whimpers, her skin flushing a deep red I know I see this time. "That's ..."

Smirking, I lean in and steal a kiss. "Hot? Duh."

"Jesus," Cedar sighs, her rigid frame finally softening in my grip as her sight darts between mine. "Such a fucking caveman."

I snort and snag another kiss from her swollen lips before tugging her around me until she's clinging to my back once again. "When it comes to you?" I toss over my shoulder. "Absolutely."

Engaging the key, the engine roars back to life and all too soon we're back to heading off in the direction of the ass kicking I'll gladly accept so long as it means the woman at my back is safe.

Chapter Twenty-Four

Cedar

THE SOUND OF THE bike tires crunching up the driveway has my stomach dipping with each passing foot that leads us closer and closer to the lit up porch, the only obstacle between Fin and my dad.

Because he always waits up.

Shit.

Working a swallow down my drying throat, I squeeze Fin tighter for a split second before he rolls the bike to a stop in the same spot where Peach parked not that long ago. I hop up from the bike, yanking the helmet off as the shakes start and my breath quickens.

They already fought once.

How the hell do I explain this to my dad, when I don't even know what we are?

"Sweet?"

But here I am bringing him home at … I glance at my phone with trembling hands. *It's four in the morning …*

Jaxon Jones wakes up at four in the fucking morning.

Oh, fuuuck.

"Cedar, what's wrong?" Fin's hot skin touches mine when he takes the helmet from my grip and sends a shockwave straight up my arm. The contact makes me jerk away instinctively.

"Um…" I poke my tongue out to lick my dried lips, my sight darting to the dark silhouette standing the in doorway. "Shit."

"Look at me," Fin whispers as he grabs my wrists and dips to meet my unfocused eyes. "Sweetness, look at me."

Digging my teeth into the inside of my lip, I let my gaze settle on Fin's furrowed brow.

"I've not—" I blow out a heavy breath and grip Fin's calloused hands harder than I need to. "I'm not—"

"Is your dad cool?" Fin's jaw clenches when I cut myself off, his eyes sharpening. "Like he's good to you, yeah?"

"Fuck," I breathe out on a humorless chuckle that does nothing to ease Fin's rising blood pressure I can see, thanks to the thick veins popping in his neck. "He's cool, Fin. I just …"

God, why is this feel so hard to admit?

Shaking my head, I meet Fin's gaze when he tugs me closer and wraps those massive arms around me. "Tell me."

"Jesus." I roll my eyes and bury my face into his delicious smelling chest because it's the only thing that's helping me focus right now. "I've not come home with anyone." I gulp down the shame, the guilt. "In, like, a long time, Fin."

His frame physically relaxes under my touch. "Thank fuck," Fin breathes into my hair and squeezes me so tight I think my ribcage might collapse.

But it's the best damn hug I've had in my life.

"Not since …" I sigh into the warm fabric of Fin's shirt and hook my arms around his waist with what feels like a thousand pound anvil sitting on my chest.

"Not since fuckface." I feel Fin's nod at the same time I hear the storm door creak open and heavy boots hit the wooden slats of the porch. "I'm piecing it together." His lips press to the top of my head in the gentlest gesture I don't feel deserving of, which only makes me squeeze him tighter and that pressure holding in my heart a little looser. "You don't have to say a word."

"Ahem."

Like a shotgun blast into the night, the clearing of my father's throat echoes around my ear drums and has me shooting back from the warmth I don't think I've ever felt until him and a rush of a different kind of guilt washing over my now heated skin.

"Cedar," Jaxon *Atlas* Jones growls into the early morning dew like I am every bit the teenager I feel and takes another menacing step closer to the edge of the porch. "In the house."

"What?" I scoff. "No '*princess*' this time?" I say because mouthing off to the brute of a father I was blessed with has totally always got me what I wanted.

Not that I know what the fuck that is this wonderfully intense too-early morning.

"Get your ass in this house. *Now.*" His voice booms off of the surrounding trees and sends some creature in the distance scurrying away to safety and my defiant hands to my hips.

"Cedar, listen to him." I swing my gaze at Fin, who's focused solely on the porch where my dad stands with his arms crossed over his puffed chest and his feet holding his stance wide.

"You both are ridiculous." Scoffing, I shove Fin's shoulder as I stomp across the lawn and up the few stairs to stand in front of the man that has saved my life more times than even he knows. *If only he knew the truth.*

The snort is almost inaudible from between his pinched lips, my dad's shoulders only giving a slight bounce in the dim light where, up close, I catch sight of his bruised brow and the heavy bags under his eyes that flick to me for only a moment before returning to Fin's position in the driveway. "Go grab some sleep, princess."

Growling, I shake my head and flip both of them my middle fingers as I sidestep my overprotective father and slam my way into the house.

The fresh scent of brewing coffee smacks me at the same time the exhaustion does, and even though there's a part of me that would love to just stay up with a warm mug of life, my feet don't take me past the couch where I collapse.

I try to listen for yelling. I strain my ears for thudding fists or the kick of Fin's engine as he speeds away from all the crazy that comes with me and my baggage.

But the peaceful silence, with only a mild timbre of deep voices in the distance, lulls me into the dark abyss of sleep before I'm ready to let it claim me.

S UNLIGHT FILTERS THROUGH MY eyelids, the sound of a door creaking open and then closing in the distance bringing me closer to awareness until I'm shooting up and my chest is heaving with a panicked race of my heart.

"What happened?" It's immediate, slurred with sleep as I whip my head around with stiff muscles and a grimace at the ache built up from the weird angle I passed out in. "What time is it?"

My head pounds as my eyes finally adjust to the wickedly bright light and the sight of my father in the recliner, his forearms propped on his knees, filters into my brain and has my stomach dropping. "What did you do to him?"

"Who?" It's gruff, almost hoarse sounding.

"Fin," I snap and swing my legs over the side of the couch to push to my aching feet and beeline straight for the window, where I yank back the curtains and find the driveway empty. "What did you do, Jax?"

"Princess," my dad nearly whispers, his sight trained on the floor and his roughened hands scraping against themselves with just the right amount of noise to have my mouth going dry.

It's in that moment that my panic kicks up, my chest going tight and my brain fogging with each detail I notice of the man I have loved my entire life. The way his dark hair is tousled like he ran his busted hands through it too many times to keep the waves brushed back. The uncharacteristic bow to his overly large shoulders. The fact that the sun is up and my dad isn't in his shop doing the thing he loves almost as much as he did my mother.

"What did you do to Fin?" It's a growl, something I learned from watching the very man I question, whose knuckles are bloodied. The one who loved with a passion and fought with soul. "Please tell me you didn't."

"Cedar." It comes like a plea when his head finally raises and his piercing eyes meet mine with a look that slices right to my heart. "Why didn't you—" But his words cut off as he shakes his head. "Sit down and talk to me, princess."

"What?" I throw my hands up as the emotional roller coaster rails me with an upside down turn I'm in no way prepared for.

"The coffee is fresh. Sit and talk."

Blinking at the man that refuses to look at me now, I run my own hands through my hair and search for the mug on the coffee table like it might have the answers.

Where. Is. Fin?

I scoff and stomp over to flop into the seat I was asleep in merely minutes ago and snag the steaming ceramic by the chipped handle. "Okay, I'm sitting and I'm fucking talking."

I pause for a sip that burns all the way down and pin my father with a glare. "Now where the fuck is Fin?"

"He's fine," my dad grumbles and runs his callous hands over his face. "Headed back to his brothers or something."

Immediately, the tension in my chest eases, and I suck in a desperate breath. "Okay, you didn't kill him. That's all I was asking."

"Cedar," my dad breathes as he leans back with a straightened spine and a clenching jaw. "Why didn't you tell me about Jeremy?"

My stomach drops and my jaw goes slack at the intensity staring back at me. The anger radiating from across the living room lands square in my chest and all that weight I was able to forget for just a moment comes crashing right back on me again.

"No." Shaking my head, I hop to my feet and drop the mug to the table with a clash I didn't entirely intend that has solid brown liquid bounding over the sides. "No way."

"Sit," Dad demands in that fatherly tone that grates on my nerves and has my own jaw ticking.

"I'm not having this discussion." Scoffing, I plant my hands on my hips and growl at my father. "I don't know what Fin told you, but he doesn't know *shit*."

My dad follows my lead and jumps to his feet to face off with flaring nostrils and a growl of his own. "He knew e-*fucking*-nough."

"Nah." I shake my head with a humorless smile because I know that no one knows the truth about Jeremy except the therapist I really need to call. "He's made assumptions."

"So he's wrong?" It's my dad's turn to scoff and shake his head as he spins away from me and talks to the ceiling. "So you're telling me the man decked me, on my own property, for no *fucking reason?*" As each word leaves my dad's lips, it gets louder, more intense, along with the look I catch from his profile shining in his eyes. "And I didn't deserve it?"

Wait ...

"He hit you?"

The tense jaw and flared nostrils are enough of an answer when all my father does is spin back and stare at me with an odd mix of anger and desperation clouding his eyes.

Blue eyes that look just like mine.

Blue eyes that stare at me with an admiration, and a level of disappointment, that have my chest tightening and my own sight misting over.

"Why didn't you tell me, Cedar?" His voice is thick, raw with the emotions as his hands flex and the man I've looked up to as strong and defiant of all things bad stares at me through a watering gaze. "I mean, I knew he wasn't good for you. But why didn't you tell me how fucking bad he really was?"

Years of built-up pressure and emotions, years of compartmentalizing all the bad things, years of taking the trauma and stuffing it so far down I thought I'd never have to feel it again, comes rushing in and knocks the breath right from my lungs.

"I could have made it better," my dad chokes out.

Panic fills me and my throat closes up as I swing my wild gaze around the room in search of something—any fucking thing—that will get me out of this.

"Princess," my dad says, his voice sounding far off and garbled through the heart rate that races in my ears and threatens to pound out through my skull. "Cedar, come sit down, please."

"I ca—" My lungs heave, desperate for a fresh fill of oxygen the emotions are denying me.

"Fuck." The curse comes only seconds before warmth surrounds me and my knees decide to quit holding me up.

I don't know when the sobs start. But I make it to the couch and cry into the arms of the man that has saved my life already and leave trails of snot over his never-really-clean shirt.

"Cedar," Dad attempts to soothe, though I can feel the rage radiating off of his skin like the glow from the sun. "You are never going to have to worry about that prick again. I'm going to make it better."

"Dad, no." I grip his shirt and sob, desperate to keep him from ruining the life he hustled so hard to build. "No prison."

"Never. Again. Cedar."

Chapter Twenty-Five

Fin

"WHERE THE FUCK HAVE you been?" Exasperated and throwing his hands up, Leo paces the floor of the RV living quarters with his normally meticulously styled blonde hair poking in all different directions and his pressed white shirt covered in wrinkles. "Just like Toby over here with the god*damn disappearing acts.*"

I raise a brow at the band manager and set my helmet that still smells like her down on the marble countertop next to the door that slams shut behind me. "Well hello to you, too, Le," I mock with the nickname we all know he hates.

"What the fuck, Fin?" Leo spins to me, rushing up close to my face with wild eyes and a heaving chest. "I called a meeting two hours ago."

"And?" I scoff and brush past the abnormally obnoxious band manager. "I'm here now."

"And?" Leo laughs, the sound on the verge of exposing the crazy. "This shit and we have a show in less than six hours. And you fuckers want to change shit up?"

"Yup." I plop my tired ass into the leather cushion of the couch between Rex and the arm. I haven't slept in ... shit, I don't even remember the last time I actually passed out for more than ten minutes, only to roll over and find Cedar's ass high-tailing it out of the bed in the very back of this same bus. The thought alone makes my cock stir with memories of her hot pussy wrapped around me, the southern part of my brain counting all the ways to get back there again. "I had to check something out."

"Bro," Rex chuckles quietly and shakes his head at our brother, who goes back to pacing. "How was she?" he whispers to me with a furrow to his brow, his clasped hands covering his mouth, his elbows braced on his knees when he bends forward.

"She'll be good," I mutter back. "But I'm going to need a hand."

"Name it." I meet Rex's hard stare and grit my jaw at the sincerity I see echoing back. Jutting my chin in acknowledgement and appreciation I know he picks up, I let out a tight breath.

Because I also know that Leo doesn't lose his shit over nothing.

The *put together, keep all of us in line, take none of our shit without giving it back tenfold* band manager is still pacing the space like the tile beneath his feet will show him the answers to whatever has thrown him into a panic so long as he wears it down enough with his Oxfords.

This can't be good.

"Are you *fucknuts* listening?" Leo growls from his power stance at the front of the group when my gaze swings to him.

"Nah," I attempt to jest with a shrug that feels forced. "Can you start from the top?"

"Okay, listen here, you assholes." Leo brings his hands together in a thunderous clap that jolts Toby back to life from a dead sleep—which is probably a drunken stupor—and has the man that looks on the verge of homelessness snapping straight in his seat and wiping the sleepy drool from his bearded chin. Glancing around at the rest of the group—Rex and then Mac on his other side, Ian standing cross-armed at the helm of the bus with Jordan on his heel and Peach leaning against the frame that leads to the bedroom—we all swing our concerned glares on the manager and wait.

"Alright," Rex grunts and rubs his hands together. "You got us, Le. Let's go. What's got your panties all twisted up?"

Leo shakes his head, his arms falling loose at his sides when Ian steps forward, his fancy go-go-gadget tablet in his grip. He taps the screen and spins it to show us a picture that makes my stomach fall through my asshole. The photo is dark, because it was taken at night—last fucking night—and filled with the very stage we're supposed to play on in less than six hours.

But it's not the stage that has me thrusting to my feet and snatching the device from the brick shithouse of a bodyguard with no regard for my own safety if I piss him off.

No.

It's what's on the stage that has me pinching at the screen and zooming in.

"Who?" Red hot anger rips through my veins and tightens my already tense muscles, the tablet creaking with the force of my grip when I raise my heated gaze up to Ian's.

"Pure speculation is floating around on who has a pair of legs wrapped around them on stage after hours, but it won't take long. I picked it up right away when the photo flagged."

"The fucking guitar," Rex growls from my left.

My guitar.

The candy red Manson MB-2 with an ebony finger board and the controller screen built right into the slick as hell body that shimmers in the stage lights.

The piece I bought right before the Road Trip tour because I wanted it and because my last one was so broken in that the neck actually started splinting and leaving little painful reminders in my already calloused thumb.

Rex pulls at my arm to get a look at the screen I tilt in his direction because at this point, Ian's right. It's only a matter of time before the internet calls me out on it.

Where am I?

On stage, fucking someone.

With her pale legs on either side of my hips, her boots at my elbows and my guitar hanging loose against my ass, there's no mistaking what's going down in the wide shoot of the Setlist's main stage, including my back that lights up the tablet and makes its way across the internet.

I'm just lucky her face and naked as fuck state is hidden behind me.

"I wanna know where it came from, Ian," I snarl and dump the tablet in Rex's grip when he stares at it too long, as if confirming it is who he thinks it is.

"I have a fucking guess," Rex mutters and presses the button that blanks out the screen before handing the device back over to As Above's head of security.

"Yeah," Leo drags out from behind us, his humorless chuckle filling the cabin, and has me spinning on my heel with a tic to my jaw and a clench to my fists. "Or we could have just … oh, I don't know. Maybe kept it in our fucking pants?" Leo's voice echoes off the walls and settles in the center of my chest like a kick straight to my ribs.

And that just won't do for me.

Stepping up to one of the men I've considered a brother for the better part of a decade, I wrap up the collar of his fancy shirt in my fist and yank his ass up close and personal to the sneer on my face.

"Or maybe you could have done your job." With a growl, I shove Leo aside and throw a look over my shoulder as I move. "I'll take that hand now."

I don't wait for a reply because I'm already out the door, helmet in hand, my thudding footsteps echoed behind me.

The kick of my bike's engine roaring to life feeds the adrenaline already coursing through my veins and has me twisting my neck to relieve some of the pressure before slapping my helmet on and peeling out of the service entrance and onto the main road with one of As Above's security blacked out SUV's in my rear-view.

Cutting through the crowded street, I bank a left off of the main road where all the festival goers jam up the traffic and hit the calmer surface streets to open the bike the fuck up.

The engine roars to life when I engage the throttle, the SUV making the same turn just a few seconds behind me and the driver gunning it to catch up.

Inhaling deep, the earthy scent of Cedar fills my lungs and pulls a deep growling yell from the recesses of my chest.

He was right there. So close to Cedar, possibly seeing her body again.

All because I couldn't keep my hands off of her.

And I had no fucking idea.

Bile races up fast and burns the back of my throat when the rage rips apart my nervous system and the only thing I see is pulsing red waves filtering out the pavement in front of me.

I pull onto the street leading into the dump of a trailer park I tracked Jeremy down to only hours ago, the SUV on my tail. I pass the rusted bucket of a car, the cracked and barred windows, the shambles of houses left behind to rot or become the next meth lab.

My jaw tics as I ride past the overturned flowerpots, the piles of trash and broken bicycles left abandoned on the destroyed driveways.

This is the life she almost lived.

I feel the ache of Cedar's disappointment down to my very soul. The lasting pain Jeremy caused her that just echoes now in her strikingly blue as fuck eyes.

I'm gonna do so much better by her.

I can still imagine those eyes now—watering, puffy, and so full of pain—when I pull my bike right up to the last trailer in the deep recesses of the park and dump it.

My feet thunder up the decaying steps to the broken storm door. The glass shards from the busted door have been left scattered across the wooden porch and crunch beneath the sole of my boot with each calculated step. Lifting my knee, I raise my foot and slam it right below the doorknob.

The panel springs free from the jamb, smashing into whatever's behind it and hangs loose on its hinges.

"Where the fuck is Jeremy?" I snarl into the darkness of the trailer that lets loose a smell so pungent I almost don't go inside.

Almost.

"Wait, what the fu—"

"I'm looking for a cock-sucking gutter rat," I demand.

Scattering, like roaches in the light, several bodies take off like the cops just pounded in the door, dropping bottles of all varieties and other paraphernalia.

But I don't give a fuck about the ones that make it out the door before it's filled with Ian's tall frame and Rex's halo of wild hair.

I don't give a fuck about the guy getting a blowie from someone on the couch that doesn't stop, even though the door was just smashed in. Or the spilled liquor adding to the stench of the place. Or the mounds of blankets and foil and drapes covering every bit of the windows to block out all light.

I have my sights set on the greasy rat cowering in the corner with a needle stuck in his arm and a thumb to the plunger.

"No—wait," Jeremy screams when I stalk across the worn out carpet I'm certain was never meant to turn this shade of shit brown and maneuver around more piles of straight up rotting garbage.

Trash that reminds me of the smell of a dumpster just outside of a particular tattoo parlor. With a particular artist that could have lived this life if she's stuck around this filth. Filth that would have ruined my girl.

My. Girl.

I kick away the needle from Jeremy's arm because the thought of touching whatever he's trying to inject himself with makes my skin crawl and my fists rage to stab it in his eye instead.

Jeremy howls when the needle snaps from the body and leaves a prong hanging from his loose arm. His other going limp at a weird angle thanks to the contact of my boot and the force of my kick.

"Get the fuck up."

"What did you do?" He howls into the trailer, real tears streaming down his dirty, pitted face and leaving clean tracks in their wake.

"I said," I growl and reach down to wrap his stained shirt around my fist so tight it chokes him. "Get. Up."

"Okay, okay," he whimpers on a choking sob, his good hand coming up to wrap around my wrist and claw at my skin as I raise the fucker to his feet anyway. "I'll get you your money."

"Money?" Chuckling darkly, I shake my head, the movement loosening the waves on top of my head enough to fall over my eyes. "I'm not here for money, Jeremy."

"But," he half chokes when I lift him straight off of his feet and his glassed-out eyes go over my shoulder. "He gave me money!"

"Oh?" I take a second to glance over my shoulder at a shrugging Rex, only for my heated gaze to swing back on the filth in my hands. "Rex," I call. "Get the rest of them out of here. Get them help."

"Aye," Rex affirms and I hear his boots stomp away from the pleading look in Jeremy's eyes that follow each movement with a level of clarity I didn't think this druggie could possess.

"But I've got the money—I swear I haven't spent it."

Growling, I shake the ragdoll of a man in my hand and slam his back up against the wall with a crack loud enough to put a smile on my face when he howls.

"I told you, Jeremy." I slam him again, only to bring him close enough that the only thing he sees is the rage in me. "I'm not here for money."

"Then ... what ..."

"I'm here *for your balls.*"

Chapter Twenty-Six

Cedar

"I TOLD YOU SO," Aria mutters.

Scoffing with a grin at my best friend, I shake my head and lean over the human canvas in my chair to get to the shading part of the ink.

When I got here this morning—while later than I should have been—I tore out the pages of samples waiting in my portfolio book and replaced it with a photo of Rex's neck tat under the premise that today is a day for original pieces only. No duplicates, no pre-drawn shit.

Only fresh new designs that were gonna cost more in change and in time, but worth the wait.

I needed the freedom.

Especially after bawling my eyes out in front of my dad for the first time in so many years that I feel cleaner. Lighter.

On the verge of free from the sins that aren't mine to carry.

Or at least that's what my therapist calls it.

Not that it dismisses my own actions that I've taken because of them—like lying or omitting the things from the people that I love most—but instead trying my hardest to move on from them with a little less weight baring down in my chest.

Then there's Fin.

He deserves to get whatever he wants from a person that shares his life, if that's in the cards for a rock god like him, and that just isn't me. Not right now. Possibly not ever.

I'm not sure I'll ever be good enough for a guitar legend like him.

But for now, I've decided to start with Aria, my bestest friend in the whole wide world who deserves to know the whole truth.

"Whatever," I reply to Aria and wipe away excess ink.

As soon as I muster up the courage.

The concentration on the piece at hand is what I blame for not remembering what the hell we were even talking about.

"Seriously, C." I catch my best friend rub her protruding belly from the corner of my eye. "You said the kiss was fucking nice." More hypnotizing circles around her larger-than-one-baby belly. "And Rex said there was some kind of photo or something. That's why the meeting this morning."

"Wait." Aria's words seep into my subconscious and have my hands backing off of the piece I'm almost done with. "Back the fuck up."

"What?" More circles and a crease to her sculpted brow. "Wasn't Fin with you?"

"Uhhhhhh…" I drag out on a breath. My hands threaten to shake, so I set the tattoo gun down on my little side table. I tap the client in my chair to make sure they're still sleeping with their headphones in, and when they don't stir at all, I rip off my gloves and stand. "I mean … shit—"

"You totally were." Aria points a manicured finger in my direction and snickers. "That's why you didn't answer me!"

"Fuck." I blow out a breath through puffed cheeks and rub a hand over my forehead that feels hotter than normal. "Okay, I was." I can admit that without her judging me, right? "For a little bit but he left."

See, I didn't die, and she doesn't know it all.

I can do this.

So why does my chest feel like it's on fire?

"What picture?"

"Oh." Aria pushes up from her lean on my toolbox and pulls something up on her phone. "Even I found it online. Ian's slacking." Facing the screen my way, Aria continues talking despite my heart stopping in my chest and my knees going weak at the sight. "Looks like Fin, but if he was with you last night, then there's no way it's him."

Oh my God.

"It's kinda hard to tell cuz it's so dark." Aria turns the phone back to herself and pinches at the screen to zoom in. "I mean, there's more than one guitar like that in the world, right? Or maybe someone took his?"

"Oh, fuck." It's out of my mouth before I can stop it when she flashes the zoomed-in version and the room spins. "Oh, no."

"Cedar?"

"Ohhhhhh, *no.*"

Both of my hands come up to bury my burning face in them.

"C?" I feel her too-cold hands on my bare shoulders thanks to the simple racerback tank I opted for today instead of the showy shit and my pregnant best friend is guiding me across the tent until my ass hits a stool. "Did he leave you early last night?" I hear the anger filtering into her voice as she tugs my hands from my face. "Did he really leave you and go sleep with someone else?"

I shake my head—at least I think I do—as I stare at the ground and wait for a pit to open up and swallow me whole.

This is all wrong.

So wrong that the heat of angry realization washes over me and my breath comes in pants. "Do they know who took the picture?"

My voice doesn't sound like mine as flashes of the who that would give a fuck about me sleeping with Fin fill my mind and fuel my rage.

"I don't know. All I got was that there was a pic." Aria dips to catch my gaze when I stare my seething heat at the concrete and hope that a pit does open up and teleport me right to the shithole place I know Jeremy's holed up in.

He was way too eager with Rex last night. Too pointed about being back.

The fucking cash.

"It was me, Ari." Filling my chest with the almost chilled air my portable AC unit tries to keep up with, I steel my chest and meet my best friend's eyes. "That's me. In the picture."

"Hot damn." Aria's grin appears on her rounded out face, but her brow stays pinched. "No one is going to know it's you." Her hands rub up and down my arms soothingly, even though there's no way to soothe this ache in my chest. "They aren't even sure it's Fin yet."

"Doesn't matter, Ari." I shake my head and stand on steady feet as I run a hand through my hair to get it out of my sticky face. "Someone will figure it out."

"Well," Aria sighs and keeps a hand on my bicep as I step forward. "Can't say I know what to say to that. Especially with what happened after the video leaked."

The video that got Jordan banished for supposedly getting head and made Mac all pissy.

At the same time that Rex's tat got leaked, and the internet went wild with As Above secrets.

Shit.

My hands go to my head when my chest feels constricted and I suck in a breath as I pace the small space around my sleeping client and my preggo bestie.

All the while, my head swims with so many emotions I can't even catch one long enough to feel it before it changes again, all of the feelings merging together and morphing into some weird numbness.

"Fuck," I hiss. "It was me. All of it." The words rush out of me into the humid air of the tent before I can stop them. "I bagged Fin on stage and I'm pretty sure I know who took the picture. I didn't think he was fucking smart enough, but I guess it doesn't take much to just upload a pic of the right person and the internet digs in its talons and takes off."

"Whoa, C ..." Aria steps forward like she might try to stop my angry paces, but backs away at the last second. "Slow down. Who would do that to you?"

I freeze mid step and spin so fast it makes my head tilt. I drag my hands down my face and meet my best friend's worried gaze, knowing that there's no way around telling her. "Fuck, I know you remember Jeremy."

"Hated him, actually. So glad when he left." Aria shakes her head. "I know it was hard for you, though, but I'm so glad he disappeared."

"He was bad, Aria." The words fall between us as the ambiguous meaning furrows the already deepened vee between her brows. "Like bad."

"Uh-huh." Aria nods slowly like her hormone addled brain is taking a second to pick up what I set down. "Bad how?"

"Like bruises I hid, emotions I can't process, and the reason I keep a bat in the shop."

Her jaw grits and her fists ball up as tears build in her pretty green eyes.

And my chest splits open just a little more.

"No." She shakes her head as the tears crest her lashes and she swipes them away from her cheeks with her free hand. "But you never told me."

I drag in a shaking breath and rub at my face again to distract myself from the tears that prick the backs of my own eyes. "We weren't as close until after it all. And I never wanted to relive that shit again."

"So." Aria sniffles and wipes at her face with flared nostrils and a ticking jaw.

"He called me," I cut in before she can ask, before the roll I'm on screeches to a halt. "He called. Showed up here demanding my attention, which isn't the first time he's tried since we broke up. Rex scared him off last night, but this pic suggests he never left." I gesture to the phone still in her hand and exhale a hearty breath with a shaking snicker that lacks all of the humor. "I panicked, Fin was there. We hooked up, he took me back to dad's."

Aria's eyes widen at my summary of the events.

"The festival's been a real roller coaster," I say on a forced chuckle and shake my head as I step up to my best friend.

"Do you know where he is now?"

My shoulders lift on a shrugging sigh. "I would assume his parent's old trailer. I have no idea." Hair falls around my shoulders when I shake my head. Resolve settles in around the ache in my chest and holds me together with the plan formulating in my mind. The visions of Jeremy losing body parts and screaming my name for the last fucking time make the corners of my mouth tip up. "But I am going to find out."

Aria stares at me, her green eyes wide in what I presume is shock, and puffs out her cheeks. "We should call someone."

"Like who?" I scoff and spin back to my chair that's still filled with a passed out client. I snap on a fresh pair of gloves and nudge the participant that has managed to sleep through this whole endeavor that continues, even when I prod them with another set of needles.

It only takes a few more minutes of stunned silence to finish the piece and shake the client awake to pay. Once the chair is empty again, I meet Aria's determined gaze.

"Ian. He can help."

"Nah." I finish the cleanup and toss the trash. "I just need to go talk to him. Set him straight before I let anyone go after him."

"Cedar, you really think I'm going to let you go alone? To that same guy who used to abuse you?" Aria's voice shakes behind me, her words slicing right down to my soul at the realization of their truth.

"I'm not the same girl I was then."

Or even two nights ago.

But I don't say that last part out loud. I don't go into all the details of how my life has managed to change the moment that Fin rushed in and demanded I see him.

As if I didn't already see the man that saved me once.

Fuck, does he know?

"I have to take care of it, Ari. Alone."

Chapter Twenty-Seven

Cedar

THE THING ABOUT BRAVERY is that it's also terrifying.

I pull up to the ransacked shack that used to be a decent place to hang out at on my Frankenstein of a motorcycle and heel down the kickstand.

My hands shake. My heart races faster than any other nightmare that's woken me out of a dead sleep at the memories.

But my determination wins out over all of it as I step up onto the rotting porch for the first time in almost ten years.

The last time I was here, it was empty of people and for a therapy thing that Sara thought might help—go back to the scene, see that I get to walk away from it all in one piece, and replace the memories with stronger ones.

It worked for a while, but then the nightmares came right back.

Except I was older thanks to having seen the place as an adult and Jeremy was just as vicious as ever.

We'd gone on to try something else, but I'd already gotten to the point where I shared that I just wished he was dead. Gone. Never to be seen again in the light of day. That's what I needed to get past the trauma. That's what I needed to know that he was never coming back for me for sure.

But then the worst happened. He showed up again, coerced me into being with him again out of guilt with all of his mind tricks, and my stupid, immature heart agreed because maybe this time was different. Maybe this time he'd grown up and changed.

Maybe this time he would love me like I needed to be.

Except it was different.

He was worse.

Far worse than any horror flick I've fallen asleep to, worse than any walking red flag, or villain.

This fucker was my real life, full-blown gaslighting manipulative abuser that made all those good-deep-down characters seem like angels.

That time, I was the one to disappear in the dead of the night and never looked back after he put his hands on me for the final time. I ran to my dad's—the one place I knew he'd never come back to—and hid until I heard a rumor of him moving out of town again. To follow another dream on a whim, which was really just code for drugs.

Jeremy was all about chasing the next high. It took me too long to realize I was just another conquest, another hormone boost to satisfy his seriously messed up brain.

I promised myself then that I'd never see this side of town again, let alone Jeremy. Not willingly anyway.

It sent me into another spiral that required more therapy, where I became this version of me that refused to let anyone else in besides those who were already there—Aria, her sister, and my dad.

And it was working just fine. I was fine.

Until Fin showed up.

With his pretty-boy eyes and sexy as hell smile and that sound he makes when he cums

...

Sucking in a deep breath that's filled with the scent of pungent garbage, I steel my shoulders and face the broken glass of the storm door with a grip on the handle.

The worn release button catches on the pad of my thumb when I yank it, the scent of propane filling the air in place of the garbage I was expecting the moment the front door creaks open.

Having seen every horror movie on the market, I know stepping into the house—alone, without a weapon of any kind—is one of the worst ideas I could act on, but I'm resolute. Resolved to whatever happens. Ready to put this chapter of my past behind me where it belongs.

I step inside and see the drenched couch, the spilled liquor and pill bottles spread out over the furniture. A layer of trash on the once-blush-colored carpet that's now some fucked up shade of shit brown. The scent of booze is almost as strong as the garbage and gas as I step deeper into the house. Dust clings to every flat surface above eye level almost as much as the foil and drapes stick to the nicotine covered windows.

Then I hear the rattle of chains—like this is one of those stupid movies—and I go for the bat I know Jeremy's mom used to keep behind the door.

Please still be there …

Yes!

My fingers wrap around the grip of an aluminum baseball bat and I drag my new weapon with me down the narrow hallway in the direction of the sound.

With every step closer to the back of the house where the kitchen is, the scent of propane permeates the air so thick it feels like it's the only thing I'm breathing. It makes my eyes water and my mouth go dry as I walk across the worn path in the carpet that veers off into the bathroom and then continues the rest of the way to where I had my first dinner date.

The sound of chains rattle again, this time right next to my head. And while I subconsciously jerk at the sound, the walls don't come crashing down and nothing flies in my direction. Sucking in a deep breath and regretting it, I lift up the neck of my shirt to cover my nose and mouth and turn to the smaller door set into the wall next to me.

I don't remember what's on the other side. And while my mind conjures up all kinds of tormenting things that might be on the other side of the panel, I reach for the knob anyway and jerk the door free from the jam with my bat cocked at the ready.

Not that I could get a good enough swing in the confined space, but the thought makes me feel better.

"Jeremy?"

Soft, pain-filled moans escape past the shell of a man's bloodied lips, one of his eyes swollen completely shut while the other is on the verge of the same. I step back and take in the sight of the one that controls my nightmares handcuffed to the pipes leading out of the water heater. One of his hands is bent in an unnatural angle that makes my stomach clench and his too-big pants hang loose around his thighs. Blood stains the exposed purpling skin of his chest, some spots appearing as sores broken open, while others look like fresh track marks.

Are those fresh bruises?

"Ce—Cecilia?" He groans into the space, his puffy jaw leaning into his shaking twig of a bicep, as red-hot anger rips through me.

I feel my face heat, my ears burn, my hands clenching the handle of the bat in my grip almost as hard as my teeth grit.

Cecilia.

The bitch he cheated on me with.

The one who encouraged him to chase after more highs, more stars, more dreams.

"You came for me?"

"Nooo," I drag out and let out a humorless cackle as the man of my nightmares stands helpless at the mercy of whoever left him here, defenseless and beaten.

Like he left me.

A calm washes over me as he muddles on, murmuring about the woman he always wished I was, the one that died from an overdose about two years ago in a town on the other side of the country.

"Who was behind the photo, Jeremy?" I lower my bat across the front of my body and snarl in his direction.

"I already told him," he screams, tears streaming down his pitted cheeks. "I told the man with the money. Ask the one with the halo. I told him."

God, he sounds high.

"Jeremy," I snap and flick the bat into the doorway, the thick end landing against the tank next to him with a resounding *thunk*.

"Oh my God," he screams into his bound wrists, his words echoing around in my ears and tipping up the corners of my mouth with each passing second of torture he endures. The man sobs, his bloodshot and swollen eyes wheeling on me and widening a fraction, as if I see the realization settle into his fried brain. "Cecili—*Cedar.*" My name comes off on a growl, his sneering lip losing all intimidation in all their busted glory once I glance down and realize the old and fresh wet spot on his crotch. "You fucking bitch."

Jeremy's face splits open with a sound of pure rage escaping his bruised throat.

"Who told you to take the photos, Jeremy?" I tilt my head, my chest loosening with every second the man stays chained up, just like in some of my dark fantasies, the thought tipping the corners of my mouth up in a wicked grin.

"Your fucking dildo of a boyfriend," he screams and lunges, his pants catching just as his wrists do. "You did this to me. You whore."

I grit my jaw at the sentiment, the name calling, the growling yell that sends me right back to a ball on the floor with this man standing over me. His hands on me, his fists hurting me.

His dick I didn't ask for.

With flaring nostrils and a racing pulse—an adrenaline spike that screams at me to run—I raise my gaze from his dirty and bare feet in a slow perusal of the monster that haunts me with a cemented stance.

I will not run.

With each rewriting detail of his brokenness, each faucet of his downfall, each detail of his almost demonic-like possession of my thoughts, I take in this version of Jeremy now.

I will not run.

Taking in his busted and bloody state, I let my brain rewire the neurons that redirect the pathways of my fear and commit each detail to memory.

Time to fight it.

"Who had you get the pictures?"

"Fuck you, slut."

Lifting my chin, I let a small smile tug back onto the corners of my lips as I give a small nod. "I like sex, Jeremy." Reaching into my pocket, I fish out the Zippo he gave me before he went crazy. The one with a little *J* carved into the metal sleeve that he destroyed a tattoo gun carving it with. "Just not with you."

I have a fifty-fifty shot that flicking the flint doesn't blow the trailer up, considering the amount of propane that has been feeding into this space.

But, considering the pilot light on the water heater hasn't blown us up yet, I have a minute or two before it all goes boom.

Except, I have this nagging in my mind that this man—the torturer of my sleepless nights—hasn't suffered quite long enough.

"You slutty ass bitch," Jeremy growls. "Get me the fuck out of here, you whore." His tone escalates to a piercing yell with each word that rings around in my head and draws my eyes up to meet his for the last time.

Flicking open the lid of the lighter I used to love, I poise my thumb over the roller and raise my eyes to the demon that haunts my thoughts for the last time.

"Rot in hell, motherfucker."

Dropping the thing, it falls to the brown carpet at my feet and I spin away from the crackle sounding somewhere else in the house that builds along with Jeremy's screams.

"Cedar." He curses as I seal the door closed at my back and stalk across the rotting porch to where my bike sits.

I can still hear his screams as the snapping cracks get louder, the widows illuminating through the fog of dust.

"Cedar. Come get *me*."

Ignore.

Ignore.

Ignore.

My chest fully expands with the breath of fresh air, my head slightly swimming from the inhalation of the gas, coupled with the emotions that rage inside me.

"*Cedar*. It was *Ar—guhhhhh ...!*"

But none of it stops the smile from reaching my lips.

Chapter Twenty-Eight

Fin

ADRENALINE RUNS FAST AND hard, pumping my muscles up and protruding the veins I've been told stick out when I'm pissed.

It's almost like I can feel them pulsing beneath my too tight skin.

Craning my neck one way, then the other, I wait for the inevitable pop that sends a rush of warmth down my spine and growl when it doesn't give the relief I'm looking for.

I need to see Cedar.

Then I need to fuck her.

And I need both now.

I stalk across the festival mats, through the main crowd, and make my way to where I know Cedar will be, with cracked open knuckles and a sense of relief that she's close.

I can't tell her.

My chest is tight with the need for her, for release, but lifted with the knowledge that Cedar won't ever have to be fucked with again. At least not from someone like him as long as I'm around.

As long as she'll have me.

I'm sure she'll hear about what was done, maybe feel some type of way about it. But she'll never know the whole truth.

Which is the price I'm willing to pay for her.

And right now, I could give two fucks less about any media rumors or the news segments that are going to cover the incident.

All I want is her.

"Cedar!" It's off my lips before I even reach her tent, the flap drawn closed and what feels like a million festival goers between me and getting to her.

I need to see her.

To fucking get inside her.

Make her fucking mine.

"Cedar ..." Whipping the deteriorating canvas back without a care of who might be inside getting ink, I step inside and blink away the sudden plunge into the much darker tent. "Sweetness?"

Silence echoes back, the lack of noise ringing around in my ears as I wheel around and take in the sight of Cedar's setup all packed up.

The wrap now gone from the chair, the cleaner bottles stashed somewhere out of sight, the array of colored ink she'd left out for ease missing.

Even the trash is empty when I peek in to check.

What the fuck?

Even the music has stopped in her absence, the crowd a calmer buzz in the background of the festival that I don't hear over the sound of my blood rushing and my heart beating in my ears.

Where is she?

Flexing my fist with a ticking jaw, I check the final spot in the tattoo tent to know for sure if she's gone.

The cash drawer.

Stalking around the little podium-esque stand and smashing around the shelves I've seen Cedar hide shit on, I come up with nothing.

Nothing.

It's gone, too.

A wave of cold rushes over my torso and snakes its way into my gut with such a sense of finality that I want to scream. Yell. Smash something.

She's gone.

And I've gotta fucking find her.

"Yo."

Practically seething with the roller coaster this woman continues to put me on, I turn my pumped chest to my bodyguard, who looks a lot like someone I want to punch.

"Where have you been?" Peach growls at me through gritted teeth and a day old shirt.

"I am fucking sick of people asking me that question." I shoulder check the orange-haired wall of man standing between me and my path to find my woman. But he stands against the movement and forces me back with palms to my chest.

"You don't get to fucking say that to me." Peach's light eyes bore into mine, his heavy hand landing on my shoulder, his fingertips digging in. "Not after what we all just left."

"Don't you ever bring it up again," I growl menacingly and jerk from his grip.

"Fine," he scoffs out and steps right into my space, close enough that I might explode. "Your disappearing acts need to stop, Fin. The world knows it's you."

The picture.

The cold grip of anxiety digs its artic fingers into my stomach once again, and I have to take a step back as the realization sets in.

Cedar.

"Peach?" His head dips but shakes, and my features fall. "What about Cedar?"

Is this what it feels like to love someone?

And then lose them?

"Where the fuck is she?"

Chapter Twenty-Nine

Breaking News

G UITAR GOD ISN'T SO godlike now, is he?

Recently nominated, and recipient of a musical award, was found with his pants around his ankles.

ON STAGE.

But who is the mystery groupie caught in Finland Montgomery's grasp?

Subscribe now to find out.

Chapter Thirty

This just in.

L EAD GUITARIST OF As Above found on stage with his dick out.

Finland Montgomery has refused to make a statement to the public, but the public wants to know.

Is this as serious as known Roadie, Doll, and what does Doll think about someone stepping on her turf with the man?

Click and subscribe to find out who is this mystery woman with her legs wrapped around our beloved Guitar God is.

You only get the best info here!

Chapter Thirty-One

Toby

THE LIGHT FEELING OF being perpetually buzzed leaves me floating on a cloud of numbness that I've long ago preferred as my permanent state of being.

Everything is better with whiskey.

It's easy, cures everything, and the rest you just don't remember.

So when my best friend and brother shows up to the bus with that look in his eye—the one that begs for relief from the world—I hand over the bottle I've been nursing.

I know the world has tilted on its axis when Fin accepts the bottle, takes a long pull and swipes across his mouth with the back of his liquor holding hand. Couldn't recall a time he didn't reject a drink right before a show.

"Who ate your Wheaties?" I ask and eye the man.

"Wheaties are fucking gross."

"Uh-huh." I nod—I think—and reach to take the whiskey back from the lead guitarist. But I miss. Or maybe he moves away faster than I make it to him. Because that just seems to be our thing now, him moving fast and leaving me behind. "So, it's about the chick?"

"Shut up, Toby," Fin growls and kidnaps my bottle to go sit and brood on the couch with a huff. "Did you see the fucking picture, too?"

"All over the internet, my man." I purse my lips, the hair of my mustache tickling my upper lip as I tilt my head to the tablet left set up on the table. "Who is she?"

Fin's chin drops to his chest, the frame of him bowed in more than normal as he mumbles. "Maybe they'll be able to find her."

I think.

"What?"

"Just get fucking drunk with me, yeah?"

"Done, brother."

Considering I was already on my way to plastered when Fin walked in, it doesn't take long after I settle into the couch with him to get his lips loose and moving without any help from me.

"You ever caught feelings, Toby?"

My tongue swipes away the liquor from my lips and I pass the bottle back across the couch to Fin.

"Nah," I shake my head, my long hair tickling my bare shoulders. "Sounds messy."

"Right," Fin snorts and takes a long pull from the bottle. "Messy." He props the glass against his thigh, his fist tight around the neck as he stares at the wall for a beat. "But undeniable."

"What's that mean?" I reach for the whiskey, which serves to shake Fin's tight gaze from the wall to me instead. His eyes, blue and intense, make me pause.

"Means," Fin sighs, the side of his jaw jumping even though his eyes soften, "that there's no running from it. Even though she's not here, they are. They're infectious and painful with nowhere to fucking put 'em."

I don't have time to compute my bandmate's words before he's on his feet and digging out his phone. The thing is to his ear, and he's mumbling shit I don't get as he turns away from me to speak.

"Just *find her*."

Chapter Thirty-Two

Cedar

MY LIMBS ARE HEAVY. My eyelids heavier.

My chest is on fire. A soul deep ache that calls for the last person it should.

But maybe it could ...

If it was really over, maybe I could be that person that's deserving of someone like Fin.

The wind whips through my hair that spills out of the helmet, chilling my exposed skin. A shiver rakes over my body and has the handlebars in my grip jittering. I straighten the bike before it dumps me into the ditch, but my vision blurs and the tears streak down my cheeks.

I can't let anyone see me like this.

And that leaves me with exactly nowhere to go.

Asphalt fades into the tree line as I slow the motorcycle, the hills melding into the sky with each passing minute that the sun fades on the ripping pain in my chest.

Wide open and raw, I hold on to the handlebars for dear life when the tires skitter and debris kicks up enough that I lose the ass end of the bike before I can correct it.

I slide, dumping Frankenstein on its side and bailing from the machine before it can crush my leg. The move skips me over the road like a rock on the surface of the water, the pavement tearing into the moto jacket I'm grateful I thought to throw on before lifting the bike from my dad's garage.

Skidding to a stop with a heaving chest and my back to the ground, I let my arms flop off to my sides and a maniacal laugh escape from between my chattering teeth into the helmet I'm also glad I remembered.

"Fuuuuck," I breathe into a laugh that shouldn't be happening, given the fat tears still rolling down my cheeks and fogging up the face shield.

It's finally over.

I'm not sure how long I lie there before I reach, slowly, for my pocket with hope that my phone is still intact. With as little movement as possible, I fish the device from my pants and engage the button to trigger the voice command. The familiar ding of recognition from the thing has a relieved breath pushing out past my lips and the commanding words rushing out.

"Call Aria."

"Calling Aria ..."

The ring fills my helmet, the Bluetooth connection making me wince with the volume when the line clicks and a voice sent directly from the heavens replaces it.

"Cedar Savin Jones, you better be fucking alive and not out there doing stupid shit."

Snickering, I let my arm flop back to the pavement beneath me and stare up at the darkening sky I can see through the fog still taking up most of my field of vision. "Only a little bit."

"It's been hours. Tell me what happened." There's a hope in her voice that I almost wish I didn't have to crush, but alas, that is the life of a best friend, right?

"Oh, God, so much," I breathe into the mic, a slight hitch to my breath. "I don't even know where to start."

"Um." Aria's voice flitters over the line with a slight tremble I try to ignore, the hummed response one I've seen enough times that I know she shrugs right along with it. "How about where you left off?"

That conversation feels like weeks ago now, not just a few hours. The one where I was finally giving in and avoiding my avoidance tendencies.

And my therapist's words settle into my brain from my last session where she was hell bent on providing the logic of why that method was definitely the wrong choice. That long-term avoidance was never going to get me to the healing stage of shit.

But why the hell not?

It can work, right?

"You think Jeremy had something to do with the photo leak. And Fin?" Aria says into the phone matter-of-factly, like she knows exactly how to get me back on track.

"Damn you, Aria."

"So, you slept with the guitarist. So what?"

Oh, boy.

"Well," Snickering, I force my torso up off of the pavement, my lips peeling back with a grimace at the ache that answers my move. My ribs hurt along with my neck and lower back, but I can't tell if it's from emotion or the wreck. The tension of walking away from a man who was going to burn to death, or from the hours and hours I've spent both bent over bodies for work, and bent over for Fin.

So I sit, and I regale the tale of my life to my best friend with a shaking voice and stiff muscles.

How I ran into Fin and the way he held himself even from that first meeting back at the *Saltwater Skulls* show. Then how he was so sure of everything that first night back at my parlor that made me want him even more. Enough to break my one rule and let him chase after me anyway. And how that chase makes me want to keep running *to* him instead of away.

How Jeremy returned to torment me, popping in my life throughout the years, and how my dad showed up just like he always has to protect me when the scum called this time. And then I had Rex find me in the lot of the venue when Jeremy tried to leverage me with my phone, and Fin made sure I got back to my dad safe.

Then how I found the subject of my nightmares cuffed to a water heater inside of a trailer that I knew was going to go up in flames and I did nothing to prevent it from burning him alive. And maybe I added some fuel to the fire by leaving my lighter behind.

And once I'm done sharing way too much with the woman on the other end of the line, I'm met with a silence I didn't expect.

"Aria?"

"Cedar."

"Say something."

"Hmm," she hums, the sound of her tapping pen echoing over the line loud enough that I can almost see the sketches in front of her for her next creation.

"Hm? That's it?" I scoff into the mic and grab a handful of the gravelly dirt by my feet just so I can throw it.

"Well," Aria sighs into the phone.

"Well?"

"Considering the breaking news now flashing on my task bar, I'd say that the real-life nightmare is definitely gone."

I don't hold back the sense of relief that washing over me. Even when I know I shouldn't. "No way."

"I know now how much of a fucking threat this man was to you. Probably others." Aria blows out a long breath that replaces that tension right back in my beating chest. "You feel better?"

"Yeah, but that's fucked up, right?" I push up to my feet and brush off the dirt from my hands against my thighs. It hurts, but I manage.

"Maybe it is, maybe it isn't." Aria pauses long enough to have me looking around the street I stand beside to confirm I'm still alone. "Listen … I'm glad that he's gone. Period. And that you're fucking here, okay? The guilt that man made you feel is all his to carry. Not yours."

"Shit, okay." I blow out a breath and pop open the face shield to suck in the fresh air. "I know you're right. It'll take some time to sink in, I think, but you're so fucking right."

"Exactly," Aria chuckles, pulling a forced chuckle from my aching ribs. "Now tell me what you intend to do about Fin."

"Guh," I scoff and roll my eyes. "Way to go for the jugular, *bestie*."

"Hey, this is what I'm here for." There's a light chuckle on the other end of the line that has some of the tension fading away. "So Fin, … we like him. We slept with him. How long has it really been?"

"Ummm."

"Right. A long damn time. So now that you've slept with him, what are you going to do?"

"God, Aria, I don't even know." I pace around in the dirt, kicking small rocks as I reel from the roller coaster of this conversation that is my life. "I know what I want to do, but I don't think that's an option."

My best friend scoffs. "Why the hell not?"

"Because what if he doesn't love me back?"

"What if he does?"

Chapter Thirty-Three

Explosion

REPORTS ARE COMING IN from all across town with the sightings of the smoke cloud forming over the trailer park where a home burst into flames beneath the afternoon sun.

Crews are on site battling the blaze now at what reports are calling the known drug house.

Was this an accident or was someone after their goods?

Check back for more information in just a little bit.

Chapter Thirty-Four

Fin

WITH A SWIMMING HEAD and a complete lack of anything but static from the thing beating in my chest, I step up on the stage and prepare to muddle through this show with enough enthusiasm to get it over with.

For the first time in my career as a musician, I am dreading the sight of the titty flashing, the moshing and the gathering to get as close as possible.

For the first time ever, I'd rather be anywhere but here.

And I don't like that.

Somewhere around half of Toby's bottle, I called Peach. I don't entirely remember what I said, but I know that I asked him to find her.

We should have just finished it.

My mind works overtime with the whys and the whats despite my best attempt to distract it, to numb it, and hope to forget.

Even the barely dressed chicks in the crowd that bounce and get those around them amped up have lost every bit of the appeal they once had.

I don't want to see them.

I want Cedar.

Pulling in a deep breath that expands the ache in my chest that even the liquor couldn't completely touch, I hover my hand over the neck of my cherry red Manson MB 2.

The stand is just off the side of the stage where I left it next to my main show piece. Another Manson. Another red one.

But it's not that one.

The moment my fingers graze the ebony neck of the MB-2, I lift the piece from the rack and shrug the strap across my torso that pumps with a thumping heartbeat. Stalking with a gritted jaw, I take my place beside Rex on stage right and jam an extra pick between my gritted teeth.

The red body gleams back, catching the lights that flash across the stage as Mac pounds out a beat behind us, and right as the he changes the tempo, I raise two middle fingers to the crowd in the biggest *fuck you* to the world.

A *fuck you* to those that forwarded my picture, to the ones that spread that shit across the internet. To the media outlets that reported it, all for a few clicks.

A *fuck you* to the industry that allows the behavior. A culture that promotes the sharing of misinformation or shit that doesn't belong to them.

And an even bigger *fuck you* to the garbage that led to Cedar jumping every time I go to touch her and damaged her enough that she had to run from me.

Again.

Camera flashes catch me, document my statement to spread the narrative and say they were the ones that saw it firsthand.

But this time I want that.

I want the world to know that I don't give a fuck what they think.

Slamming the cords, I make the instrument against my hips sing along with Rex as the brand new lyrics come off his lips.

"*Wringing our angels so tight, the devil comes out.*

"*Dragging behind me the bodies of my mistakes,*

"*Bury the cadavers before I can be tainted again.*"

The vocals burst out through the speakers, the amplifiers pushing the sounds farther out across the masses of stunned patrons prepped and ready to take on this packed venue just to see us.

"*Swimming through the ages of who I used to be,*

"*Finding my way, crawling through the darkness,*"

The crowd cheers from beyond the broiling stage lights, a sea of bobbing heads throbbing along with the beat in waves.

"*Clawing through the end.*

"*I'm coming home to you, the light.*"

Rex stalks across the stage, his arm out wide, the grill of the mic to his lips.

"Wipe away the decay, sing me your songs of praise.

"For the man you know I'm not."

The words seep into my bones and leave goosebumps in their wake, the fucking truth of them, and pulls a wicked tip to the corner of my lips.

"Wipe away the decay.

"Sing me your songs of praise."

Traveling fingers and strumming hands, I step up to the edge of the stage with a sweat slicked brow and nod along to the fresh song with a renewed ache in my chest.

And that's when I see it.

The lights change from a green glow that blends everything together to a blanket of soft white that illuminates the first several rows of people watching with rapt attention.

The highlight of glowing orange hair manning the crowd control between me and them comes into view as he's pulling in surfers and pushing back people who press too close to the fence that protects them from us.

But it's not Peach that has my head cocking to the side as I strum.

No.

It's a tatted wrist that lifts up above the sea of heads in front of him, with horns poised and ticking to the beat I keep.

A flash of night sky inked into pale skin I've had my lips on illuminates in the ocean of bodies like a beacon in the storm as they're bathed in a wash of red.

Cedar.

She's here.

Smashing the heel of my palm into the controller screen built into the shimmering body, I engage the riff to repeat the string of cords I play and slide the piece around my back until the body is smacking me on the ass and I move.

Cameras catch my palm as it meets the platform. Flashes capture my body catapulting off of the stage and my boots hitting the no man's land between me and the screaming fans. Screams that amplify when my fingers wrap around the barrier and haul up onto the platform midway up the fencing. Hands grab onto my shirt without the guitar as a deterrent and tug me closer to the crowd, but I don't see a single one of them.

I don't register any of the faces that yell, scream, chant, and cry when I look down and motion with my hands for the mass to split.

Bodies press into others as a hole opens up with just enough space for me to toss my legs over the barrier and land with a thud I feel in my bones.

The movement is echoed by the beat racing off my back and the axe landing against me with a smack as I push forward a step and the crowd separates a little more.

Enough that when I trail my gaze across the faces looking at me, mine locks on a set of blue eyes that are going to haunt me for the rest of my life.

"Sweetness."

In that moment, I don't care about the elbows I catch, or the shoulders I check as I step closer because I don't dare take my eyes off of her.

My torment.

And my salvation.

I know I'm running out of time. My recording will only last so long before I need to make a change to keep the show moving. But I refuse to turn around without her.

So I reach across the opening space and wrap my fingers around the back of Cedar's neck.

The sea parts for her as she moves to me, the feeling of her in my grasp breathing a warmth back into that bruised spot in my ribs as her hands meet my pecs.

Cedar's body against me, her smooth skin in my hands, and the rush that comes with having this woman anywhere near me has the rest of the fucking room fading away like nothing but her and I exist right here, right now.

"I've been looking for you." My eyes flick between hers, our foreheads nearly touching, my other hand making its way to her hip and tugging her closer when she doesn't push me away. "Fuck, where have you been?"

"I ... um, I didn't know where else to go."

"So you ..." My brow furrows when she sinks her teeth into that red bottom lip of hers, and I almost lose my train of thought. "So you came to watch us?"

Cedar shakes her head, her black locks moving across the fingertips still curled around the nape of her neck. "No."

"Sweetness," I growl and tighten my grip, bringing her closer still. "I don't have time for games. What did you come for?"

"You, hotshot."

Cedar's lips meet mine in a crash that sends shocks right down my spine and has me wrapping her hair up in my fist to keep her close.

It's like a piece to the puzzle of my life has finally clicked into place. Like the missing segment appeared in the last place I ever expected it, in a way that I certainly never knew I needed.

She's here.

I don't bother stopping the groan that escapes when she parts her lips and invites me in to tangle our tongues. And I definitely don't stop her hands from snaking up my chest and burying themselves in my hair.

She tugs and I pull until there's no space left between us and just as I think she's going to pull away, she's hopping up to wrap those sexy as sin legs around my waist and forcing me to catch her.

"Goddamn." I'm all out of breath when I pull back, my hands firmly planted on her ass and absolutely copping every feel as she stares down at me with a wicked as hell grin and a smear to her colored lips.

"A little birdy said I should." Her hair falls around us, encasing her face in a darkened halo that blacks out her eyes and only enhances that sexy as hell grin I'm definitely getting hard for.

"Should what?"

"*Wipe away the decay,*" Cedar recites, one of her palms pressing to my jaw. "*And sing me your songs of praise.*"

I fight the grin that wants to break free but lose when Cedar leans in to run the tip of her nose along mine. "I wrote that."

"Uh-huh." Cedar nods. "It's about me, isn't it?"

Schooling my features when she leans those blues just enough to catch my sight, I purse my lips. "Nope," I say on a rising grin that refuses to be held back. "Not even a little bit."

"Well," she sighs, a level of severity washing over her features. "I want to wash away the decay, Fin."

"Uh-huh." I nod and hold her close. "Will you fucking let me help you?"

Cedar shrugs, a lift of her shoulders that drops right back down. "Nah."

Scoffing when I catch the glint of mischievousness in her smiling eyes, I shake my head and take a step back. "So you weren't thinking about me all day then. I get it."

Snickering when I make another move to get us closer to the fence, Cedar leans down and smacks a lingering kiss right to my lips. "You totally get it, hotshot. I wasn't thinking about you one bit."

"You are so fucking mine when I'm done here, sweetness. I hope your ass is ready."

Cedar wiggles against me, her grin glued to her lips as my boot taps the barricade we need to get on the other side of. "Just avoid my ribs."

My brow furrows, but I don't have time to process her words before the crowd is pushing at us and pulling me out of the bubble this woman creates.

"*Calling Finland Montgomery back to the stage, please,*" Rex mimics a nasally tone over the speakers, loud enough to grate my nerves and kill the boner I was sporting. "Finland, please return to your post, sir."

Laughter fills the air and has me snorting as I slide my guitar around to settle between me and my girl and haul us back over the barricade only to come face to face with a giant screen showing me and Cedar all wrapped up.

"Damn, I hope you weren't trying to keep us on the low." Shaking my head, I grind my teeth together at the utter lack of privacy, pissed that the option has been taken from Cedar because I wasn't thinking when I saw her in the crowd.

I just went to her.

"No," Cedar sighs and cups my jaw with both of her hands. "I wasn't."

And just when I thought I was all out of surprises with this woman, she leans in and plants another kiss to my lips, hot enough that the crowd cheers and hoots for us.

"Fuck," I breathe into her hair when she pulls back only to wrap her arms around my neck and press her cheek to mine. "I swear you knock my feet out every time, Cedar."

Chapter Thirty-Five

Cedar

W HEN I TOLD FIN that we could hold up together after the show—surprising the both of us—I never expected this.

Damn Aria and her seed planting.

'Maybe it's really love, Cedar,' she said.

'Maybe you could give it a try, Cedar,' she said.

When I said yes to trying to figure out whatever the hell this is between us, I thought we'd go to a hotel, terrorize the staff for a few days and then maybe realize we weren't compatible and move on with our lives, even with the pictures of us from the show plastered all over the internet.

He's a fucking rockstar after all.

They'd forget about me eventually.

I thought that we would burn out. Flare up, then fizzle out.

Easy. Quick.

But the last two weeks have taught me better.

Finland Montgomery is not an easy man. Nor is he quick or simple.

And the thought of not having him hurts even worse than I ever thought possible.

The man takes what he wants, stopped asking questions after the first morning he woke up to find I was still by his side and is thrilled to try all the things I've ever wanted when it comes to sex.

And he doesn't make me feel like a freak to want them.

I'd showed up at the headlining show for the *Setlist Music Festival* with every intention of saying my goodbyes after a night of fun. Walking away and letting my heart break over a man I never really had and moving on with a poor emotional state over ice cream and more ink that I don't need.

But Fin had other plans for me. For us.

Instead of all that catastrophizing coming to fruition, the man I've always known was more than meets the eye, shattered all of the expectations, pulled out all the stops, and has shown me every night since what a real man does with a woman.

He hasn't let me down once.

Except right now.

Paint covers almost every inch of the bedding, my body, and even some of the floor.

I think there's even a painted handprint on the wall.

Correction: *Body Paint.*

The non-toxic, safe for sex kind.

Yet another one of my things I've always wanted to do—*paint a picture with sex*—and instead of jumping on me like I've asked for him to, Fin sits naked in the corner of the room with his now tainted guitar and a smeared notebook.

And a vibrating wand left pressed to my exposed pussy.

"Fiiiiin." I roll my head to the side and lick my lips—*is that cherry flavor?*—and lift my hips from the mattress we are definitely going to have to replace after this. "It's not gonna fuck itself."

Fin smirks and snorts and lifts a colored brow, but not his eyes. "Beg like I told you to, Cedar."

Ugh, I hate him.

Not really.

In fact, it's more like the exact opposite.

I just don't have the courage to tell him.

"C'mon, hotshot," I taunt on a pant to hide the moan that threatens to crest my lips and pull on the restraints that prevent me from doing the shit myself. "Come get me."

I'm losing the gumption I started out with. Lost to the sensations of my body climbing ever close to that cliff, but not so close that I dive off.

Not without him.

"Beg, Cedar."

"Nuh-uh." I shake my head against the pillow, my hair collecting static and clinging to my sweating face. "Just come fuck me, hotshot. Show me you can."

Snorting is the only answer I get to my goading when Fin leans back over his notebook and scribbles something with marbled fingers.

A growling groan vibrates through my body and challenges the vibrations already going on between my legs that are set to drive me mad.

And if I get too close, guess what distinctive feature this fancy little toy has?

That's right. *Bluetooth.*

So the fucker doesn't even have to get up to ruin my orgasm before it can happen.

Ughhh.

"Fin." I shudder as the vibes increase and my back arches at the sensation. "God-damnit."

"I want to hear you beg me for it, sweetness."

"No."

"Then ink me and I'll do whatever you want."

"Also, no." I catch his shrug as my eyes roll and my body threatens to cave without me.

"Then you're going to be stuck there for a while."

It's a power struggle between us. Hellbent on making sure one of us will cave.

It's not going to be me.

Determined to win this match that I've completely made up in my mind, I ease into the vibrations set to drive me wild and, well, I let them.

Because while I know that I won't be able to hold out much longer, even if it's just a touch, I know that Fin won't be able to watch me lose it for long either.

Grinding my hips into the toy between my legs, I let the moan overtake me at the hardness the toy provides against my clit. "Oh, God," I hiss when I ease up and the vibrations take over the friction. "I'll just do it myself then."

"Cedar," Fin warns, his eyes snapping to what's happening between my legs and darkening.

"Hotshot," I moan into the open air and grip at the restraints holding me down as my eyes slide closed. "It feels so good."

Growls echo through the haze of bliss taking over my body, which only drives me closer to the edge.

The bed dips at my side, my body sliding closer to Fin, his scent filling my nose, and forcing out everything except him. His rough hands feather over my thighs, the warmth radiating from him as he maneuvers from my side to between my spread legs.

"Tell me how good it feels, sweetness."

"Mmmm," I moan and suck my bottom lip between my teeth. "Not as good as you."

Fin's dark chuckle flits over my chin and leaves chills in its wake, his heat blanketing my body. "Then say it, Cedar," Fin demands on a growl, the bed dipping by my head as he leans over me, his pelvis warming the insides of my thighs.

"No ..." I breathe into a moan when the vibrations change and the pressure increases.

"Tell me," Fin whispers over the shell of my ear, the hot breath making me shudder with need. "Tell me how bad you want me to fuck you."

"Oh, G-God," I stutter and suck in a breath.

"I want you so close that all I have to do is touch you to set you off."

Doesn't he know he already could?

"Fin," I groan as my body tightens, my spine arching up off the mattress only to slam into all of his gloriously hard muscles that make me gasp.

"Say it, Cedar," Fin demands and rotates the wand over my clit, the sensation enough to have my eyes rolling back. "I don't hear you begging for my cock."

Oh, God.

I can't keep up. The feel of his weight pushing into me, teasing me with that dirty-as-hell mouth and arousal covered toy between my legs. The way he heats me in places that he touches, but leaves the exposed bits cold and desperate for his touch.

The emptiness I feel without him inside me.

"Oh, God," I moan.

"Sweetness," Fin growls above me, drawing my eyes open only for them to roll back at the sight of his hardened jaw and parted lips. "You say my name when I fuck you."

"*Unggg.*" The vibrations disappear, a faint thud registering in my brain milliseconds before I feel the tap of his pierced cock against my clit that sets me off like a firework.

The contact starts the headfirst dive into an orgasm that only intensifies when Fin slams his cock into me so hard I feel his pelvis meet mine. Deep and punishing, his thrusts hammer into me with enough force to keep me against the bed and my mouth popping open in a silent scream.

"Say it," Fin growls on a pant, his cock swelling inside me. "I wanna hear that scream, sweet."

"*Oh ... ahhh ...*" I choke out as I come undone beneath him with an orgasm that feels never ending enough to curl more than just my toes. "Fin."

"Beg, Cedar," Fin breathes over my ear. "Say it."

It's too much. Too much sensation. Too many dirty words. Too much *him*.

"Oh, God, Fin," I gasp. "Please."

"Please what?"

"Please fuck me. Harder, Fin." I feel myself clench even harder around his cock, my spine bending painfully to him like a magnet to metal. Like the tides responding to the moon's pull. "Please, Fin."

"That's my girl," he growls, his hips slamming me in pressured thrusts until I'm moving up the bed with the force, the restraints pulling at my limbs and digging in. "Cum again, sweet. On my cock."

"Please, yes." Stars taint my vision of the dancing headboard, my pussy clenching around his hardness in response to him without me even trying. "FIN."

"Shit, yes, Cedar."

I feel his roar of pleasure more than I hear it, the vibrations of his voice bouncing around in my chest like a tattoo straight to my heart as his cock explodes inside me.

"Fin," I choke out with a hoarse voice and a pulsing pussy, the sound of his ragged breath echoing around my ear drums from what feels like somewhere in the distance. "I'm in a tunnel."

His husky chuckle overtakes his panting when he pulls out of me, leaving me shuddering with aftershocks. "Good."

"Nuh-uh." I race to catch my own breath and blink away the spots that fill my vision. "No good."

"Sounds like ..." Fin's far away but deep-as-fuck voice pauses as he leans one way to release my wrist, then the other. "I did my job."

"Mmmmm." It's all I can muster as Fin removes the bands from my limbs and pulls me to my side and curls around me.

He looks ridiculously hot with the paint smears on his jaw and brow like some form of sexual warpaint as he settles his head beside mine and wraps his arms around my still sore ribs along with hooking his massive thigh around mine.

It feels like home.

I've never felt so comfortable being pinned down, the weight of this man tethering me to him like gravity to the earth.

And it's like the love I know I've been hiding from shows itself in a way I can no longer ignore.

I am lost to all that is Finland Montgomery.

My hands find their way into his hair and Fin's lips find their way to mine in a kiss so passionate and sweet it makes me want to weep.

I guess I can have this, too.

"Gimme a minute to hold you, sweet." Fin cups my jaw, his thumb feathering over my bottom lip that holds his brilliantly blue gaze in a way that I feel the caress down to the butterflies that flutter in my belly. "Then I'll get you cleaned up."

"And tacos." My voice is just a whisper, the emotion sticking in my throat. His gaze flits up to mine and I know he sees the mist gathering there. I try to hide it, to blink the building tears away, but Fin has this way of knowing all the words that stick to my tongue and refuse to let loose.

"And tacos." He nods in confirmation and slides on an easy grin that stretches his face. "I meant what I said before, Cedar."

"What's that?" I clear the frog from my throat and furrow a brow at him with a shaky sigh.

"You're safe with me, sweet. *Always.*"

I let out a long and heavy breath, a release of tension leaving me along with it, my head nodding in knowing as I grip at his hair and drag him close enough to bring his lips a breath from mine. "I know, hotshot."

And I kiss my man like my life depends on it.

Chapter Thirty-Six

Fin

EVERYTHING HAS CHANGED.

It doesn't stop the drop to my heartrate when I notice Cedar's mask fall back into place at times, but I find that the last two weeks have had me living for the moments when she takes the armor off and sets it aside just for me.

And waiting for that satisfying buzz of her tattoo gun.

She jokes, deflects shit she probably shouldn't, but I still see the woman beneath the mask and I don't think there's anything on this planet that could stop me from finding her in everything around me.

Her scent between my sheets after I've shown her what it's like to be treated right, that way she wants to be in the bedroom, and out of it.

She's in the sunrise we stayed up long enough to watch, and the moon she admires most nights its clear enough to see. Even more so on the nights where it looks like one of those horror werewolf movies and the damn thing shines bright and is half covered in just the right amount of darkened clouds.

She's in the way I now share my food because she never wants to order enough for herself for fear of judgment.

And she's there in the soft touches in the middle of the night, or in the crowd of the day, where she no longer jumps at the contact, but instead smiles at me like maybe I made that fancy werewolf moon she likes.

I know there's still a long way to go, but ... we're getting there. Together.

Now ... it's the smell of her shampoo filling my place after I ran the water hot enough for her to summon her demon friends from the pit of hell to join her and the itch of fresh ink on my hip, right along my Adonis belt.

Of a damn taco.

The first meal we shared, just us.

I snicker and pad my way across the now clean—*ish*—bedroom to the cracked open door where steam billows out when I push it open.

"Sweetness," I call into the echoes of the water falling like pulsing streams and smacking off of skin and tile.

"*Hotshot,*" Cedar mimics a deep voice that makes hers crack and pulls a chuckle from my throat.

"I'm coming in," I say to her silhouette that darkens the steam-covered glass I slide out of my way. "Hope you're ready."

Cedar smacks her lips and spins to me beneath the spray with wet skin and a grin she can't hide. "It has not been ten minutes, liar."

I shake my head and don't hide my husky chuckle when Cedar's gaze slides down my naked body.

Parts of me are still covered in cracking paint, the shit drying in places I'd rather not discuss, but none of it matters when her eyes slide easily over my torso to my junk that jumps at the attention and back up to my face with a smirk.

"Hmm," I growl and push the door closed behind me to keep the rest of the hellfire warmth inside the massive shower with us. "Looks like my timing was perfect."

Cedar's tongue darts out to lick her curved lips that hides none of her wicked intentions. "Seems so, hotshot."

Meeting her grin with mine, I move across the warm tile to wrap my arms around her wet body, her skin running with paint streams that fade into the bottom of the shower and disappear down the drain. "Seems that you could use a hand."

Cedar's face breaks open with a smile I would do anything to keep on her pretty face as her arms come around my shoulders and her hands find the dampening hair at the nape of my neck. "Yes, please."

I feel my lips quirk up at the corners when I lean down to press my droplet covered lips to hers, my tongue lolling out to swipe across her swollen lip.

She kisses me back with a fervor that has my hands trailing down her hips to the backs of her thighs and gripping her just hard enough to lift her until her legs are wrapping around my waist and my cock is standing at attention between us.

Not that it's ever stopped begging for her attention.

This time, I go slow. Soft. And step us up to the wall I press her back into as I line the head of my cock up with her entrance.

"Fiiiiin," Cedar sighs as I slide my cock inside her tight heat until I'm bottomed out. "Yes, fuck."

She's swollen and sensitive, her pussy pulsing around me as I pull out and press back in. "You feel so good wrapped around me. *So sweet,*" I groan and press my forehead to hers, my hips picking a tempo that's boarder line torture as my cock slides in and out of Cedar's pussy.

"Mmmm," she moans, her head tilting back against the tiled wall, exposing her painted throat. "Yes, so good, Fin."

Leaning down, I press my lips to her thrumming pulse and nibble her flesh until she's tightening around my cock and gripping at my hair. "So sensitive, aren't you."

"Uh-huh," she mewls with a nod against the tile. "So full."

I can't help the chuckle that eases into a groan of my own. "You gonna cum again for me?"

"Yes," she breathes and clenches around my sliding cock. "Oh, God."

Burying my cock deep inside her, I rock my hips against her as she clamps down on me and rotates her pelvis into mine. "That's it, sweetness. I love it when you cum on my cock."

"Fin," Cedar half sighs, half moans into the easiest orgasm that leaves her like jelly in my arms.

"Shit, that's hot." My chest heaves with need, my balls tightening up as I draw back from her body. "Can you stand up?"

Easing her back to her feet, Cedar nods despite her shaking knees. "Maybe," she snickers.

Snorting, I hold her around her waist with one arm to keep her from toppling and wrap my free fist around my cock. I pump and groan into the water that rains down on us, my grip on Cedar's waist tightening the closer I get.

My head falls back as my orgasm races closer, only to shoot farther forward when Cedar bats my hand away and replaces it with her own.

"Fuck," I groan and gasp. "I'm gonna cum."

It's the best warning I can give before my muscles are tightening, and my cock is shooting thick ropes onto her belly.

I'm cupping her face in my palms before my cock can stop pulsing, my hungry lips finding hers in a kiss so hot I want to be back inside her again. I feel the head of my cock slip against her skin in the mess I made, the water slowly washing it away and replacing it with just Cedar's silky skin.

"You're amazing." I kiss her lips between my words, my own refusing to come down from the grin she causes.

"Stop." Cedar snickers and bats at my shoulder with no real effort.

With a lightness to my girl that I've caught more glimpses of over the last few weeks, I step back and snag the body wash from the shelf and lather up a deep purple loofah with little bat sponges stuck inside the mesh.

I take my time worshipping and washing every inch of her skin, making sure all the paint is gone and all that's left is the woman I know I'd admire, even if she was always covered in paint.

Cedar returns the favor, washing my body with a cloth I snag from the stash just outside of the shower, her hands taking special interest in lathering up my face. I think it's just so she can look at me without having to look at me, but I don't care.

Her eyes are on me.

And that alone is enough of a rush to have my heart skipping beats.

"You ready for me to feed you, sweetness?" I ask as I towel off her body despite the chill that takes over my droplet covered and fully exposed skin once the water is off.

"Someone promised me tacos."

Snickering, I wrap her up in the fluffy terrycloth and slap her ass on her way out into the bedroom. "I know a place not too far from here."

I snag a towel for myself and wrap it around my waist as I follow Cedar out into the room.

"Do I have to wear clothes?" Cedar almost whines, her perfectly plump bottom lip poking out in a pout that's coupled with a shy tilt of her foot and the fluttering of her lashes.

She's so damn cute it makes my heart hurt.

"Yes," I say, even when my cock screams otherwise. "And not that skimpy shit that looks like nothing but thread covering those tits," I growl and aim my pointer finger in her direction, only to set the fire alight in her growing evil grin.

"You sure about that, hotshot?" Cedar challenges and spins on her heels with purpose to her bag. "I thought you liked it."

Growling, I move across the room to fist her towel and yank her to my body. "For *my* eyes, yes." I grip her hips and grind against her ass. "Not for others."

"Mm," she hums in response, her hips swaying back into me as I wrap a hand up in her wet hair and tug her head to the side. "Sure, I'll wear something like that for you."

"Good." I lean down to capture one of the rings through her lobe with my lips, the feel of her ass rubbing against my cock making me groan. Her wispy gasp turns into a chuckle that has my dick filling and my heart racing.

"I'll wear the green one. Just for you, hotshot."

My cock is almost completely hard again when she spins out of my grip, her hair sliding easily between my fingers and her towel whipping off her body as she goes. I catch her devilish grin as she flips the long black strands over and gathers it all in the towel she wraps on top of her head.

I'm too caught up in watching her nakedness, my hand reaching down to grip at my length through the towel when she straightens and that wicked grin plastered to her face seems ... too wicked. "Wait—"

"Nahhhh, hotshot," she drawls on a tsk as she moves to her bag and pulls out a piece of clothing that's nearly non-existent. "You said to wear it *for you.*"

I'm struck speechless as the woman is dressed in what feels like a millisecond with only a sheer layer covering her torso, her nipples barely concealed by the dark green embroidered ivy vines that look like tattoos rather than a freaking shirt.

Or whatever the fuck that is.

Why is it fastened between her legs like a fucking onesie?

And when she bends over to feed her feet through a set of matching dark green cut-off shorts and exposes the thong that's not at all covered by the vines, I growl. "Damn you, woman."

"What?" she asks innocently as she straightens and fastens the button of the shorts at her waist. "You said to wear it *for you.*"

"You're fucking killing me," I groan and scrub at my stubbled jaw.

Cedar bites her bottom lip to try and hold back the grin on her face. Tries. "Aria made it for me."

"Can you at least …?" I gesture to her chest with a defeated sigh and resign myself to the fact that I'm just going to have to keep fighting off other men for the rest of time. "I don't know, throw on a fucking jacket or something?"

"Pfft," she scoffs with a roll to her eyes and pads across the room back into the bathroom. "That's like asking to wear a coat over a costume, hotshot," she snickers as things clatter against the vanity and I'm left struck stupid in the middle of the floor. "No thanks."

"Goddamn." My cheeks puff out with the breath I force and I shake my head.

This is it. This is her.

Vibrant and bold. Beautiful and challenging.

I swipe my hands down my face as I turn to my dresser in search of my own clothes and I can't fight the tip of my smirk rising as I ruffle through the items I have clean.

And I fucking love her.

Letting the terrycloth drop to the floor when her hair dryer kicks on, I jab my arms through a muscle shirt that's seen better days and snap the elastic band of a pair of boxers against my waist. With a pair of jeans holier than Jesus on a Sunday, I tuck my wallet and my keys into the pockets and snag my phone that's riddled with notifications I ignore.

They can wait.

I turn to the mirror hung on the wall I definitely intend to bend Cedar in front of later and run my fingers through my waving hair only to give up trying to tame it.

I freeze when I spin around to see Cedar standing in the doorway watching me.

"Holy gothic gods, I owe you a sacrifice," she mutters more to herself and bites that fucking lip in a way that does things to me.

To my cock.

"Sweetness," I growl at the sight of her, my brain catching up to what my eyes are seeing and my cock waking the fuck back up at how easy it would be to strip her naked all over again.

Cedar is hot. In make up and out of it.

She leans in the doorway, her lined eyes tracking down my body and back up again as she runs a hand through her straight black hair and sinks her teeth into her lip that's so deep a red, it's almost black.

"*Goddamn.*"

Chapter Thirty-Seven

Fin

I CAN'T KEEP MY eyes off of her.

Halfway through the wait for tacos at the bar just two blocks from our place, I stopped trying.

God, I am so gone for this woman.

I watch her over the high top table between us as she takes in the sight of tiki-themed shit plastered all over the walls of the open-air bar and sips on the fruity cocktail that came in a sugar skull shaped glass. Her tongue darts out to flirt with the straw in her drink, drawing my eyes to the motion she uses to tease me.

Fuck, I'm in love with her.

A ping of ache settles in my chest at the notion as the swell of need gets bigger with each passing day that I don't tell her.

In my head, I run through all the reasons why *not* to say anything. Not yet. It's not time. It's so soon. She's just coming out of her shell enough to stop fucking jerking when I reach for her.

What if I change all of that?

The risk is too great to challenge. Too heavy to toss out without knowing where she is in all of this.

Her former abuser was buried yesterday.

Well, what was left of him.

Does it weigh on her?

Shaking myself out of my head, I find myself picking at the label of my beer bottle. Nervously, I bring it to my lips and take a pull. It's almost warm thanks to the hot humid air still floating around the darkening skies and definitely isn't helped by the hand I've had wrapped around it since it was placed in front of me.

I don't even like beer.

I'm a whiskey man.

But when my girl ordered a nice tall drink with a stupid amount of alcohol, I knew I needed to keep it slow and light.

Hence, beer.

Too much in my head shit anyway.

"How do you just …" Cedar gestures around the bar, drawing my eyes around us, "not get noticed?"

I shrug and set the unwanted beer on the table. "Hide in plain sight, sweetness." Sick of waiting, of not touching my girl, I step around the table we've been standing at until her elbow bumps into my chest and her eyes flick up to meet mine. "Helps if you know the patrons."

"Huh?" Cedar's gaze whips around the space in search of familiar faces, only to come back to settle on me with a lifted brow.

Tilting my head to our left, I say, "That's Dreadful Souls in the corner." I lift my gaze, meeting the lead singer from across the room with a subtle jut of the chin that he returns, then goes back to his friends. "And over there." I nod to the standing tables lining the door, similar to the one we stand at. "That out-of-place fucker is one of the top photographers in the states."

"Wait." Cedar's hand lands on my forearm as she whips her head around takes in the faces around us. "G?"

"Yep. The one and only," I snicker when her jaw drops and gesture to the bar. "Most of the guys in the back know Sentry or Ian in some way."

"No way." She shakes her head. "The bartender?"

"Lugh's brother," I answer easily about As Above's second-in-command security member that has been noticeably absent the last several weeks. But I guess in order to keep the roster rotating, Sentry would need other clients to protect when we aren't on tour or causing scenes.

"Shiiiit." Cedar's dark locks flow around her shaking head, her gaze coming back to mine. "So, you just know people."

I chuckle and slip a hand onto her hip, tugging her body into mine. "Yeah, sweet. I know people." With a grin, I dip down low to place my lips against the shell of her ear. "But not as well as I know you."

I feel the shivers rake over her body as she shudders into my chest and I can't help the way my hand possessively travels up from her hip to the back of her neck, her silky hair threading through my fingers. Fisting the strands, I tug her face in my direction and grip her jaw with my free hand when her heated gaze meets mine. Her plump lips part in a pant that washes over my face only moments before I'm pressing my lips to hers and swallowing her breath down.

She opens for me like the starved fiend I know I am and I'm lost in the way her tongue tangles with mine, tasting and teasing, until I'm breathless and completely ignoring the silhouette that darkens my periphery.

When the shadow refuses to disappear and my girl's gaze keeps darting in their direction, I roll my eyes and glance at the waiter's waiting hands.

"My apologies. Your food." With a subtle nod, the waiter drops the platters of tacos on the table and disappears.

"Guh," Cedar groans and nearly tosses me aside to get to the source of the delicious scent wafting up from the waiting meal.

Snickering, I plant a kiss on top of her head that she dismisses, her hands already going for the meat-filled floppy tortillas topped with cilantro and fresh onion.

I step just to the side of her, giving Cedar enough room to eat freely, but not enough space that I can't reach out and touch her when I want to, and dive into my own platter of food.

The plates are huge, as usual, and lined with more tortillas underneath the street tacos to catch all of the droppings and produce more deliciousness at the end without having to build it.

The first bite has my stomach growling in recognition of the lack of a lunch and my plate is cleared in a matter of minutes.

"Jesus, hotshot." Cedar shakes her head and speaks around a mouthful. "I didn't know it was a race."

I shrug and pluck the final bit of a taco right from her fingers and toss it into my mouth. "If you hadn't needed to be fucked right through lunch, I wouldn't have been so hungry."

Cedar's face flushes a light shade of pink at my words but burns downright red when I shoot a wink in her direction.

"You're ridiculous," she mutters low, her voice thick.

"Ridiculously yours." The words are off my lips before I can grab them and bring them back, providing me a whole new level of tension I didn't know could exist in my head about how this woman fucks with me.

My eyes drop and my hand goes to the back of my neck in a way that makes me feel … sheepish. I don't feel fucking *sheepish.*

Shit.

"Fin?" Clearing my throat and steadying my shoulders to face the music, I raise my gaze to Cedar, only to find her wide eyes stuck on her phone. She's swiping on the screen before I can ask anything, then bringing it to her face without sparing me a single glance.

And then she's fucking off.

Darting from the table, Cedar sprints to the exit as she speaks into the device and it takes me a whole ass minute to unglue my feet from the floor, toss bills on the table, and run after my girl.

"Cedar." Passing the gate outside the bar, crossing the patio filled with more outside seating, I have to jog to catch up with her trail of dark locks flowing behind her. "What the fuck?"

She spins to me when I grab her elbow, her pale face and wide, tearing eyes landing on mine. "It's Ari, Fin."

Her words, haunted and shaking, are like a spike straight through my chest.

The baby.

Without another word, I'm grasping her hand in mine and we're running back to my place where I left my bike.

By the time the garage door is open and my keys are in my hand, Cedar's cheeks are streaking with tears I wish I could make go away, but I can't.

My own chest is splitting when I plop my helmet on her head and mount the bike to insert the key and crank the engine over. It starts with a roar that hurts my ears and I'm walking the machine out onto the driveway to get the door closed as Cedar climbs on behind me.

The ride is tense, the damp air just cool enough to create chills that slice me right to the bone when I feel Cedar shake at my back. Her arms around me are stiff, and it drives me to speed faster, to get us closer to the hospital where I know one of my own brothers is waiting inside.

The echo of an engine registers in my brain when I contemplate taking the sidewalk to avoid a red light and has me checking my rear view to find a familiar bike filling the little glass mirror.

"Hold on," I shout to Cedar over the sound of the engine when the light takes too long to change, despite the lack of traffic and I swerve us up over the curb and take the walkway around the corner. She tightens around me when we bump over shit that's not meant to be driven on, leaning farther into my back.

Back on the pavement, I open the bike the fuck up, tearing up the asphalt and leaving trails of rubber behind.

It's not long, though it feels too long, when the lit hospital comes into view and we're pulling into the lot way too fast. Riding right up to the ER, Cedar is jumping off the back before I can even stop moving, my own body urging me to get the kickstand down where it is and leave it.

So I do. And I'm running after my girl in the direction of what feels like certain grief with a split open chest and panting breath.

"*Aria Scarlett,*" Cedar shrieks to the nurse's station. "*Where is she?*"

Chapter Thirty-Eight

Fin

THE WAITING ROOM IS packed.

With security stationed at the entrance, outside of the hospital, and walking the halls, it's feeling more and more like we're trapped in a box of emotion.

It's making me even antsier than when I walked in here.

Rex has paced the entire length of the sterile tile without saying a fucking word to anyone since we were led back here.

Mac filled us in when we arrived on a bunch of shit I'll never even begin to understand about pregnant women and hospital policies, but has resolved to sitting in the corner with a view of the entire room. He set his sights on his twin that arrived just after us and hasn't moved except to follow his brother's pacing with his eyes.

Aurora and Cedar sit together in the only other chairs in the room, holding on to each other and whispering shit to keep each other calm. Judging by the constant bounce of Cedar's knee and the damp Kleenex in her grip, I'd say that it's not working.

And this is another moment where I feel like she needs something I'm not.

With my hands threading through my hair, I blow out deep breaths as often as I can force them to keep from raging all over the nurse's station for some damn updates.

Something to ease the ache in everyone here.

And each time the door is opened, every one of us jerk to attention, only to be let down by whoever steps inside that's not covered in scrubs.

I have to do something before I go mad.

All the waiting around, all the tension and unknown, is driving me insane.

But I'm torn.

Go to Cedar…

Or to my brother?

With my heart in my throat, I take one look at Rex's red rimmed and unfocused eyes and know that there's not a single thing I can do or say that will make the man feel better.

How would I feel if it were Cedar back there without me?

The notion slicks over my knotted stomach and has me turning toward my girl, whose eyes are already on me, watching me.

And what I see rips me up enough to have me dropping to my knees in front of her.

"Sweetness," I croak, my hands going to her thighs as she unravels herself from Aurora and leans to me with a tear soaked face.

"Why aren't they telling us anything, Fin?" Cedar asks with a thick voice and more unshed tears hanging off of her gorgeous lashes.

My chest aches at the sight, my heart splintering for her and my brother, and his girl who's all alone in a hospital bed.

And that just won't fucking do.

Shaking my head, I reach up and swipe away the streak from her cheeks as she sniffles.

"I don't know, sweet." I take her hands in mine and kiss her knuckles. Breathing in her scent fuels me, expands my chest and increases the reckless anger I've been trying to hold back for quite some time. "I don't know, but I'm going to find out."

What started out as anxiety pumping my blood fast morphs into rage the longer I see Cedar's fallen face. The more I hear Rex's thudding paces wear a pattern in the tile without answers as to why the fucking father isn't back there with his future wife.

Fuck hospital policy.

I'm pushing to my feet with a lingering press of my lips to Cedar's forehead only to spin and catch Rex's body, forcing his feet to stop with my hands to his chest.

"Let's go get your girl, Poppa." His bloodshot eyes focus on me, his jaw stiff with tension, but he nods in determination and lets me spin him back in the direction of the blue clad staff.

It takes some convincing, with only minor threats to the hospital security that shows up for the assist, before we finally get a white coat in front of us spewing words in what seems like another language I hope that I never have to hear again.

Something about patients being under anesthesia and unable to answer specific questions that allow certain family members to enter the room during a difficult delivery.

Or in this case, emergency C-section.

Especially when the patient is high profile.

Ian was the one to get Aria into the emergency room while Rex was stuck by a horde of fans at the damn grocery store, meaning he was just a few minutes short of getting the clearance he needed to enter.

All of the noise we make gets my family escorted out of the general population waiting area to the neonatal wing of the hospital where, just down the hall from them, I get to watch my brother throw his massive amounts of curls into a knot and scrub up through a pane of glass.

I can't hear but see the sink spray the water I'm certain would be hot enough to make Cedar happy as Rex washes up, or the paper gear they cover him in, and if the circumstances were different, it would be a funny sight to behold. But not today. Not like this.

The nurses rush around him, making sure things are tucked and tied and covered long enough that I see his snarling growl make them jump straight out of their skin and have them ushering him off toward the door.

He plants an elbow into the panel, only to pause and take one last look at me through the window.

That's when I see it all shining in his blue-green irises.

The fear.

Pride.

Hurt and guilt.

Love.

I firm my jaw and hold that gaze until he settles on determination and juts his chin in my direction.

It's go time, Rex.

I return the nod, and watch my brother disappear through the second set of doors with his shoulders squared and his head held high.

Rex Thompson is about to be a father.

Chapter Thirty-Nine

Cedar

A URORA HAS BEEN PLASTERED to my side, providing me some semblance of comfort in the fact that she hasn't stopped leaking from her eyeballs, not once, and has been a constant reminder that it's okay to let others see the emotion.

Doesn't mean I have to like it.

Because when I look around the room, every other person also here is in some state of *holy shit, what do we do* for the very same reason.

It's fucked up, but it's giving me some level of peace with the tears that collect on my lashes.

My best friend is both having her baby and is having a really fucking tough time with it.

Pulling in a deep breath through a chest that would rather cave under the weight of what I refuse to accept as possible, I uncross and cross my legs enough that it jostles Aurora's head on my shoulder. Her eyes peer up at me, red rimmed and raccooned, and I see something else shining in her irises.

Curiosity.

"He called you '*sweetness*'," she states with an air of disdain tainting her question and wings her brow. "Or did I imagine that?"

I purse my lips and shrug the shoulder she still leans on so that it fucks with her head placement. "And?"

"Ew."

I almost snicker at her response. "You mad, bro."

"Um," Aurora drags and blows out a heavy breath. "Fuck, I wish I could be."

Blinking at her unexpected response, I pull back and palm her shoulders to force her upright. "What's that supposed to mean, squirt?"

She shrugs and lets out a sigh. "I don't know. I guess I want to be 'cause I don't want you assholes to leave me all alone, but I spent all those weeks being mad at Ari before and now she's—" Her eyes well up with a fresh batch of tears that make my own itch. "I just ..." Aurora lifts another shoulder and reaches up to swipe her used tissue beneath her nose. "You deserve happiness more than anyone, C."

My shoulders inch down from my ears, my head tilting to the side. "You really mean that, don't you?"

"Duh," she says on a roll of her watering eyes and a shake of her head. "I know I'm fucking selfish sometimes, but I also want you guys to be happy. For real."

She drops her head and fiddles with the tissue in her hands. "Squirt," I say and squeeze her biceps to get her eyes back up on me. "You'll get there one day, too."

I watch Aurora's eyes trail over my shoulder for a moment to where I assume Jonathon is stationed only to return to mine, the air around us shifting away from the jealousy Aurora is known to hold. "So you really love him, then, huh?"

"Fuck, baby sis." I shake my head and can't stop the small lift at the corner of my lips. "I really fucking do. I don't know how. Or why, but yeah." My grin grows slightly at the thought of Fin's warmth cradling around me just this morning. "I love him."

Aurora returns my small smile, her eyes going back over my shoulder as she leans in close to stage-whisper. "Then maybe you should tell him to his face. He looks like he could use it."

"What?" I hiss with wide eyes and a snicker from Aurora as I slowly turn to find the man that holds my heart staring down at us. "Hotshot? *How much of that did you hear?*" I ask with a grit to my teeth on that final bit.

Fin's hands are on me, pulling me to my feet and crushing me to his chest in the warmest bear hug I've ever gotten. His lips are on my forehead, breathing me in as I lean into the wild beat of his heart in his chest. "Just enough, sweetness."

I bite my lip to hold back the flood of emotion that threatens to overtake me once again, only to lose the battle and have my tears soaking into Fin's shirt.

God, he smells like home.

"Cedar," Fin nearly whispers, his deep voice thick against the crown of my head, tickling the strands of hair there. "God, I love you."

"Fin." I barely choke out and grip his shirt. "Stop it."

"Never." I feel the subtle shake of his head against mine when his lips refuse to leave my hair and his arms tighten around me. "I'll never stop. You are my salvation. My destination. My home."

"Oh my God," I cry harder into his chest, but his words don't stop praising me, reassuring me.

"You challenge the shit out of me," he chuckles and leans back to cup my wet face in his massive palms. "*But what is music without the staff to keep it all together?*"

"Fin." My heart splinters in two and bleeds a rush of warmth into my chest for the first time in ... well ...

Ever.

This moment. This segment of time.

This *rush* as I stare into the loving blue gaze of the man that stole my heart when I wasn't looking. It's what I will forever recognize as the moment that my life changed for the better.

"Say it, Cedar," Fin demands in that tone that sends chills—the *great* kind—down my spine. "Tell me I'm not crazy."

"Pfft," I scoff on a watery chuckle. "You're definitely crazy, hotshot."

"Cedar," he growls in warning.

With a wicked grin and a zip across my lips, I lock it up tight and toss the imaginary key over my shoulder.

I might love him ... but I'm still me.

"*Sweetness.*"

Chapter Forty

Fin

I OPEN MY MOUTH to demand she say those three little words to my damn face, only to have it all set aside for the man that walks back through the doorway covered in paper scrubs and enough blood to make me growl.

"Rex?" I spare a glance for Cedar, including a lifted brow that promises we'll talk about this later, and step up to my brother that looks like hell chilled over. "Man, say something."

"She's—" Rex's bloodshot and glassy eyes lift to mine and shine with so many emotions as he babbles and wobbles on his feet. "They're—"

When he topples a little too far to the side, I catch him by the biceps I've seen lift amp stacks without breaking a sweat, and his grip latches onto my forearms with more force than I expected. "Goddamnit, Rex. Spit it out," I growl at my brother while I silently hope that what I see is not what my brain wants to tell me it is. "Is she ok? Are they ok?"

Swaying and unsteady, Rex's eyes mist over as his fingertips dig into my arm. "Fin," he chokes out on a sob that breaks my fucking heart when he launches forward and wraps his massive arms around my shoulders.

"Rex," I demand and grip him right back. "You bastard, *tell me they're okay.*"

I feel his head move against my temple as the shakes take over his body and a relief I refuse to believe just yet washes over me. "They ... it's them, Fin."

"Them?" I ask with a thickness to my own voice, the lumps building higher and heavier in my throat. "As in Aria and the baby, right?"

His head shakes against me. "Two."

I rip Rex's iron grip from my body, his hands landing on my shoulders to keep himself upright while I hold him steady by his ribs. "Two?"

The man nods with a tear-streaked face and a lift to his thinned lips. "Yeah, Fin. We got twins and they're okay."

"Fuck."

"Oh my God."

Arms are all I see before the both of us are submerged in all of those that have sat around us and waited for the words to finally come out of Rex's mouth.

Cedar crushes to my chest when Aurora bounces excitedly beside her and Rex as more arms snake around us and bring us all closer together.

"Holy fuck, bat dick, you scared the shit out of us." I chuckle at Mac as his bandana comes into view over Leo's head and Toby's beard scratches over my arm.

"Me?" Rex scoffs halfheartedly and shakes his head as best he can as the center of our giant group hug.

"You're right." Mac nods somewhere behind his brother, his flopping hair all I catch. "It's baby girl's fault." His head pokes up over the group and he rests his chin on his own twin's shoulder. "Can I go tell her?"

Chuckling, Rex nods his head. "Aria needs her rest, bro. So two at a time. And be *chill.*"

"Oh, then it's me and you, baby sis. Let's go." Mac breaks off from the group to hook his arm with Aurora. "I'm not giving those babies back once I get them."

The rest of our group breaks away as Mac and Aurora disappear down the hall, leaving me to hold Rex back up from the grip I never released.

"Can't believe my girl wants to see this fucker," Rex pauses and drags in a deep breath before leaning farther into me and Cedar, who still clings to my side. "You two are next." Rex shakes his head, but chuckles when I scoff at him.

"Next time, I'm letting you eat the tile. *This fucker,* my ass." Rolling my eyes, I haul Rex into my side as he drapes an arm across my shoulders. "How's some coffee sound?"

"Like magic," Rex answers and I maneuver us through the waiting family members to the short and private hallway where a single coffee machine stands, guarded by Jordan, with Cedar tailing us but hanging back.

"Congrats, man." Jordan tips his head and Rex returns the sentiment in a true testament to how exhausted the man must be.

"Thanks," Rex mutters at pokes at the buttons until the smell of roasted beans fills the air.

We make it back to the waiting area in time for Mac to be announcing that Ma Thompson's plane has landed and needs a pick-up.

"Ma's lucky that I love her," Mac grumbles.

And then he steals the cup of Joe from his twin, drinks half even though it's scolding hot, and shoves it back into my free hand.

Huffing, Mac steps aside and clears the path as Cedar slides in on Rex's other side and lifts his arm across her shoulder much the same as I have.

I keep all of the weight of a snickering Rex that he can't handle as the three of us step in stride down the long hallway that leads us back toward the sterile room I left him in. "By the way, fucker, this better not be vagina blood on me."

"Fin," Cedar snaps.

"What?"

Rex snickers and shakes his head as we reach the door just down the hall from the windowed room. "They had to cut her open to get them out, man. Once the first one was out, it was pure chaos. Doc let me cut the first cord, but then something happened and he went to hand the baby over to a nurse that wasn't there, I was. So it's ..." Rex shrugs and reaches for the handle that lets us into the washing space and bathroom area of Aria's room, the rest of it cut off by a privacy curtain. "It's *something*."

Cedar laughs, the sound like music to my ears, and leans over the sink to scrub in clear up to her elbows as Aurora peeks out from the opposite side of the hanging fabric.

"Damn nurses stole them for footprints and you're back already," Aurora curses and disappears for only a moment before snickering her way out of the room.

"Love you, too, squirt," Cedar calls at her back and snags paper towels to dry her dripping hands.

Rex and I follow suit while I try my damnedest not to think about what the hell transferred from him to me and I snag one of the stupid paper scrub covers that Cedar ties at my back before we slide back the curtain that leads us into a room with bustling nurses. "You don't want to give that back to the baby."

"Babe," Rex sighs and goes straight to the bedside that holds a pale Aria connected to way more wires and tubes I don't want to think about. She's sweaty and ashen enough that I might end up with nightmares.

"Rexy," she sighs and takes his hand in a grip even I see is painful. "We're not doing this ever again."

Rex chuckles and nods. "Whatever you say, baby." He reaches up with shaking fingers but a smile as he swipes sweaty hair from her face. "God, I'm so glad you're okay, babe."

"Gross," Cedar mutters on a snicker, drawing Aria's sight to the two of us, standing off to the side, waiting for … well … I'm not sure.

"C." Aria reaches her free hand up, beckoning her best friend to her other side and my girl goes without question. "So glad you're here."

"Of course, I'm here." Cedar rolls her eyes, but she can't hide the tears I see building as she grips her best friend's hand and settles in beside her.

"And Finland." Aria's tired eyes land on me. Her head tilts to the side Cedar has taken up, and I follow the silent instruction.

Swallowing the lump in my throat, my boots move me across the tile, close enough to see the pattern on the hospital gown Aria wears, though my eyes don't translate what's actually there.

"How you feeling, Aria?"

She drags in a breath that puffs her cheeks when she blows it out. "Been better."

"So," Cedar starts. "Twins, huh?" She snickers when Aria shoots her a look. "Where dem babies at?"

"I blame you. And you—" Aria's lethal gaze whips to her future husband who tries and fails to hide his prideful smile.

"Anyway, babe," Rex snickers when her grip tightens down on his hand again. "You gonna ask them or you want me to?"

"Cedar." Aria's head slides easily over to her best friend with an emotion I can't read sitting in her green eyes. "Did you do the thing?"

Cedar burst out into a laugh that has me settling into this edge that Aria has me on and willing my heart rate to slow down. "Jesus. Yes, ok?"

"Good." Aria nods and lets her head fall back into the pillow. "Tell them Rex."

I meet his eyes over the top of his girl's battered body and cock my head. "You guys are killing me with the suspense here."

"Well," Rex starts with a grin. "Mac is forever going to be their uncle. Him, Ma, and Aurora would be first in line."

"Okay," Cedar drags, her gaze shooting to mine for a moment and landing back on Rex. "For what?"

"If something were to ever happen to the two of us," Aria clarifies as her eyes flutter closed and she pokes a tongue out to wet her cracked lips. "We want you guys to take next in line."

"As in …?"

"The babies' godparents," Rex amends and has my sight snapping to him.

"God …?" I look down at Cedar to ensure I heard right and when her same shocked expression meets mine, I feel my chest break open a little more. "Godparents?"

"Us?"

"Yep." Aria nods against the material beneath her.

"Which is why you two had to come in. I didn't wanna wait."

Rex stands from his crouch at his girl's side and comes around the foot of bed to clasp a hand on my shoulder, stronger now than he was ten minutes ago.

He remains silent when his eyes scream it all, and as he walks away, I realize that he hasn't called me *'newb'* in quite a while. Instead, he leaves me with the pride in his eyes, the trust, the fucking love for his family.

Including me.

I hear a door snick closed somewhere in my shock as I stare off into the space around Aria's feet and it's then that I recognize the feel of Cedar's hand in mine. It's warm and comforting. Strong and steadying.

"Holy shit, Fin." In a daze, I follow Cedar's gaze to the door that Rex walks back through in fresh scrubs and two bundles cradled to his chest.

One in fucking pink.

And one in goddamn blue.

"Guys." Rex beams as he steps up close to Cedar and me, his thick arms holding the swaddled balls against him in a way that makes them look tiny. Fragile. Small. "Footprints all done. They're all ours now."

Too fucking small.

"Oh my God," Cedar half whispers with a thickness in her voice that has me dragging my attention to her.

But then Rex's forearm bumps into my chest and demands I take the micro human covered in pink. "Meet Aurelia Savin Thompson." He grins at me when I gingerly slide my hands between him and the baby's back, my hand cupping the tiny skull to keep her head from flopping back.

"Savin," Cedar whispers, "As in …?"

"Yep," Aria says from behind us and I cradle the little girl closer to my chest.

"That's it," Cedar exclaims on a watering laugh. "I'm keeping the receipt."

Aria chuckles lightly behind me, but I'm already walking away from the group, my eyes set on the pudgy little cheeks and the light tuft of hair peeking out from beneath the pink cap on Aurelia's little head that's settled into the crook of my elbow. Her baby scent wafts up to tickle my nose and pull my heartstrings when I lift her closer, her lashes fluttering against those fat little cheeks.

"I take back what I said," I mutter to the little girl in my arms with a grin pulling up the corners of my lips. "I love you instead, Aurelia."

"Hey," Cedar scoffs. "Fuck you"

"Language," Aria snaps.

"Already? Seriously?" I hear Cedar's sighing scoff, but I don't dare take my sight off of the little girl in my arms. "Now both of their first words are going to be *'fuck'*. You're welcome."

My barking laugh bubbles up out of my chest before I can dampen the sound, the loudness of it jolting Aurelia and making me instantly regret even breathing too loud.

Except her little eyes only flutter beneath her still closed lids and her mouth makes a little suckling motion, but then she just settles right back in and begins snoozing again.

"Thank fuck," I mutter, my gaze lifting to those around me with an easy grin when I'm met with Cedar's eye roll and Rex's snicker despite his future wife's evil stare down. "You knew us before you asked us." I shrug. "You get what you pay for."

Snickering, I lift my chin when Rex's arms lift the blue bundle in offering to Cedar.

"And this is Macalister Finley Thompson."

My breath catches in my throat and my brow furrows deep.

Finley?

As in Fin-ley?

"Me?" It's off my tongue, quick and questioning as I step closer. "Rex?"

"Yeah, man." Rex sighs with a smiling nod, his now free hands coming up to land heavy on my shoulders. "It was hard to choose. But once we found that one, we knew it was right."

Shit.

My eyes burn, my chest set alight.

The breath I drag in shudders more than I'd ever admit, which only pulls Rex's grin higher.

"You helped me, Fin." Aria's cracking voice travels lightly from her spot on the hospital bed. "And while Rex'll never admit it, you've helped him, too." I drag my gaze from the heavy set in Rex's blue-green's to Aria. "And we love you for that."

Nodding, I clear the emotion building in my throat and avert my misting sights back to the little girl in my arms that shares a namesake with the woman I love. "Do you realize how many big-ass uncles you have now, girl?" I whisper to Aurelia with a chuckle. "Anyone that ever messes with you is so fucked."

"Jesus Christ, can you at least *try*?"

"Nah," Cedar drags from beside me with a lean to show off Macalister. "Tell your mommy *'fuck'*. Say it, Makkin."

Rex snickers and leans down to press a kiss to Aurelia's pudgy cheek. "Don't you dare go giving them nicknames, C. Mac'll be so pissed."

"Ugh," Aria growls. "Get out. All of you!"

Sniggering, Cedar leans Macalister closer to Aria, only to blow a raspberry in her direction. "I'm calling him Makkin. It's fucking cute."

A fist flies, landing with a solid thump in Cedar's bicep. "Hey," Cedar shrieks and curls her body protectively around Macalister and away from his mother. "You meanie!"

Laughter bursts out of Aria only to be cut off with a wince and a grip to her gut. "Ahhh, shit."

"Babe?" Rex rushes to her side, his hands going all over her. "You ok? You need the doctor?"

Aria shakes her head and breathes through her clenched teeth. "Laughing hurts. Let's not make me do that."

"Okay, no laughing." Rex nods and brushes more hair back from her face. "Got it, babe."

"Hey hotshot," Cedar says. "Trade me. I wanna meet my goddaughter."

Goddaughter ...

Fuck.

One look down at Aurelia in my arms and the only answer I can give pops off my lips when I see her little blue eyes staring back up at me. "Nope."

Her lids close and flutter open slowly, her tiny tongue poking out between her lips that begin lifting in a smile.

Yep. I'm fucking done for.

Chapter Forty-One

Cedar

*M*Y BEST FRIEND IS *glowing*.

Despite the pale complexion and the bags under her eyes, she's so full of pride for her new little family as she watches my ...

Boyfriend? Lover? Partner? Man?

Whatever. It's Fin. Just fucking Fin.

As Aria watches *Fin* saunter around the room with the pink swaddled bundle of tiny human held tight to his chest.

That makes my heart rate kick up with nerves beyond anything I've ever felt before.

He said he loved me.

Right?

I'm not dreaming?

Looking down at the little coo that comes from my own chest, I lock eyes—fucking brilliant *green* ones—with Macalister and can't stop the corner of my lips from tipping up. With a pudgy nose and puffy cheeks, Makkin greets me with a little half grin I just know is going to stop someone's heart one day.

God, he's so fucking cute, it might be mine.

I bounce the baby softly and shake my rising head, my sights settling on the woman of the hour and my thoughts rotating to all the freaking questions that no one has been able to answer yet.

I also need to stop thinking about what the hell Fin and I are supposed to be.

"Ari," I half grunt to get her attention to redirect from her man. "So what happened with these two?" I hold Makkin up and sniff at his new-baby smell before ghosting a kiss on his capped head.

Well, if that doesn't swell the fucking heart.

"Oh, um." Aria licks her lips and clears her throat. "I got so dizzy, I couldn't stand up. Ian panicked when I started having what I thought was Braxton-Hicks, so he brought me in."

I cringe, Fin's hiss echoing around the room as he spins on his heel and walks away from the conversation. "I really don't wanna know."

Snickering, my best friend continues. "So, when I got here, the ultrasound showed the umbilical cord around one of their necks, and they told me the only option was to cut them out. Definitely not the original plan."

"Lalalalalalala …" Fin murmurs, making me chuckle.

"My heart rate got too high, and they had to get them free." Aria shakes her head and lets out a breath. "They put me under before Rex could get here. It was hospital policy or something stupid that kept him out until the very end."

"But," I start and glance down at little Makkin, whose making my arm sweat with his head but feels like he weighs almost nothing. "It's too early, right? Did you know it was twins?"

"Well, they couldn't stop the labor, because of the cord. And I guess they kept hiding in the ultrasounds I had, their heartbeats synced enough that we didn't hear it. But …" Aria clears her throat and picks at the blanket covering her legs. "I also miscalculated the timing." I furrow my brow when Aria's sight shoots to her man that hovers attentively at her side. "I guess I was pregnant sooner than I realized. The babies are on the smaller side because they are a little early, but were also sharing everything."

"Babe?" Rex's fingers brush over the hand he holds, his face showing something akin to what I'd guess mine looks like.

Utter confusion.

"Jesus, it was around the night I met your mom, Rex."

His eyes flare wide for only a moment before a shit-eating grin nearly breaks his face in half. "Fuck yes, babe. I knew it." Rex's deep chuckle rolls over the room.

"Shut up," Aria mutters, her face showing the first level of color and it's red.

Like beet red.

"Huh." I scoff with a grin. "Didja get your freak on at the mom's house, Ari?" I bounce my brows when she turns another shade of darker red. "Get it in while Ma wasn't watching?"

"Ew—" Aria covers her face with her hands while her man laughs at her side. "God, stop."

"Something like that," Rex mutters on a chuckle, earning himself a backhand to the chest.

"Rex!"

"Go ahead, babe," Rex rumbles on a smirk that I really should look away from. "Say my name and see what happens."

"Ugh, you're insatiable."

"Good God, it's time to go." Fin's skin warms my side, his voice filling my ears and drawing goosebumps down my spine. "Before they start making the next one right here."

"Oh, no," Aria forces, hands up and all. "Nope. Never again." She winces and grips at her stomach. "Cedar, don't do it."

Snickering, I shake my head and lean closer to hand little Makkin over to his ridiculous parents. "Ari, I don't even know if I have a boyfriend or not. Pretty sure babies are a hard *no* for me."

"Ahem." I hear the correction in Fin's tone, but I shrug him off and lean down to kiss the cap on Makkin's head.

"Oh, boy," Rex mutters as he accepts the transfer of his daughter from Fin's solid arms I pay a little too much attention to when they ripple and pop veins beneath the ink.

"Um," Aria states as she straightens herself up in the bed with only a slight wince and one arm. "You better lock that shit down." Her pointer finger comes up just when I open my mouth to smart right back, only for the pointer to land over my shoulder. *At Fin.* "And you better do it *right*."

The fierceness I see makes my chest ache and my stomach warm over. "Ari ..."

"I'm dead serious. Fin," Aria speaks solidly, clearly. "Don't fuck this up or I'll have your nuts."

"Damn, babe," Rex sniggers. "I think I'm even a little nervous right now. *I like it.*"

I turn just in time to catch Fin's clipped nod and his eyes flit to mine. "C'mon, sweetness." He holds out a hand I accept and I allow him to tug me to my feet. "Time to have a little fucking chat."

"What did I do?" Fin's solid arm I was just admiring rests across my shoulders and pulls me in tight to his side.

"Call me later, C," Aria calls to my back, her crazy switch flipped back to the normal person that doesn't threaten dude's balls. "I want all the details."

God, I love her.

Snickering, I hold up a thumbs up with my free hand in answer when Fin refuses to loosen his grip.

Our steps fall in sync as we walk, his lips sealed up tight, and his warmth sending little spikes of adrenaline through my system.

Fuck, I'm nervous and excited.

We leave the room, the washing station where Fin dumps the paper smock, and once we round the corner to a cleared hallway, my back hits the wall before I even see him move.

Thick arms cage me in against the sterile white walls, my chest heaving against Fin's as he pushes in real close and dips low enough to meet my eyes with an intensity that has me biting my lip.

"You're right, sweetness," he breathes, that air washing over my face as he reaches up, using his thumb to pop my lip free from my teeth. "You don't have a boyfriend."

Wait, this is not going how I thought.

The last few weeks of amazing sex and connection have been for nothing? It was just a fling with a rockstar?

But he told me he loved me.

"You have a fucking *man*, Cedar." I blink up at the near snarl on his face, it's so intense. So serious.

So hot.

"And when a man tells you he *loves you*, that's it. Full fucking stop."

What?

"You're it, sweetness."

I blink, struck dumb as my heart thunders in my chest.

"Call me whatever you want. I don't care. But know I'm all fucking *yours*."

"Mine?" I reach up because it feels wrong not to touch him and plant my palms against his adrenaline fueled pecs.

"Yeah," Fin says tenderly, his tone a complete contrast to the shit he just delivered, his heart pounding so hard in his chest that I feel it in my palms. "Yours."

"Mine." I test the word on my tongue, the weight of it weird, but somehow ... good.

Because Finland Montgomery is giving himself to me.

"So when someone asks you," Fin leans down, making sure his shining eyes capture and hold mine, "what do you fuckin' say?"

My lip finds its way back between my teeth for a good nibble when my eyes start to itch and my chest fills with this foreign feeling I've carrying around for a while now—the one that Sara called love when I panicked and asked her about it. "That you're mine?"

And God help me, I fucking believe my therapist with my whole being.

"That's right." He nods, one single curt tilt of his head. "All fucking yours."

"Okay."

The softness of Fin's features slide enough to let that wicked smirk shine through and shoot straight to the spot between my legs.

"Let's get out of here." Fin pushes off from the wall and snags my hand in his massive one. "It's time for me to worship my queen."

Epilogue One

Fin

MONTHS LATER ...

Staring at the paperwork in my trembling grip that Cedar had me hold on to—because her dress doesn't have pockets and 'just in case, Fin'—I shake my head on a stiff neck and chuckle to myself.

Of course she really did.

That's my girl.

I reach up and tug at the stiff collar of my dress shirt. Then I tug at my tie that's tied way too fucking tight around my neck and amplifies the nerves battling in my stomach. I'm soaked in a perspiration that's probably going to ruin my chances of getting the deposit back on this rental.

God, why is it so hot?

Swallowing down at the lump threatening to build in my throat, I catch sight of my girl rushing across the dance floor. She's got a trail of shimmering purple material following close behind her tight ass I know I left handprints on this morning.

Because what sane man can turn down the request of '*spank me while I ride your cock*'?

Not I, that's who.

Then I see the one who's got me twisted and shuffling from foot to foot. The one I need to speak to before we leave here tonight.

Jaxon Jones.

Being at weddings is a thing, right? It gets people all lovey and open and soft, right?

Including me, because, *damn,* was I proud to finally see Rex and Aria at the altar together, with my girl as the fucking minister that bound them. Hence the paperwork I'm holding on to.

Just in case.

But right now, I'm biding my time, hoping that Jax gets enough alcohol in his system that this will either go smooth as silk, or complete meltdown that ruins Rex's wedding.

I do not want to see Aria if that happens.

So we're not hoping for the latter.

While also simultaneously avoiding an astute Cedar so that she doesn't figure it out before I can ask her. She's been paying too much attention to the little shit, which really isn't her paying attention to shit but more of me not knowing how the hell to hide shit from her all that well.

Maybe if I fuck her brains out first ... then she won't notice.

Kicking off from the wall I've been propped against watching the reception go on around me, I stalk in the direction Cedar disappeared to in hopes of catching her.

Who knew that the minister and maid of honor would be so fucking busy?

And why the fuck is the co-maid of honor not helping since she didn't bring a date?

I round the corner that leads into the hallway and get my answer as to why little miss Aurora is notably absent from her MOH duties.

That girl, I swear.

With a shake to my head and an averting of my eyes, I slink past the bride's little sister and follow the trail of purple fabric I want.

"Sweetness," I growl when I finally catch Cedar's wrist and spin her to me, making her release a little gasp that makes my cock jump when she crashes into my chest.

Yes.

"Oh, hey, hotshot." Cedar's chest pumps with her labored breath, successfully drawing my eyes to the way her tits nearly spill out of the top of the glittering fabric, her hand landing on my pec, her earthy scent filling my nose. "I was just—Jesus." She heaves in a deep breath and jabs a thumb over her shoulder.

"Just gonna ... suck my cock in the broom closet? *Sure thing.*" With my lips tipped up in a smirk, I trail a hot glance up the sides of her exposed neck to her parted pouty lips up to her darkened gaze. She's got all kinds of makeup around her eyes, some kind of smokey shit that makes the blue look electric and normally I wouldn't give a fuck about it, but that coupled with the way she's eating me alive with just a look?

Fuck, it'll definitely do.

Leaning in close enough that I feel the heat rising off of her dewy skin, but not close enough to touch except for the fingers still wrapped around her wrist, I dart my tongue out and trace it around the shell of her ear. Cedar shivers so hard that she's pressing into me and biting her lip to stifle a noise.

That won't do.

"C'mon." I hear the huskiness in my own voice and plaster my body to hers, pinning her against the wall. "Someone's gotta christen the party."

A weak snigger rolls up her throat, her hands latching onto my shoulders, her nails digging in just the way I like. "Bathroom, just down the hall."

I lean back just enough to catch her head tilt in the direction and we're off on a jog, Cedar's giggles echoing off the walls with her hand clasped tightly in mine.

Still can't get over hearing that fucking laugh when it's aimed at me.

The outside door to the bathroom we end up in doesn't have a lock, but the bigger of the two stalls does. It's fucking small, so I have to squeeze in behind my girl as she cackles and tries to get the panel closed around us.

But this one has those silver handles attached to the walls.

I shed my blazer and hang it on the hook, but I don't let much more than a tilted smile crest my features.

"Oh, God, you're doing the thing." Cedar points at my face, hers flushed a perfect shade of arousal pink I've been looking forward to seeing since it left her face this morning.

"Turn around, Cedar," I say with an even tone and a tilt to my brow. "Hands on the railing."

"Oh, shit," Cedar muses with a smile that's almost too wide for her face and gathers up some of the material around her waist as she turns awkwardly and plants her ass right against my already hard cock. "Big bad Fin's here."

My cock strains against the thin fabric of the dress slacks, chasing the heat of her as she bends at the waist and braces her hands on the railing just as I'd demanded.

God, I love it when she listens.

My hands find her hips and latch on, grinding my hardness against her. "How wet am I going to find you, sweetness?"

"Uh, very."

My chuckle rings darkly over the open space and I reach between us with one hand to undo my belt.

"Good," I growl and tug my zipper down.

With my cock free and her ass still covered by the ridiculous amount of silky fabric, I release her hip and drag the material up in a bunch at her waist.

"Fin," Cedar mewls, giving her ass a little wiggle when I slip a finger between the thin strap of her thong and the heated skin of her ass.

"Hm." With a snap decision, I yank on the underwear until it tears in my hands and has my girl yelping at the way the elastic rebounds and slaps against her skin.

Why push it to the side when I can have her panty-less for the rest of the night?

"Oh, God."

"Cedar," I growl and grab her hips in a punishing grip. "What have I told you? Huh?" My grip slides to her ass, my fingers digging in and spreading her, making her hiss with anticipation. "Whose name do you say when I fuck you?"

A breathy groan leaves her lips, and she pushes back against me like the dirty little girl she is. "*Yours.*"

"That's right, sweet." Angling my hips, I flex my cock and smack the head against the ring through her clit, making her back arch. "My name only."

Fisting the base, I apply enough pressure on my girl's slicked clit with the head that she moans in response. "Please Fin," she murmurs, all needy and ready for me.

"Tell me how you want it, Cedar," I demand, my cock a relentless tease against her heat.

"Oh, um." She pants, her hips following my motions when I direct my cock from side to side against her sensitive flesh. "*Fuck*, fast and hard."

Smirking—because I knew that's what my girl needed, I just wanted to hear her say it—I line the head of my cock up with her entrance and switch my grip to her shoulder with one hand and her hip with the other.

The feel of her open and hot for me, sitting just against the tip of my dick, has me groaning before I even enter her. "Say when."

"Now, Fin. Now."

I sink inside her in one solid thrust that has her stretching up on her tiptoes despite the heels on her feet and gripping the railing to keep from bashing her head into the wall.

"Fuck," I groan out and withdraw my hips when she gasps, only to slide back inside her, deeper and harder this time. "So fucking tight around me. So good."

"*Yes.*" The feel of Cedar's pussy wrapped around me has me tightening my grip when she moans and slamming harder into her until we're nothing but the sounds of skin slapping skin and moans echoing around the bathroom.

There's no denying the sounds coming from this stall, and I don't give a fuck if anyone can hear us outside of it because as long as I have my girl's pussy, hands, or mouth wrapped around my cock, I'm a happy fucking man.

She's all mine.

"Fin," Cedar drags out when I arch my hips and pass my piercing along her G-spot, over and over again. She tightens, her dewy skin a nice shade of flushed as she grips the railing and angles her hips up to match my punishing pace. "I'm gonna cum, hotshot."

"That's right," I growl and pull at her shoulder until her back meets my chest and my hips slam against her ass. "Cum on my cock, Cedar."

"*Ung...*" She sinks her claws into my arm that snakes around her shoulders and holds her in place while she takes my cock. "Gonna..."

"Now, Cedar," I growl when my balls draw up tight and my abs flex and the orgasm crashes into both of us in dirty waves of filthy words and the sounds of skin on skin.

Easing her back over, I make sure her hand is back on the railing before rolling my hips and thrust my still leaking cock inside my girl. She flutters around me and groans, her walls tightening with the aftershocks of a solid orgasm.

"I want you to go out there," I say, my voice deep when I pull my cock from her heat and wrap my fingers in her loose dark locks as the material at her waist falls back down around her legs. "With my cum dripping out of that sweet, *sweet* pussy." I drag her in the upright position by the strands in my fist, her back flush to my chest, her lips parted in a pant I don't wait to taste.

"Fin." Cedar shudders against me, but I don't stop.

"And tell your daddy he's been *replaced.*"

Epilogue Two

Jaxon

Sitting alone at the bar of a wedding that my little girl officiated, with a smooth tumbler of tequila warming in my grip, is not where I thought I'd end up.

But that's life, isn't it?

Never expecting the outcome of where things lead you—like Cedar's mother and me, for example.

Meeting and falling in love with such a fiery free spirit was never part of the plans when I signed up to go to war, and I certainly didn't expect that same free spirit to stick it out, being a military wife and all, and give me the best thing that's ever happened to me.

That woman was the love of my life.

She'd be so proud of our little girl. Pissed at herself for missing the signs like I did, but damn proud of the woman Cedar has become in spite of it all.

Considering I'm still haunted by my late wife's dulled eyes—the very same ones I see full of life in my kid—I think I did pretty good raising our daughter on my own.

See, Cedar never really had any chance of a relationship with her mother because my kind and loving Melany's mind took her way before her body decided to it was time. Her mental health took a dive during the pregnancy and the woman I fell in love with never came back to me.

It's been thirty years and the ache in my chest still sits wide the fuck open.

I got to watch it all happen, in slow motion, like a bad movie on repeat. Melany refused help, pushed me away to the point of locking me out of our bedroom on a regular basis, and finally took matters into her own hands the night of our little girl's third birthday.

After that ... all I could do was channel my grief into protecting my daughter.

She was all I had left.

So when I found out about Jeremy, it was like a kick straight to my heart. Another instance where I'd missed the signs. Another place I'd failed, except I didn't.

My little princess braved that shit and got out before it took her from me, too.

And while I found out the truth of it all way too many years later, I was finally able to do something about it and know that my little girl would still be surrounded by love and protection, even if I wasn't around.

That's all I needed.

I found the boys at the trailer that day, roughing up the shit stain that put his hands on my little girl in ways she didn't like, and it was then that I knew for sure that my princess had found her next chapter. That she'd be safe without me if need be.

I made sure they all got out before I handcuffed the dirty stain of a guy to the water heater and turned all the gas burners on full blast minus the flame. I knew it wouldn't take long to get enough gas in the house to either cut off the shit stain's final brain cells or blow.

What I hadn't expected was my little girl storming that house with a level of determination I'd never seen before as I'd settled in to wait it all out. Just as my heart was about to stop and my feet were carrying me forward with nothing but thoughts of getting her out before the trailer blew and took her right along with it, my little girl emerged from the shithole.

Now, she'll be forever free of the threat of that fucker coming anywhere near her.

And I'd accept any sentence in any jail just knowing that my little girl is safe and protected and surrounded by a love that reminds me of my Melany's early days.

Finland Montgomery is good for my daughter. He looks after her, cares about her.

Loves her.

But that doesn't mean I have to like what I see, even if I know it to be true.

"Hey, Poppa Bear." *Speak of the devil.* I throw back the contents of the glass I've been nursing as he continues to speak without my acknowledgement. "So, I love your daughter."

Gritting my jaw and pulling in a deep breath to keep my fists on the table instead of planting in the kid's face—again—I remain stiff as I catch the bartender's gaze with a lift of a finger to signal for another drink.

Because if Fin's tone is any indication of what he's really after, then I'm going to need a shit ton of alcohol.

"Don't call me that."

"Fine," Fin concedes and settles into the stool next to me as if he'd been invited. "So, about the second thing I said."

A growl is the response he gets when the bartender slides a glass down the length of the bar and it smacks against my waiting palm. "I know this. It's why you still have your head attached."

"Why do I get the feeling you're not talking about this one?" I catch him tap his inked pointer finger to his temple in my periphery and shake my head on a sigh.

"Spit it out, kid."

It takes a long tense moment of the man flexing his jaw like the words are getting stuck in his throat and me slowly sipping my fresh drink, if only just to drag out his torture even more.

A father knows things.

Things that happen when people fall for each other.

That and Cedar beat him to the punch two days before she left on her girl's trip. It was a quick comment she threw out, more to herself than the room while she tossed her laundry into the machine in my house because the studio above her shop doesn't have personal washing machines. It's something my princess has done since she moved out—come over on Sunday with an arm full of shit to wash and a dire need for caffeine before someone loses their head.

She wants them to move in together. But only if he asks her.

I'd only shrugged when she looked up from the mound of clothes in her hands with those big blue eyes that got her out of so much trouble as a kid. So soulful. So innocent.

And then I made her promise to still come over and do her laundry every Sunday, whether she did or didn't.

Fin clears his throat and nods to himself, like he's psyching himself up before he speaks, and reaches over my forearm to pluck the tumbler right from my grip.

This mother—

Throwing the drink back like a shot, he hisses and slams the glass back against the bar before looking me dead in the eye.

"I'm moving her in with me, Jax, and while I don't give a shit if you approve or not, I know my girl does."

Hm.

"Moving her in, huh?" I work my jaw and rap my knuckles on the bar top for the bartender's attention. "Did you try asking her that, kid?"

"Uh, well—"

"Not up to me," I cut off his words and accept the next tumbler the bartender slides my way, a second coming in right on its heels. I lift my arm in time for Fin to catch the glass with a furrowed brow and a tick to his jaw.

"Well, no shit, but—" He fiddles with the glass for a moment before tossing the drink back again and letting loose a loud hissing exhale. "I'll take that as a yes." The tumbler smacks against the bar with a crack, and Fin is spinning away with a grin. "Make sure you hide the bat."

Heat grazes my side, the opposite of the one that Fin just vacated, as I chuckle and a melodic voice fills my ears.

"Aren't they the greatest?"

Working my jaw, I keep my attention on my glass and take a sip to hide the smile I'd rather keep to myself. "Not in the slightest, ma'am."

The snicker that responds has my own lips tipping and the tequila finally warming that hole in my chest as I turn to address the woman at my side.

But then my words get stuck in my throat and my brow furrows at the sight of her.

With hair so light, its borderline silver, pulled up in some weird updo that makes it look like a French braid that's raised up off her head and the tail of it running down her shoulder to rest on top of her freckled chest on one side. A chest that's plump and fits so nicely into the top of her sparkling dress that I have to clear my throat and try my best not to shatter the glass in my heavy grip.

"Fin came to me late in life." She chuckles out as she holds up a manicured hand for me to shake. "I did my best with them."

I guess I've been struck dumb because instead of taking the offering like a gentleman, my sight darts back up to her flushed face with hints of crow's feet edging her lined eyes and I swear I lose a brain cell or two at the sight of the gorgeous blue-green irises and thick burgundy lips smiling back at me.

"Name's Marie." *Marie ... Marie ...* Her words bounce around in my head until they finally stick to something and I get my composure back—kind of—and clear my throat. "Marie Thompson." She shoots me a wink when I finally accept her offered hand and the slide of her smooth skin against my callouses sends little shocking tingles clear up my elbow. "But my boys call me '*Ma*'."

The End!

Acknowledgements

G UYS, WE FINALLY MADE it.

If you're here, then you've made it to the end of the very *second* book I've ever gotten into the physical universe! *Yay!*

I hope that Fin gave you hope, Cedar reminded you that there's more to life, to healing, and Peach let you laugh along with him.

Did you enjoy the cameos and updates on Rex, Aria, and the rest of the gang? I'm so glad they showed up for our characters in this book, and continue to do so in the next one.

I have fallen in love with this band to the point I even see them, in my mind's eye, playing on stage to certain songs that come on the radio. It's like my own little movie I'm so glad I get to share with all of you.

Figuring out how to accomplish all this as an indie this go round was no easy feat. There were a lot of curses, tears, and long hours making this book baby happen and I'm so fucking glad it's finally here.

My first acknowledgement is Mr. Stone. Forever my ride or die, my rock, my babe, my tough love king. I love you, babe. And I like you most of the time ;)

To my besties with your undying encouragements, never ending cook outs, and constant jokes. I love you guys.

For my momma giving me this love of music. My sisters. My niece and nephews. To the moon and back.

Next up are my beta readers, Brooklyn and Bev! Your comments, feedback, and unwavering support are paramount. Thank you for loving Fin and the rest of the band like I do.

To my editor, my proofreader, and my cover designer— thank you for making this book baby shine. He's so damn pretty.

A quick thanks to Wander for taking sexy af photos! The Fin on the cover is soooo the Finland in my mind.

To my readers for all of your support, your reviews, your kind words about my guys. Thank you, thank you, *thank you*. None of this would mean anything without you!

And finally ... to the younger version of me. I wouldn't be here, in the place, writing these books without you. Thanks for not giving up, even when you thought you might.

<3

Content Warnings

*C*ONTENT *W*ARNINGS INCLUDE ON *page panic attacks, mild insomnia, references to past abusive relationship, verbal abuse (not between main characters), return of the abuser, violence, and pregnancy concerns (not between main characters).*

*References made for **off page** content include non-consensual events (only mentioned, not between main characters), traumatic birth, therapy and therapist.*

This book is character driven and *not* meant to be any kind of reference to self-help. Not everyone deals with trauma or mental / physical abuse in the same ways. This is just a representation of how my characters have dealt with their situations / mental health and is no way any sort of reference for real life use.

The Rush is meant for audiences of 18 years or older.

Also by Rae Stone:

As Above series

The Moment

The Rush

Turn the page for a sneaky peek at what's to come …

Sneak Peek

THE FOLLOWING PAGE AND a half is a snippet of As Above, book 3. This is unedited, subject to change at any point, and includes copyrighted material. (Copyright © 2023 by Rae Stone) Which means no sharing!

If you prefer to go into books blind, then skip these next two pages. If not then I hope you enjoy this little teaser for what's to come. The band, the banter, the *tension* ...

This is your final warning :)

"DIRTY FUCKER," SOMEONE MUTTERS from one of the other couches in the space that's also covered in packages. Probably Rex, our lead singer, song writer, and twin to the drummer I flick another envelope in the direction of in hopes that it sticks in his ever-present bandana headband.

Today's is white.

And for some reason, so are his nails.

It'd match perfectly.

"What?" I chuckle and pour a fresh taste from the bottle at my elbow. "Like you bastards didn't enjoy the shit, too. Y'know, before your balls sagged so much you needed assistance holding them up."

"Some of us *like* having our balls handled."

"Oh, I like my balls handled. *Fondled.*" I hold a cupped hand up and wiggle my fingers. "Tongued. Just not by the same set every night."

Shaking my head when all I get back is a round of grumbles, I take a drink and lean back, no longer interested in the handwritten letters proclaiming love and sacrifices for people they've never met. *We've* never met.

Of course they love us. We're As Above.

My latest drink settles heavy in my gut, the tension in the air thickening thanks to damn near all of my band mates and brothers completely ignoring that this used to be fun. Getting bras thrown at us was funny and sexy. Getting laid in a different city every night was our life. And letting the world drool all over us was our only way.

Not anymore.

Me and Leo are the only bachelors left in our group and I'm beginning to think that As Above's days of chaos have officially come to a screeching halt.

Show nights have stopped including after parties with booze and girls and blow.

Tours are over for the foreseeable future.

Even writing new music and practices have been capped.

All thanks to the permanent pussy these bastards decided to pick up.

Grumbling to myself, I push up from the stool with a swimming head that tilts me to the left just a little bit and wrap a fist around the bottle I've been nursing.

I'd rather be drunk off my ass than to sit here any longer with a bunch of old bastards that have given up on this rockstar life we were all so desperate for as kids. Dreaming and planning about, *together,* since fucking grade school.

We couldn't fuckin' wait to get our hands on it.

Now look at 'em.

<u>About the Author</u>

Rae Stone is native to the Midwest, from a town called Springfield, OH. While she no longer resides in the City of Roses, Rae is definitely a misfit of Suburbia that would rather paint her nails black and annoy the neighbors with her loud rock music.

When she's not elbows deep in writing, Rae can be found attending concerts with Mr. Stone, consuming romance novels like water, and letting her fur kids run wild.

Wanna connect? Find Rae on socials below!

Facebook | Instagram | Tiktok | GoodReads | BookBub | Newsletter | Rae's Reader Group

www.ingramcontent.com/pod-product-compliance
Lightning Source LLC
Chambersburg PA
CBHW032350310726
48973CB00007B/1949